MW00412584

Amazon US

5 stars: Read this awesome novel–you won't be sorry!
A captivating story, beautifully written, and SO much fun!!
I loved the twists of the plot. It was like a painting, the
lovely scenes of Barcelona and outskirts and of Sitges, and I
could almost taste the food and the cava. Truly enjoyable in
every way. I hadn't read a full-length novel in so little time
in ages–very hard to put this one down!

5 stars: I really enjoyed this book
I enjoyed this book on several levels. Living in a
community similar to Kingsbay in the US, I savored the
character development and description of that waterside
community. Being a sailor, I enjoyed the author's insight
into the world of pleasure boating. About a third of the way
through the book, the storyline takes an unexpected twist
and I could not put the book down. I have not visited
Barcelona, but it is now on my bucket list. McPhee
provides the reader with a great comparison of the cultures
and life in the upper middle class in the US and Spain.

Amazon UK

5 stars: Highly recommended
A great first novel - the characterisation and the scene-
setting at the start were meticulous and allowed the reader
to get to know the characters. However, once the storyline
was revealed the action grew apace and some prior
assumptions were challenged! I particularly loved the
section on Barcelona, which again showed great attention
to detail by the author, who created a wonderful sense of
atmosphere–and menace. By the end, I couldn't put this
novel down–now I can't wait for his next one!

5 stars: Gripping debut

'Bunco' crosses continents in the wake of a man whose sinister nature rocks the quiet community of Kingsbay. A fast moving story fuelled by lies, lust, money and shocking crimes cleverly balanced with friendship, trust and love. The narrative captures character, time and place with skill and credibility. A gripping read with a nasty twist in the tail.

Amazon International

4 stars: Read the book from start to finish in less than 3 days!

Most enjoyable...connected with the characters and the feeling of 'place' was well described in each of the locations. Will be recommending the book to my book group here in Sydney, Australia. Look forward to reading more from this new author.

4 stars: Bunco

A great holiday read. It begins with a scene well set out in the USA that becomes a mystery that you follow from the USA to Europe with the places so well described that you can almost feel you're there. An interesting mix of characters, with the villain getting his comeuppance in the end.

Available in paperback and as a Kindle e-book.

EMPRESS

BRIAN MCPHEE

Copyright © 2017 Brian McPhee

All rights reserved

Published by Entente Publishing

www.ententepublishing.com

hello@ententepublishing

2.001

Dedicated to the men of the British Merchant Navy
who, in the 1940s, kept
the United Kingdom armed and fed.

And in particular my father,

John McPhee

M.V. Egidia &
R.M.S. Strathnaver.

THANKS

Many thanks to my wife Sheila, my daughter Marianne
and my cousin George Dunn for ideas, comments,
corrections and encouragement.

Once again, my talented brother, Stephen, provided
the cover art.

Thanks also to James Thomson of The Diving
Museum in Gosport.

See also the author's notes at the end of this volume.

IMPORTANT DISCLAIMER

With the exception of some prominent historical figures, all persons portrayed are entirely fictitious and bear no resemblance to any persons, alive or dead. Any apparent resemblance to actual persons or places is entirely coincidental.

See the author's notes at the end of this volume.

West of Scotland vernacular

Clatty – filthy

Close – the common entrance and stairways in a tenement building *(pronounced like 'close' meaning near, not 'close' meaning shut)*

Eejit – idiot

Factor – a landlord's agent

Flit – to move house

Ginger – any sparkling soft drink

Isnae – isn't

Range – a simple coal-fired, cast iron cooker built into a fireplace

Steamie – the public washhouse (laundry) where clothes and linens could be steam washed then dried by passing them through the heavy rollers of the 'mangle'.

Sweetie – Sweet/candy

Tatties – potatoes

Weans – children *(rhymes with 'planes')*

Wheesht – be quiet!

Wisnae – wasn't

For American readers, a 'quid' is a pound (£); during the war, equivalent to $4. 'All found' is a job with free meals and accommodation – *We pay £5 a week, all found.'*

For all landlubbers; when facing forward towards the bow of a vessel, your left is 'port'; 'starboard' is on your right.

**This novel was inspired
by a true story**

*From the Wikipedia entry for the
Empress of Britain:*

'In 1995, salvagers found Empress of
Britain…The bullion room was still
intact. Inside was a skeleton but no
gold …'

Extracted June 2017

1962

UNDER THE ATLANTIC OCEAN

Steve eased his head and right arm through the jagged opening, mentally cursing his bulky full-face mask. His powerful flashlight cast a cone of cold illumination across the interior surfaces of the ship's strongroom.

There was nothing to see.

He drifted a little further into the hole, mindful of the sharp edges threatening to rip his dry suit.

The room was starkly empty except for a small pile of debris in the far corner.

No gold. Nothing.

Gingerly Steve began to back out; frustrated, disappointed; all-in-all, thoroughly pissed off. He added up the hours and money wasted on this fruitless quest.

'A total waste of fu…..'. He felt something brush the back of his head.

"Oh God! Oh God! Oh, sweet Jesus!"

With one panicked heave, he shot back from the opening, arms thrashing wildly, a maelstrom of silver bubbles bursting from his exhaust vent, heading exuberantly for the surface. His abandoned flashlight swung at the end of its thin tether, casting weird shadows to dance and sway around the scene of devastation.

"Steve, Steve, calm down. Think about your breathing. Come on, man. Breathe."

Andy came alongside his boss and saw he was regaining control; his breathing returning to normal.

"Look, look at the bloody thing."

Steve's trembling finger pointed to the dark opening.

Andy turned to look, and his own stream of bubbles ceased for a long moment.

Dreadfully slowly, the head of a corpse was falling past the jagged hole. It was not quite a skeleton; here and there ragged strips of pale flesh clung tenaciously to the skull. As they watched, appalled but spellbound, the head drifted out of view, followed by the rest of the body, clad in a black diving suit, much like their own. Seconds before the ghastly apparition disappeared, they glimpsed a rubber swim fin trailing from a skeletal foot.

1928

CLYDEBANK, SCOTLAND

The women leaned heavily on their windowsills, strong arms red and chapped; hand-rolled cigarettes held lazily between nicotine-stained fingers. They had paused their assorted conversations; words thrown from one window to the next, or all the way across the street or, by twisting unnaturally, to a neighbour on a higher floor.

The taxicab had stopped thirty yards from the end of the street. The women stared as the sole passenger unfolded himself from the cab and looked up at the serried windows. The women stared unflinchingly back.

The stranger was aware of the silent watchers following his progress along the uneven pavement. They were carefully calibrating his meticulously crafted appearance; the shine on his shoes, the subtle sheen of his hat, the flash of white above a grey-gloved hand carrying a soft leather briefcase emblazoned with a golden crown. He had the polished look of someone born to privilege and power.

The stationary taxicab radiated sharp clicks from its cooling engine. It would wait for its passenger's return journey to Glasgow Central Station and the early evening London train. The man's visit north would be as brief as he could possibly make it.

The visitor reached the corner and froze. After a beat, he slowly raised his gaze to properly take in the leviathan before him. The enormous, unworldly hull soared high over the grey tenements, dominating the mean streets around, even the sky itself. It was truly an awesome sight, vastly more imposing than he had pictured in his wood-panelled Whitehall office. The cliff face of steel was taller than Nelson's Column, as long as three rugby fields.

He had seen the pyramids of Egypt, the great cathedrals of Europe, New York's majestic skyscrapers; but they were all planted firmly in the earth. The colossus before him was designed to glide across the oceans under man's direction. It struck him as preposterous that something so massively solid could possibly float.

As he slowly walked towards the behemoth, the man briefly caught, then lost, a panorama of the entire vessel. He retraced his steps to appreciate it properly. But he looked in vain: There was simply no way his imagination could grasp the entirety of the hull—its immense scale defeated him.

The cranes looming over the abandoned hull were themselves enormous, the largest ever constructed. There were eight of them marching down each side of the ship, towering over it, spanning its width; each ready to hoist materials inboard to be lowered into the depths of the great vessel.

But for now, the huge cranes were motionless—silent sentinels awaiting the command to spring to life.

As he approached closer, the civil servant picked out details in the scene before him. Most prominent and revealing were the mournful streaks of rust staining the massive sheets of metal cladding the ship.

It was ten o'clock on a Wednesday morning, but the shipyard was eerily silent. No men clambered over the hull, driving in red-hot rivets; no incandescent sparks cascaded from welding torches. The great iron gates barring the rail tracks were padlocked. The powerful yard locomotives, which should have been operating continuously, ferrying materials to the work crews, stood sullen in their sidings. Scraps of metal, shards of broken bottles, shattered wooden cases; all were reflected in fetid black puddles. Great wooden beams lay scattered carelessly around. Scrawny grasses and rank weeds exploded from ominous black crevices; finishing touches to the scene of desolation.

In the echoing distance the man could hear the faint cries of children; there was a school somewhere nearby, he surmised. But the fathers of the schoolchildren were sitting silent at home or were milling around the Labour Exchange; a soulless place where hope came to die. Even highly skilled craftsmen, men who had long ago swallowed their pride, were lucky to pick up a couple of days' labouring work now and then.

Hull 384 spoke to everything wrong with the times and the country. Conceived as a monument to national pride and wealth, Hull 384 had instead become the manifest symbol of the decay of a community and the dizzying decline of a once-proud empire–and a silent howl of rebuke to politicians and business leaders.

The man from the Finance Ministry lifted his eyes once more to the magnificent bow, looming high over his head. As if on cue, a shaft of sunlight sought out a patch of bare metal and the reflection illuminated the detritus and decay around him.

To a curious watcher, the man was tiny, insignificant; but the papers in his elegant briefcase would transform Hull 384, the yard, and the lives of the families in the rows of tenements.

For Hull 384 was to be resurrected. Steelworkers, joiners, painters, engineers, plumbers, electricians – thousands of men of every trade and none would be employed once again to realise the dreams of her designer. She would be launched and fitted out here, on Scotland's River Clyde.

Then the fastest, most elegant, most luxurious liner ever built would bear the rich, the famous and the powerful across the oceans and around the world.

1929

CLYDEBANK, SCOTLAND

The pregnant silences between the anguished cries were longer now. Alex could still hear his wife's pain and fear, but he sensed she was tiring.

Yet another agonised moan from the room next door tore at his heart. This was his Annie, the rock of their family.

This was her sixth confinement. The others had gone easily, what could be wrong this time? She had been so confident; just that morning she had been reassuring him, commanding him not to worry. She would have her sister, Kate, with her, and the midwife if need be; everything would be fine. But three hours ago Alex had been sent to fetch the doctor. And now, after an interminable delay, he was with her at last.

The bedroom door opened, and the doctor stepped into the kitchen – the all-purpose room where the family cooked, ate, played, talked, read, bathed in the big zinc bath kept under the bed in the bed recess, the alcove in the wall opposite the single sash window.

"Your wife is very ill, Mr Campbell, she should be in the hospital, but we can't move her now. We need to get the baby out immediately. Do you want to see your wife for a moment? In these conditions, without the facilities of the hospital, the situation is extremely grave indeed."

"Are you telling me my wife is going to die?"

The doctor looked down at the man seated before him, put out by the fact that Alex hadn't stood when he entered. He was accustomed to deference.

"I'm telling you she might, yes. Of course, we'll do our best, but she is utterly exhausted and…"

Alex heaved himself from the chair, his deliberate movements those of an old man, not of the vibrant figure he cut every day, working amidst the tumult and bustle of the shipyard.

He stepped to the bedroom door, paused, and pulled himself erect. Annie needed his strength now, not his weakness.

Kate was kneeling by the head of the bed, holding a damp cloth against her sister's forehead. The midwife turned from the other side of the bed and motioned Kate to follow her to the door.

"Just a few minutes, Mr Campbell; we need to act quickly to save her."

Alex and Annie were alone in their bedroom, the room where they had talked and laughed and loved together for seven wonderful years. Never a serious argument, never once going to sleep on a harsh word.

"Hello, pet," she whispered, as he knelt on the floor, taking her hand in his.

"I'm sorry, Alex, I think the baby's dead."

Tears flowed freely down her cheek. Her hair was wet and matted, her eyes sunk in deep hollows.

"Never mind that now. We just need to get you better. We'll have other children—or not. It's no matter. You just need to get well."

She gave another half-strangled cry as something tore deep inside; he could see she was holding back, for his sake.

"I love you, Alex," she gasped, "I have right from the start. Take care of yourself."

She closed her eyes; he bent down and tenderly kissed her burning forehead.

"Don't talk like that, pet. I'll get the doctor and he'll soon get you better. I need you; we all need you."

He was scared now, more scared than he had ever been.

Annie's eyelids flickered open again.

"I'll be loving you, always," she sighed, trying to smile, but failing with a heart-rending grimace.

Softly, automatically, he crooned his response, "With a love that's true, always."

It was the tune they had danced to three years ago, when Annie had decided that this would be their song, forever.

***

Annie loved dancing with her husband. The strength of his arm around her as he led her around the dance floor transported her far from the drab walls of the Co-operative Hall. Of course, the music and the crêpe paper covering the lights helped; but Annie was convinced the most glamorous thing in the room was her husband. He wasn't like the other men she saw around Clydebank. For a start, he was unusually tall; six feet one in his bare feet. He carried himself well and he danced with a grace and a light step belying his height and strength.

He was only twenty-seven, but she knew the other men looked up to Alex, and not just physically; that was why he was the youngest union shop steward ever elected in the shipyards.

Annie also saw how some of the young wives looked at her husband when he brought her dancing on the last Saturday of every month. But they didn't bother her. Another thing that made her husband different was she always knew exactly where he was. Once a week he went to the pub for two hours with his brother-in-law; and every other week he took the tram to Ibrox, to watch Rangers with his brother, Ian. Other than that, and his monthly Masonic Lodge meetings, Alex was with his family. On the Saturdays when Rangers played away from Glasgow, they would go for long walks with the children, then Alex would read to them while she made supper.

The Co-op Hall might have been utilitarian; its paint peeling and faded, but the band was excellent. There were only six of them; but the singer, a young woman with an outsized personality, was terrific. When Annie and Alex had been courting, they had gone up to the Locarno Ballroom in Glasgow, the height of glamour–red velvet, floor-to-ceiling mirrors, revolving lights, a real stage and even a proper sprung dance floor. But, Annie thought, the singer here tonight was every bit as good as the woman at the Locarno–and this girl didn't sing with a fake American accent.

Tonight, Annie was feeling especially content with her life. She smiled to herself, anticipating that later, when they were in bed, she would tell Alex her news: She was pregnant again. A brief shadow passed behind her eyes as she thought of Willie, her first born, who had died more than three years ago, aged only two. But now her four children would have another wee brother or sister.

"What are you grinning at?" he asked her, gently.

"Nothing, everything; I'm just happy."

Alex smiled at his wife and held her closer.

"Alex! Listen! She's doing that song again, the one I liked. Oh, I just love this song! This is going to be our special song, pet."

Annie didn't know all the lyrics yet, but she hummed along and sang a few snatches. The next time she heard it, she would know all the words.

I'll be loving you always
With a love that's true, always

When the things you've planned
Need a helping hand
I will understand, always.'

***

The doctor and midwife came back into the bedroom and Alex was ushered out to join his sister-in-law. The two of them sat in silence, listening as Annie's cries tailed off as the chloroform worked its magic. After what seemed an age, but was probably less than fifteen minutes, the doctor came back into the kitchen. Before he had said a word, Alex's heart was breaking.

He would not cry, he would not.

"I'm sorry Mr Campbell. Perhaps if I had been called earlier."

The doctor threw a glance at Kate, who was now sobbing.

Alex shot out of his chair and stood chest-to-chest before the medical man.

"Don't you dare, don't you bloody dare. It wisnae Kate's fault; and if I hear of you saying otherwise, you'll have me to deal with; d'yeh hear? It wisnae Kate who made Annie wait."

Alex pushed past the startled medic with a final glance that made no attempt to mask his contempt.

"You can see yourself out."

The second Alex's hand touched the door handle, his mood changed—anger at the doctor set aside. He stepped slowly into the bedroom.

The midwife had pulled the blanket up to Annie's chin and had closed her eyes. For a fraction of a second, Alex glimpsed a tiny wrapped bundle on the floor at the far side of the bed, but instantly he looked away.

Alex knelt once again at his wife's side.

"It's still you and me, pet. Always," he whispered, as once again, for the last time, he leaned in to place a kiss on his wife's head.

The following day Alex was back at work. The funeral would be on Monday, when he would take the morning off, with no pay of course. But there was still rent, food, clothes to pay for; and now a funeral. His workmates would ensure Alex had an easier time for the next week or so. In particular, they kept him away from the most dangerous jobs, the very tasks that, as a rule, Alex was first to tackle. The high platforms were no place for a man distracted by grief and concern for his weans.

Alex was smart enough to know what his mates were doing, and wise enough to accept their help. Even the foremen and managers gave him a clear berth. They knew how much he was respected by the men, and they had no wish to stir up trouble by adding to his problems, for this week at least. Anyway, Alex had earned the right to a few easy days, earned many times over by his efforts and leadership since construction of 384 had restarted over a year ago.

Alex was the shop steward for his section of the workforce. He led the Black Squad, the men of the Boilermakers Union—the welders, riveters and platers—the most important union in the yards. He was one of the most respected shop stewards in the huge enterprise. He wasn't an agitator. As long as he believed his men were being treated fairly and with respect, he would be reasonable. He had no time for the communists in the yard, but he had learned from bitter experience that the union had to stand ready to fight the bosses every day; they would get nothing that wasn't demanded from strength, solidarity and a willingness to stop work if required.

Alex had led his men out on strike the previous year, when the managers tried to recruit some Catholics as riveters. He couldn't have told you what he had against Catholics, he knew next to nothing about their religion, except it was full of superstition and ignorance.

It was a tribal thing. The skilled jobs belonged to him and his and they would be defended. Anyway, everyone knew the Irish brought down wages. They could have the labouring jobs; but as long as Alex was shop steward, no Papist would join his union.

When it became clear that on this issue the foremen and managers sided with Alex and his men, the yard owners caved in and the Black Squad came back to work, earning overtime as they caught up with the days that had been lost.

Alex came home to a silent, empty house. Annie's body had been taken away by the undertakers, and the four children were still at Kate and Jim's. He would tell the weans about their mother tomorrow morning when he collected them for the weekend. He sat in his chair and the realisation washed over him that Annie wasn't there with his cup of tea. He welled up for a moment, but quickly dominated his emotions. He had to think about his family. There was no time for grieving.

He heard a key in the lock and his sister-in-law's voice as she let herself in.

"I'm sorry, Alex, I tried to get here before you, but feeding six of them took longer than I expected."

"Don't apologise, Kate, I'm really grateful to you and Jim. I was just thinking I'd be round first thing tomorrow to collect the weans and tell them about Annie. I tell you, Kate, I'm no' looking forward to it. Not at all. They're expecting a wee brother or sister, no' this."

She sat down in the other chair, Annie's chair. Kate was five years older than her sister and didn't look much like her. Where Annie had been a pretty and slender redhead, Kate was dark and square. But the sisters had been inseparable, visiting each other almost every day during the week. Their flats were only a few hundred yards apart. Each morning Kate would walk to the school gate, keeping an eye on her son and daughter as they ran on ahead. The sisters would meet at the school gate as Hughie raced after his older cousins.

Weather permitting, the sisters would then push the pram holding Annie's two babies to the park, three-year-old Jean holding onto her auntie's hand. The two women enjoyed their daily half-hour of freedom before starting on their never-ending drudge of household chores.

"We'll tell them in the morning, together. Hughie's the only one who'll have any idea what it all means. He's a grand boy; good with his wee sisters and brother."

"Aye, I know; he's got an old head on him."

"I done a couple of things today, Alex, I hope you'll be OK with everything. I came over this morning and picked up …"

A tear escaped, before Kate pulled herself together.

"Sorry. I picked up a dress and some of Annie's things and took them to the undertaker. I couldn't ask you what you wanted, but I chose her red dress with the spots, she loved that dress. I hope that was OK?"

"Aye, of course. The very last thing I said to her was a line from our song. She was wearing that dress when we danced to it the first time."

He smiled sadly, "She wore it every time we went dancin', it was her dancin' dress. I wish I could have bought her more dresses."

Kate was fierce with her reply.

"You loved her, and she knew it, and that's the best thing a woman can have, knowing her man loves her and is taking care of her and the family. You've nothing to regret, Alex, nothing at all."

Kate stood and moved over to the range.

"Here, I've brought you a bit of pie and tatties; I'll heat it up."

They both took it for granted that Kate would have food for Alex. He was not expected to know how food appeared on the table. He could stretch to making a cup of tea or a sandwich, but that was the extent of his domestic skills.

Kate put the food in the oven and came back to sit opposite her brother-in-law.

'He looks shattered,' she thought.

The spark had gone from his face; but Alex was strong and would recover, for his children's sake, if nothing else. Alex wasn't the kind to take to drink or to drift away from his responsibilities. And neither was she.

"The other thing; I talked with Mrs Weir. We're going to swap; we're going to do the flit on Sunday. Jim's organised a few men; it won't take long. I'll talk to the factor on Monday, after the…after the funeral, but he'll be fine. We're all good tenants, all paid up, so he'll be OK."

Mrs Weir was Alex's neighbour on the same landing. Their front doors faced each other. Now she would move around the corner to Kate and Jim's flat, and he would have Annie's sister next door, and the children would have their family beside them.

"That's really good of you, and Jim too. I don't know what to say."

"We're family, and it's what Annie would want; so nae need to say anything. I wanted it all sorted before we told the weans about their mother, I don't want Hughie worrying about who'll be looking after him; I mean for meals, an' washing, an' that."

Kate didn't add, *'And I didn't want you worrying about your dinners either.'*

But he understood and would remember.

"You might want to say something to Mrs Weir tomorrow tho'; she was very good about it. Didnae think twice when I asked her. And today was Annie's turn to wash the steps in the front close and the landing toilet, but Mrs Weir did them for her this morning."

Kate paused, and her face crumpled.

"Oh Alex, she's gone: My wee sister, she's really gone."

And she held her head in her hands and wept for both of them.

***

Alex and his crew were coming to the end of their involvement with the ship. Each week, the workforce was becoming smaller as the project progressed from structural work to finishing projects. Hull 384 had been the salvation of the yard; but the rest of Clydebank and the Clydeside, all of Scotland in truth, remained mired in the deepest depression in living memory. The government's decision to guarantee the loans to complete this one vessel was intended to galvanise the industry, but there was next to no work available for the men coming off 384. No other big liners had been laid down and the Clydeside yards were fighting each other for refits and smaller orders. At least fifty or sixty men applied for every one of the few openings that arose.

But still Alex and his mates took satisfaction from working on the most elegant ship ever built. 384 was unique, the first giant liner designed for world cruises and passage through the Panama Canal. She was a greyhound–exceptionally long and unusually narrow. The combination promised swift passages when she would be called to slice through the world's oceans.

"Knock that out and dae it again," Alex instructed the younger man.

It was the foreman's job to supervise the quality of the men's work, but Alex wouldn't abide sloppy workmanship from anyone in his section. His men were expected to demonstrate pride in everything they built. 'Clyde-built' meant the best in the world, and Alex was doing his part to keep it that way. The fact was the foremen knew they could more or less ignore Alex's section and focus their attentions elsewhere.

It was this attitude that helped keep industrial peace in the yard. When Alex asked for better tools, or more men on a shift, or more overtime, the managers were inclined to pay attention because they could see the integrity in his work and the strength of his leadership. Of course, they usually argued with him on principle, but he won more than his share of disputes.

"It's fine, an' ah don't want tae dae it again."

A few of the nearby men slowed in their work to hear what would come next–this would be fun.

"It's no' bloody fine, eejit; and anyway, 'fine' isnae good enough. Step back a bit."

Alex turned and caught the eye of a man working farther along the scaffolding.

"Tam, what rivet has this eejit made an arse of?"

"The one at his shoulder."

Alex turned again to the new man. "He's twenty fucking feet away and he can see it's wrang. It should be perfect. Every head should be the same as every other head. Didn't they teach you that?"

"Aye, of course. But the foreman's said nothing; why the hell are you gettin' on me? It's no' your bloody job."

"You're right, it isnae my bloody job: it's *your* bloody job. Don't dae it for the foreman, or the managers, or the owners. Dae it for yerself. Dae it so you can call yourself one o' the best. Or go and get a job in England or Belfast or somewhere they don't care if one or two rivet heads are just a wee bit high. Come tae thing about it, you look a bit soft, are you sure you're no' English?"

Some of the men laughed, while Alex turned and walked away. He had made his point; he didn't want to force the younger man to have to challenge him again, he had lost face already and needed time to get over it. He would learn his lesson, or he'd be off Alex's crew. It was as simple as that.

Clyde-built ships and locomotives were renowned throughout the world. The miners who hewed the coal to power them; the foundrymen who forged the iron and steel to make them; and most of all, the shipyard men who built them; these were the aristocracy of the working class. And the west of Scotland boasted uncounted battalions of these men.

But above them all were the boilermakers, the Black Squad—the princes. They were the best: and they knew it.

***

Within a few months of Annie's death, the two families had settled into their new routine. Even Hughie seemed to have absorbed the loss of his mother; smiling and laughing as much as any wee boy. His sister Jean, two years his junior, was, on the face of it, also coping. But Kate was aware of how much the little girl clung to her and to Hughie. Jean was fine as long as her auntie or big brother was close by; otherwise she would be fretful and prone to tears.

The two younger ones had little or no memory of Annie, and Alex had decided he would not make too much of trying to make them remember. The only ritual he insisted on was at bedtime, when each child said goodnight to Annie's photograph on the mantelpiece.

Kate was mother to the extended family. She fed all six children in her flat each morning and evening, sitting them around a table enlarged by her husband, Jim, a skilled ship's carpenter. Betty and Alan were still in high chairs and Kate's own children, Robbie and Jenny, had the task of feeding their two smallest cousins. Each evening the three adults ate after the youngsters were packed off to bed in the two flats. Even here they were a single unit. The two older male cousins, Robbie and Hughie, slept in Alex's flat, while the girls, and for the moment baby Alan, slept next door with Kate and Jim. Alex had already decided that, when Alan was old enough for a bed, the three boys would have his bedroom and he would move into the bed recess in the kitchen.

The children had adapted to their new reality. Life had moved on.

Each evening, as soon as he had finished his supper, Alex said goodnight to Kate and Jim; looked in on the two boys and withdrew to his chair by his own fireplace. He reasoned that husband and wife needed time alone and anyway he was happy to immerse himself in his passion—reading. Thanks to the local library and the union's education department, Alex had access to an unending stream of literature. He devoured everything Dickens had written; all of Jack London and Upton Sinclair; 'The Last Voyage' and 'The Ragged-Trousered

Philanthropists'. His father had been a voracious reader and had passed the habit on to his son.

Alex's reading fed his sense of grievance and injustice. As far as he was concerned, his wife had died because Clydebank had inadequate medical provision. After he had run the twenty minutes to the doctor's consulting room, he had been made to wait almost half an hour while the doctor attended to his better-heeled patients. And he had let Alex run the twenty minutes back home, while the doctor followed a while later in his car.

Alex's reading had also opened his eyes to just how deficient his own schooling had been and the education still being provided to his children. He might not have been a revolutionary, but neither was he a supporter of the status quo.

Once a month Alex attended a meeting in his Masonic Lodge, where he met up with his younger brother, Ian, a waiter in the Central Hotel in Glasgow. The brothers were close but work and distance meant they rarely saw each other outside of Lodge meetings and Rangers games.

One evening, a few weeks before the end of 1929, the brothers were walking to the stop where Ian would catch his tram back to Glasgow after a particularly boring Lodge meeting

"I need to find a new job, Ian. In a few months the ship will be finished in our yard and I'll be out of work."

"What will you dae?"

"I don't know; there's nothing around here."

"It's the same everywhere; the railway works are laying men off every month. Still, the rich seem to be managing; the restaurant stays busy enough, thank God. Well, here's my tram. I'll see you next week at Ibrox, it should be a great game against Dundee."

"No, I think I'll give Rangers a miss for a wee while, I need to spend as much time as possible with the weans right now. But I'll see you here next month."

1929/30

CLYDEBANK, SCOTLAND

On the morning of Hogmanay, Clydebank awoke to a hushed world. It wasn't just that the yards were closed for the holiday; the uncanny stillness was down to the dense blanket of fog that had settled in the night.

"Where is everything?" demanded Hughie.

"Everything's just where it always was, son; you just cannae see it, because of the fog."

"You cannae see the ghosties and ghoulies either, but they're out there, in the foooog," his cousin Robbie moaned, in his best spooky voice.

"Away an' wheesht yourself; there's nae such things. I'm nearly six now, you cannae frighten me, Robbie."

Hughie tried to sound confident, but Alex could see his son was just a little unsure. The fog *was* intimidating; it was so thick, you could see no further than five or six feet ahead of your face. It would be easy to get disoriented, even in your own streets. Although it was after nine o'clock in the morning, the gas street lamps were still lit. The closest lamp was little more than a faint orange glow in the mist. The lamplighter had obviously judged that the lamps would stay on today.

"Come on you two, get dressed, we've got to work today; we've got to get the flat cleaned from top to bottom, and we're no' leaving it all to Auntie Kate."

"Why, Dad? It's a holiday, why can't we just play?"

"Because it's Hogmanay: All of the dirt and dust has to be gone before midnight. We need to start 1930 nice and clean. Even the coal bin has to be cleaned."

Robbie was appalled at the prospect.

"You're kiddin', Uncle Alex; the coal bin? It's absolutely clatty, we could never clean it."

"Oh yes we can, and we will. Now come on, let's go next door for breakfast."

After breakfast, the rest of the morning and afternoon was spent in a flurry of scrubbing and scouring. The range was washed, black-leaded and polished; the door and cupboard handles were worked over with Brasso until they sparkled.

Even though the fog refused to clear, Alex and Jim lifted the carpets from both flats and took them down to the back court. They brought out the plank of wood from the washhouse and fitted it over the railings so they could drape each carpet over it in turn. They beat the dirt out of the carpets and finished by forcefully brushing them. It was the only time of the year the men did any housework, and even then only under the close supervision of a woman. Many men refused to help, even on Hogmanay, perhaps because these were also the heaviest drinking days in Scotland.

"I cannae believe Kate does this hersel' every month," said Jim, catching his breath while Alex took over.

"I cannae believe it myself. I sometimes wonder if it's fair, I mean the way the women do all the work in the house, and deal with the weans too."

"It's just the way it is, Alex; an' we work damn hard all week too."

"Aye, I know, but still, it's every day."

While the carpets were up, Kate announced that this was the time for cleaning out the coal bins. She had deliberately been running down the coal in Alex's flat, and now she directed the boys to shovel up what was left into the coal shuttle. When this had been done, she pointed at the pile of coal dust and broken nuggets at the bottom of the wooden bin.

"See, that's one of the reasons we do this–all that dross can be burned. I'll show you."

Kate laid a sheet of newspaper on the floor in front of the coal bin. All of the planks making up the front of the bin had been removed one by one to get to the bottom, where she could use the shovel to gather up the pile of dust and nugget fragments into the middle of the newspaper. Then she wrapped the package up like an oversized sweetie.

"This'll be for the fire," she explained. "Now you two finish it off."

The boys set to and soon scraped up and wrapped the remaining dross and replaced the boards one by one in the slots running down each side of the bunker. Before each board was replaced, it was carefully wiped clean, until the coal box stood once again complete, and as clean as it would ever be. They tipped the contents of the coal shuttle back in, and transferred most of the coal from next door, so they could repeat the entire exercise in Kate's flat.

Robbie sighed to his cousin, but quietly, so his mother wouldn't hear.

"See what a waste of time that was? It's completely clatty again already!"

With the dirtiest job finished, Kate washed down the linoleum floors while keeping an eye on the boys cleaning out the cupboards.

Earlier in the week she had loaded the bed sheets into an old pram and taken them to the local steamie to be washed and passed through the heavy mangle to get them dry and pressed. Now all the beds were changed with fresh linen.

By five o'clock, both flats fairly sparkled. Every surface had been dusted and washed, or polished, or blackened. Cupboards and wardrobes had been emptied, cleaned and re-filled in a neat and orderly fashion. All that was left to clean were the people; all but the toddlers were now well and truly filthy. They would need to boil a lot of water. They would start with the youngest, even if they were the cleanest. As soon as the first pot of water boiled, it was poured into the zinc bath to be cooled with tap water; and nine-year-old Jenny washed her two youngest cousins, under her father's watchful eye. Next door, Kate supervised Hughie and Jean as they cleaned themselves, their aunt scrubbing their backs and washing their hair.

There would be a break now while more water was heated.

"Who wants toast?" asked Alex, getting the expected positive yells in response. It wasn't that the children were crazy for toast; but they loved making it themselves, on an extending fork in front of the fire.

When everyone, child and adult alike, was scrubbed, changed and fed, the three youngest were put to bed. Hughie was excited; this would be the first time he had been allowed to stay up until the bells. He would get to see in the New Year with the grown-ups.

At ten minutes to midnight, Alex pulled out his most cherished possession, his grandfather's magnificent gold pocket watch.

***

Alex's grandfather had died barely three months after witnessing Alex being initiated into the town's Masonic Lodge–the fifth generation of Campbell men to join.

The day after his grandfather's funeral, Alex's father had taken him into his bedroom.

"Your grandfather wanted you to have this, son. He knew I had your Uncle Robert's," he finished with a rueful smile.

His father's older brother, Robert, had been killed in an accident at work. His watch was his brother's only significant memento of his sibling.

"This isn't just your grandfather's watch, Alex, it's a real treasure, you need to look after it for the rest of your days. Look."

Alex only wore his watch on Sundays and holidays. He delighted in its heavy weight and elegant craftsmanship, but, of course, he couldn't wear it in the yard.

"Come on, Hughie we'll go next door now."

"But why can't we stay here with Robbie and everyone?"

"You'll see Robbie in a few minutes; now we need to go to our own house."

On the stroke of midnight, there was the most almighty racket as every whistle and every horn on every ship and crane in every yard the length of the River Clyde was sounded at once. Since their tenement was directly across from the yard, the noise in the flat was deafening. Even through the fog, the cacophony would be heard the length of the river; from Greenock and Dumbarton, through Clydebank and Govan, to Glasgow itself. Most years, when the air was clear, the noise could be heard thirty or more miles away.

When the racket had died down, Alex gathered his son in his arms and whispered in his ear, "Happy New Year, Hughie."

Hughie thought it odd that his father held him so long; and for just a moment, he imagined he felt wetness on his cheek. But he must have been mistaken, he decided.

As he lowered his son to the floor, Alex turned his face quickly away to pick up the two glasses he had poured earlier: whisky for himself, ginger for Hughie. They chinked glasses.

"Happy New Year, Dad."

A moment later, there was a knock on the door.

"Go open the door, Hughie," Alex instructed his son.

Hughie opened the door to discover Robbie standing there, holding a tray with three filled glasses, a lump of coal and three pieces of Dundee cake on a willow pattern plate.

Hughie was confused. "Why didn't you just open the door and come in? And what's all this?"

Alex arrived to stand behind his son, "Come in Robbie, you're very welcome as our first foot."

"Mum said you might prefer a beer now, Uncle Alex."

"Quite right too. Come and sit for a minute and we'll drink to 1930."

When they were seated, Alex explained to Hughie.

"Robbie's our first foot: the first person to step over our threshold in the New Year. He brings us coal so we'll always be warm; food, so we won't be hungry; and drink, so we won't be thirsty. And he's tall, dark and handsome, so we'll be lucky."

"He's never tall, dark and handsome—he's Robbie!"

"Aye, he is too. Come on, drink up to a good New Year. A better New Year."

Robbie saw his uncle glance at his Auntie Annie's photo on the fireplace and had the grace to look away.

When they had finished their drinks, Alex picked up his bottle of whisky, another lump of coal and a box of shortbread, bought for the occasion.

"Can I be first foot for Auntie Kate and Uncle Jim?" asked Hughie.

Alex ruffled his son's hair as he ushered the two boys to the door.

"Sorry, son, you cannae be a first foot: You're still too wee; and anyway, you've got your mother's colouring. No girls and no redheads, that's the rule."

1930

CLYDEBANK, SCOTLAND

The mighty ship was almost ready for her launch. 384 looked less like a hull now, and more like the luxury liner she would soon become. The workers who swarmed all over the immense vessel represented an incredible mix of skills—painters, cabinet makers, electricians, plumbers, joiners, tilers, glaziers—a hundred crafts working to construct and equip a floating city. Her finishing teams had yet to begin installing the chandeliers, dressers, stained glass, decorative panelling and other fine furnishings; this would be done in the fitting out dock. But they were preparing and measuring; everything had to be planned and materials had to be ordered.

Her three funnels had not been installed, but her upper decks had been added, so she was even taller than she was during the bitter years when she lay abandoned.

But perhaps the biggest transformation of all since that momentous day when the man from the Ministry had visited Clydebank, was that the bare, rusting metal of 384's hull, was now shimmering white paint above her red waterline. On a sunny day, the streets around the ship were bathed in reflected light.

Hundreds of tons of heavy chain had been temporarily attached to her keel, to slow her passage down the greased slipway. Without this tremendous weight holding her back, at launch the ship would beach herself on the far bank of the Clyde. But the men preparing for the big day were veterans of a hundred launches of large vessels, admittedly none as huge as 384. Still, the remote possibility of beaching had been considered; tugs would be on hand to pull her free if necessary.

Temporary grandstands were built to seat 1000 invited guests, in addition to the 20,000 uninvited guests who would watch from any vantage point they could find. By tradition, when a truly big ship was launched, children were kept out of school, so wives and weans could witness the culmination of their fathers' work.

Company management and distinguished guests took up most of the grandstand; but by tradition the workforce was allocated the 200 rearmost seats. Thirty of these were given to union officials and shop stewards; the rest were the subject of a series of draws, with each craft and trade guaranteed a certain number of tickets.

Alex had decided to take Hughie with him, using the ticket that would have been Annie's. The little boy was six, going on seven and he idolised his father.

"Am I really going, Dad, really?"

"Aye, Hughie, you and me; we're going to see the greatest ship in the world being launched. One day you'll be able tell your children you saw it."

"Och, don't be daft, Dad, I'll never be that old. Mind, I'm nearly seven now, so that's quite old, I suppose. Will Jean be coming too?"

"No, just you and me. I've only got two tickets and anyway, she's too wee. She wouldn't be able to see anything."

"I'll tell her all about it after. Maybe I'll draw her a picture."

"That's a good idea, son. And remember, Hughie, there'll be hundreds of people there, you'll need to hold my hand all the time."

As the day of the launch approached, the weather turned unusually benign. It was still chilly in the mornings, but skies were blue and the air crisp with the promise of spring. There was no question of the launch date moving. 384 would be launched no matter what state she was in. There were only two tides a year high enough to allow a ship this size to pass over the sandbar in the river. There had been talk of dredging a deeper channel between the yard and the fitting out dock, but for now, until more orders came in, they would rely on Mother Nature and the accuracy of the planners.

Alex and the other shop stewards were summoned to a meeting in the shipyard office. There were only six stewards left on the site as the yard workforce had steadily diminished from its peak of 10,000 a year earlier. They had always understood they would soon be laid off until work got under way on the next project–always assuming there would be a next project. They presumed they were being brought in to hear the bad news.

To their surprise, they were ushered into an imposing boardroom, where one of the directors was waiting with the shipyard manager, John MacLeish. The room was panelled in rich exotic woods to set off the oil portraits of generations of directors of the company. MacLeish addressed them. Alex thought he looked uncomfortable.

"Thanks for coming in. As you know, the launch of 384 is on Thursday. Because of the size and unique design of the ship, there has been tremendous interest from all over the world. In fact, I can tell you that the launch of 384 will be transmitted by wireless radio to the United States and the colonies, all over the globe. But this also means there has been an unprecedented demand for grandstand tickets. I'm afraid we're going to have to reduce the workforce allocation on this occasion–to 100 tickets."

There was a collective gasp from the union delegates; but these were seasoned negotiators who knew better than to speak in haste. By custom, the most senior shop steward spoke first. At that moment, this was Jock Archibald, a master carpenter.

"You'll be giving us the use of a room for our discussions before we give you our response?"

The director spoke up, "Mr MacLeish and I will wait next door for fifteen minutes; that should be time enough, I imagine."

To everyone's surprise, Alex rapped the table for attention.

"Before you leave, I'd like to understand where the 100 tickets you hope to take from us would be going."

John MacLeish answered, "I don't think that's relevant. I explained that we have many more requests than is customary, and from all over the country, all over the world."

"We'll be the judges of what's relevant to our decision, Mr MacLeish."

As always, Alex's words carried authority.

Before a disagreement could develop into a full-blown argument, the director, his name was Ballantine, spoke again.

"It's quite alright, Mr MacLeish; I'll be happy to furnish that information."

He turned to the other side of the table.

"Around fifty are required for additional newspaper reporters and photographers from around the world and to accommodate the requirements of the BBC wireless technicians and their equipment, which is somewhat bulky, as I understand. The rest are for Members of Parliament; for the party attending on Her Majesty the Queen and for certain of our suppliers from

England who normally decline our invitations, but who have, on this occasion, accepted."

Alex nodded his acknowledgement and the two managers left the room.

Exactly fifteen minutes later, the door swung open and the two managers returned. As had been agreed with his colleagues, Alex addressed them.

"Well over 12,000 men have worked on that ship over the past few years. Seven of them died in accidents of various kinds; some of which could have been avoided if you had been attentive to the unions."

He raised his hand as MacLeish tried to interrupt. "No, you'll do me the courtesy of hearing me out.

"As is customary, 200 seats have been set aside for those 12,000 men and their families. By now, as you well know, everyone who's going has been told. They're excited, their wives and children are excited. And now you want us to inform half of them they can't come after all? Not on your life, Mr MacLeish, or yours, Mr Ballantine."

Alex paused and took a sip of water from his glass.

"Here's what we're prepared to do. We want more press at the launch; it's good publicity for the yard and for future orders. So, we'll surrender fifteen seats as our contribution to having more press in attendance. It won't be easy, mind, but we want to be reasonable. That's it. We'll have contributed more than our fair share to accommodate the press. But we don't care how many flunkeys accompany Her Majesty—that's your headache. And if you chose to invite more of your friends when you didn't have tickets for them—that's your dilemma too. You've got 800 tickets with which to fix your problems. We'll be here tomorrow morning and we'll be collecting 185 tickets. And we'll expect your gratitude and thanks."

"Now just a minute, Mr, Mr…"

Ballantine had never met the union delegation before. MacLeish leaned in and whispered in his ear.

"Just a minute, Mr Campbell. We are under no obligation to provide you with any tickets at all. There has never been a formal agreement regarding the allocation of launch tickets. The fact that we have been generous in the past, and I would suggest, remain generous today, should not be used a pretext for a dispute."

Alex responded immediately. "We're not having a dispute; we're making you a generous offer, and one which could be withdrawn, I might add. You waited until the last possible moment to spring this on us—because you thought it would be too late for the unions to do anything; the ship's finished in this yard after all. You thought you could just steamroller us, even though you must have known this difficulty was coming months ago, didn't you?"

Alex paused once more, but again he wasn't contradicted. "That was a major miscalculation, gentlemen. I guarantee that without our co-operation, nothing is leaving this yard, and certainly not that ship."

One of the other union representatives interrupted at this point,

"Someone has to knock away the chocks on Thursday, Mr Ballantine. How are you with a sledgehammer? How would you like to stand in front of 60,000 tons of ship and hammer away the only thing that's holding it back?"

Ballantine's face flushed as he spoke, "I do my job, and I expect the union members to do theirs. And I expect appreciation, not belligerence, when we demonstrate our generosity by offering you 100 seats, and, let's not forget, an excellent lunch for which there is no charge. If it wasn't for Mr MacLeish here, you would have no…"

Alex pushed his chair back with a clatter as he stood up, quivering with rage, "Don't you bloody condescend to us. You're not the lord of the manor dispensing favours to his serfs. You've never given us a damn thing we haven't earned a hundred times over. Will you be going on the inaugural cruise, Ballantine? To do your job, I expect you'll say. And what about your wife, who'll be joining you, no doubt? Will she be doing her job? And those two lovely daughters of yours? Inspecting the boilers maybe, helping in the engine rooms perhaps? And are you paying anything to take your family on this wonderful, round-the-world holiday? No? I didn't think so. So don't you bloody dare tell us to be grateful for the scraps from your table."

Alex took a breath, but no one spoke into the echoing silence.

Alex studied the two individuals on the other side of the table. He was calm now, speaking in measured tones as he looked down at his own reflection on the polished table. Everyone had to lean in to hear his words. He raised his head.

"Like most of us in this room I served in the war; and aye, I saw many gallant officers–like Mr MacLeish here."

Alex raised his head and glanced briefly at the yard manager, before moving his focus to the dapper director, holding his eye in his gaze.

"But I also saw many arrogant fools, safe in the rear, ordering their men to certain death. Well, it's 1930, Ballantine, no' 1910; times have changed–we've changed. The days of being grateful for your munificence are long over and the sooner you recognise that, the better."

He turned to his colleagues, "Come on, brothers, we've heard enough."

As the union men pushed back their chairs, once more Alex turned to face the yard manager.

"Mr MacLeish, we'll be back in the morning for our tickets. And the offer to relinquish fifteen seats is hereby withdrawn. You'll have all 200 tickets for us, or the ship stays where she is. We'll have 500 men on the slipway in front of that ship on Thursday morning, with their wives and weans; and they'll move when we tell them to, not before. See what your journalists make of that. And, Mr Ballantine, if she isn't launched on Thursday, she'll miss the tide and she'll sit here for six months. I don't expect your shareholders or Her Majesty will be best pleased. You may have to forget about that knighthood after all. Good day, gentlemen."

***

"What are you doing here at this hour, Mr Campbell? And why are you dressed…"

Alex interrupted the headwaiter, "It's my brother, Ian; he's sick, too sick to work, and anyway, the doctor said it's catching, so he knew he couldn't come to the restaurant. But he didn't want to let you down, so I'm here to work his shift, then I'll do my own. I'll be a bit late starting on the dishes, but I know I can manage."

The headwaiter scrutinised Alex. His brother's black jacket was tight across Alex's broader frame, but he could see that Alex was, as always, clean-shaven, spotless. And although the kitchen wasn't the headwaiter's domain, he had learned from the chef that Alex was a diligent worker. But going from kitchen helper and cleaner to waiter?

"Your brother is a good man, Mr Campbell, and I appreciate what you're both trying to do. Do you think you can manage?"

"Ian thought perhaps Miss Sullivan could take on his tables, and I would assist Mr Grant. That way I wouldn't have to actually take the orders. Not that I wouldn't be willing to try, but Ian explained about changes and special requests and so on, and I know I might make mistakes."

"Your brother is correct, and yes, I think his plan is a good one. Let's try it shall we? And I'll talk with the other staff: I think we can make sure you're not more than an hour late getting into the kitchen."

Alex had been laid off the week after 384 was launched and sent on her way to the finishing yard–on schedule and now christened the *Empress of the Oceans*. For the second time in his life, he suffered the humiliation of applying for the dole and facing the soulless busybody who came to the house to assess his entitlement to the meagre support available. At first the bureaucrat had insisted that the two families were a single household, and therefore ineligible for anything, since Jim Craig was still working at the fitting out yard. Eventually however, he was persuaded that Alex had to support his own four young children and he had grudgingly approved the application.

For the next four weeks, Alex tramped the streets; but there was just no work available, even for a man with his excellent reputation. He was just about at his wit's end, when his brother Ian appeared at the flat just after nine o'clock one morning.

"Last night Giuseppe Bianchi fell and broke his hip. He's the night cleaner at the restaurant. If you come in with me now, I think we can get you his job before anyone knows there's even a vacancy. What do you think?"

"What's the job?"

"You start at nine at night, washing dishes and pots and cutlery then, when the place is closed, you'd wash down all the kitchen equipment—ovens, cookers, steamers and so on. Then do the walls and floors. Oh, and you take the big bin of dirty linen round to the hotel laundry before midnight. You finish around half-five in the morning. The first tram going out of Glasgow isn't until half-six though, so you'll have an hour to wait. It won't pay great, I don't suppose, and it isn't what you're trained to do of course but, well, there's nothing else."

"No, it's fine, it's great; anything at all is great. Come on, I'll just go and tell Kate what's happening and we can get going. How did this Giuseppe guy get hurt anyway?"

"Poor guy: He climbed up on top of a counter to get to the big extractor fan, to clean it. He fell off, badly. I suppose they'll finally buy a ladder now; apparently he asked for one a million times."

Alex got the job, and a ladder. Rather than wait an hour every morning, he walked the two hours home and saved the tram fare. He slept every morning and spent afternoons with his children. He read to them and managed to get Jean reading before she started school. He supervised homework and took Hughie and Kate's two children to Glasgow's Art Gallery. He took them so often that the staff began greeting them by name.

One day, while they were standing in front of the Rembrandt painting, *A Man in Armour*, Alex heard a group of men discussing a group of paintings on the opposite wall. One of the men wore a silver-grey cravat and was talking knowledgeably about the paintings. When there was a break in their discussion Alex approached the group and addressed him.

"Excuse me, I'm sorry to interrupt your conversation, but my son has a question about one of these paintings that you may be able to answer."

The man looked at him in surprise, but Alex could see he was intrigued rather than annoyed.

"And what would be the question?"

"Well, I study each artist as much as I can before bringing the children here to see the paintings. So, I've told them something about Rembrandt and his life and how important he is. But Hughie has a question I can't answer."

"Let's by all means hear Hughie's question."

The man led Alex across the room to where the three children were waiting patiently.

"Now, who has the question?" he asked, in a pleasant, welcoming tone.

Hughie looked at him without embarrassment. "I have two questions. My dad says this might be

Alexander the Great, but maybe not. How can we not know? But my *real* question is, how did Rembrandt make it look like metal when we know it isn't, but it looks like it is? How can he do that?"

The man looked at Hughie with interest.

"Two good questions, young man. The painting used to be called *Alexander*, but all the early records have been lost, so we don't know for sure if that was its original name. All we can say for sure, is that it is supposed to be someone from hundreds of years before Rembrandt lived, because the style of the armour is an attempt to look antique. As to your real question; well, that is the essence of a great artist. He can make you see something that isn't there. Look really closely at the painting; no closer than that, put your nose an inch from the canvas. What do you see?"

"Not much, different colours. It doesn't look like anything now—it looks like paint."

"Now slowly bring your head away, slowly, slowly."

"Oh! Look! Now it's metal!"

"That's right. The skill of the artist is to trick you into seeing what he wants you to see—metal, or a flower, or a face; when all that's really there is paint. As to how he does it, well that's something you can only learn by studying lots of paintings for a very long time. That is the essence of art, to make us see something that isn't there."

"You mean like the grass in the painting over there? We studied that one last week."

Now the man was clearly intrigued. "You studied it last week?"

Now Robbie spoke up. "Uncle Alex brings us every week; we study one or two paintings then we write about them. Sometimes we copy them as well."

The curator studied the small group of children ranged around him. He could see they were well looked after, but he could also see their clothes were threadbare and patched. The man who had approached him, the uncle and father to the group, was younger than himself. He had the callused hands of a manual worker and was clearly intelligent, with ambitions for his family.

He addressed Alex. "This is my card, I'm Tom Honeyman, the Director of the museum. Whenever you come, ask for me and if I'm free, I'll join you, and we can visit the paintings together. We've got more artworks in our storeroom; we can visit those as well if you like."

Ian had fallen ill nine months after Alex started at the restaurant. For five days and nights Alex worked two jobs, from eleven in the morning until five o'clock the following morning. To avoid the journey back and forth to Clydebank he lived with Ian and his wife, Agnes, and their two young children. From then on, Alex became the relief waiter, covering any absences among the dining room staff. Gradually he learned to wait on tables himself, dealing with the foibles of the demanding guests.

Six months later, on a Sunday evening and with the children all in bed, Alex asked Kate and Jim if he could sit with them a while longer.

"I've been thinking about the future and I want to discuss something with you both."

Kate and Jim looked at each other across the table, where they sat nursing cups of tea after their meal. They had no idea what Alex was about to say.

"In three months or so, the *Empress* will be finished, and you'll be laid off, won't you, Jim?"

"Aye, that's the truth, Alex. Three months, at most."

"There's still nae work, none whatsoever. That's been on my mind. And so is something else. Robbie will be fourteen next year, but I don't want him to leave school. He's a very bright boy and anyway, he'd only be going right on the dole, and he'd get nothing. So, I want Robbie, and Hughie as well in a few years, I want them to go to the Academy."

Kate looked at her husband, clearly confused. She turned back to her brother-in-law.

"What academy, Alex? What are you talking about?"

"Glasgow Academy. I want Robbie and Hughie to go to Glasgow Academy. And then, to the university."

Alex might as well have said that he wanted his nephew and his son to go to the moon. Jim looked at his brother-in-law and at his wife.

"I don't understand what you're talking about. Glasgow Academy? What are you sayin', Alex? Glasgow Academy? That's for posh folk, rich folk. And university? Who, I mean how, whatever gave you this idea, Alex?"

"I've been thinking about this for years, Jim. Why can't our weans get a proper education? They're as smart as any youngsters anywhere. I'll tell you why—money and privilege. Well, I'm sick of it. Our boys are not going to follow their fathers and grandfathers. They're never going to sign on for the dole. Ever."

Impassioned now, he carried on.

"Listen, I've been investigating. I know you're not a Mason, Jim, but I am. There's grants and bursaries, and I think I can get one for each of the boys. That won't be enough, I'm well aware. There's books and uniforms and whatever else to be paid for. I don't want the boys to want for anything. I don't want them to be seen as charity cases. Whatever the rest have, our boys will have the same.

"I talked with John MacLeish. He's a good man. Sure, we fought all the time, he's the manager of the yard, but he never lied to me and he never looked down on us. He's been meeting with the Empress Line, the owners, about the handover of the *Empress*. He's pretty sure he can get me a job on board, as a steward, which pays well, and all found. And you could take my job at the restaurant, Jim. Between me and Ian, well, we're well thought of, and it would be easy for you to take my place. Then my wages could go for the boys' education, and more besides for the housekeeping."

For an eternity no one spoke. Kate and Jim looked at each other, struggling to embrace the scope of what Alex had just proposed. Jim pulled himself together first.

"You'd be away a lot, maybe for months at a time. Hughie will miss you something awful. And so will the rest of them, especially after the past months, when you've been with them so much."

"And I'll miss them, all of them. But we cannae let this family drift into poverty, we just can't. It's nae use putting our heads in the sand. There's absolutely nothing here; nae work, nae money, nae future. And Robbie's old and sensible enough to take the young ones to the Art Gallery. I told Tom Honeyman my plan and he's going to help. The weans'll get help every week *and* he'll support the boys' applications to the Academy. He's an influential man; it'll mean a lot when the Academy considers them."

Kate finally spoke up and surprised both of the men, as she addressed her husband.

"I agree with Alex. Yes, the weans will miss him, and us too. And I know he'll miss us; but we need to plan for the future. Glasgow Academy would be the turning point for this family. We've been stuck here for generations; working hard, doing our best and look where it's got us—facing poverty yet again. If Alex can bring himself to do it, we'll help. And another thing. It's what Annie would have wanted."

1934

SOMEWHERE IN THE INDIAN OCEAN

The humid air was heavy and still, as was the gray-blue ocean—except that is, for the sharp white line stretching back to the far horizon. For all her enormous size, the *Empress's* progress was marked by an unusually tight wake, a tribute to her narrow proportions and efficient engines, especially during her winter cruise, when she ran on only two propellers.

It was hard to be specific about the time of day. Locally, it was the hour after dawn. On the ship's clocks, it was 7:55. On a few wristwatches, it was 10:55. These were the passengers who insisted upon setting their timepieces by the *next* port of call, not the last one.

For the crew, it was five minutes before a watch change, a new shift. Red Watch had been at work since 4 o'clock. Cleaners, bakery, laundry, breakfast prep, and of course the usual complement of deck and engine room hands and an electrical stand-by crew—all of these and more were about to be relieved.

Some of the *Empress's* crew made up Land Watch, those who worked conventional shoreside office hours: hairdressers, doctors, fitness instructors, stenographers, and the like. Then there those assigned to no watch at all: first class stewards, entertainment and education staff, and, of course, the Captain; but even they lived by the four-hour rhythm of the watch handovers.

A few lucky Red Watch members had already been tapped on the shoulder by their opposite number in Blue Watch and could have been found settling down for some well-earned sleep. The decks were pristine, the panelled walls in the passageways and dining rooms glowed above spotless carpets. Breakfast buffets had been loaded; dining tables draped in fresh linen. Ices were freezing and marinades were working their magic on lunchtime ingredients.

Blue Watch crew were welcomed by the smell of fresh warm bread and breakfast pastries, but they had little time to appreciate the delicious aromas before they set about serving breakfast; producing eggs in any one of half-a-dozen ways and toast in any degree of 'doneness'; handling requests for kedgeree, porridge, sausages, kippers, all the while topping up displays of fruit and pastries.

As soon as a pair of passengers moved towards one of the dining rooms, an army of housekeeping staff assaulted their cabins; sweeping, dusting, making up beds, changing linen according to their rotation schedule, clearing away cups, plates and glasses from late-night suppers.

This was the busiest time of the day for the first-class stewards. Their cossetted passengers generally wanted breakfast served in their suites—and all at more or less the same time.

On the bridge, the Captain was reviewing the overnight reports and listening to a briefing from his Second Officer, Thomas Peters.

All over the majestic liner, dozens of crew members were checking off tasks completed or assessing what had yet to be done. There were crew whose responsibilities were keeping the *Empress* on course and on schedule and on ensuring her equipment and complex systems were working efficiently. But the overwhelming majority were tasked with attending to the creature comforts and enjoyment of passengers and doing so invisibly whenever possible.

As the minute hand reached twelve, the Captain turned to his Second Officer.

"Thank you Mr Peters, I have the helm."

1935

MEDITERRANEAN APPROACHES

By each of the liner's thirty-odd clocks, it was five o'clock in the morning; an hour before dawn, and the sea was once again serenely calm. Alex took a final pull on his cigarette, inhaling the scene with the fragrant smoke. They were almost there. He always made sure he was up early when the ship was making an early landfall, and now the Mediterranean was less than an hour away. He thought he could already sense a change in the ship's motion, a slight easing of speed as they approached Gibraltar; the guardian of another sea. This would be his fourth passage through the Pillars of Hercules, but he still felt a thrill, just as he had the first time.

He leaned over the rail and flipped the butt of his cigarette overboard. Like almost all of the crew, the lure of cheap cigarettes had tempted Alex to take up smoking. He smoked half-a-dozen a day but knew he would stop when he returned to shore life.

He had seen so much in the past three years, been to places he had dreamt about as a boy, and places he had never heard of before signing on as a steward on the

'Empress of the Oceans', as a member of her inaugural crew.

After her launch, and right on schedule, *'Empress of the Oceans'*, the former Hull 384, had been moved into the fitting out dock where her funnels had been added. Craftsmen had installed electrical and heating systems, exotic wood panelling, stained glass windows and Templeton carpets. A small, but fully equipped hospital was kitted out; along with a cinema, gymnasium, theatre, multiple kitchens and dining rooms, hair salons, a well-stocked library.

A million and one items of provisioning had been craned aboard—bed linens; crystal glasses for first class, cut glass for tourist class; champagne, clarets and sherries; silver service cutlery; pots and pans of every description; uniforms and card games; books and musical instruments; the list was seemingly endless.

Jim had arranged for Alex and Ian to come aboard the great ship in the final stages of preparation and Ian had fallen in love.

"I had no idea! This puts the restaurant to shame. I've never seen such amazing table services before. And the sculptures and paintings! You could be in the Art Gallery. I can see why you'd want to work here, Alex."

"It's very nice, but I'd rather I didn't have to work here."

"I know, and I understand why you're doing this. I'm proud of you. What will you be doing exactly?"

Alex had been taken on as a steward in tourist class, where he would be responsible for attending to the needs of the passengers in twenty-odd cabins.

Two nights before Alex left for Liverpool, he and Ian met for a farewell drink.

"Here, I want you to take this. You'll be mixing with the toffs; this'll help remind them you're just as good as they are."

Ian was holding out a heavy Victorian gold chain made to complement their grandfather's watch. It was in a wine-red velvet pouch that Ian had persuaded the hotel seamstress to make, an envelope to hold watch and chain together. The gold chain glowed, picking up the colour from the rich fabric. It would replace the worn leather fob Alex had been using.

Alex was moved by his younger brother's generosity. "I don't know what to say," he stammered.

"You'll look right smart checking the time when you're in Constantinople. And it'll keep you in mind of me and the family."

"I don't need a watch chain for that, but thanks."

He slipped the chain into its pouch and put it in his pocket. He stretched across the table to shake his brother's hand.

And now he had been to Constantinople, and to Cannes and Cairo and Colombo and dozens of other exotic ports of call. He knew the area around New York harbour almost as well as he knew the streets of Clydebank.

He had arranged for his pay to go straight to Kate. His tips would pay for cigarettes, with more than enough to spare for the little souvenirs he bought for the children when he was allowed to go ashore on the longer port stops. He sent them a postcard from every new port and they knew he expected the older ones to write something about each place he visited–he read all of their reports on his return.

All in all, the family was managing well, what with Alex's wages, and the fact he spent so little when he was at sea; which was most of the time. The *Empress* sailed to New York and back every two weeks all summer long. Alex missed every fourth trip and came home to Clydebank. In the last week of November, Alex was onboard when *Empress* left New York for her annual world cruise, picking up her European passengers at Monte Carlo, and finishing back in New York in the middle of April.

Alex was good at his job and popular with the passengers. So much so, that halfway through his second year, he had been promoted to work in first class. This meant he had only four staterooms to manage, but with the potential for much bigger tips at the end of each voyage.

As the dramatic outline of the Rock of Gibraltar came into view, Alex gently tugged on his watch chain and slid his gold watch out of his waistcoat pocket. He checked the time and, as Ian had predicted, thought fondly of his brother and the rest of the family, doubtless shivering on a cold Scottish morning. It was time to prepare for the day.

His clients on this trip were an interesting and colourful group.

When he had seen Jimmy Walker come aboard in New York with a gorgeous young woman on his arm, Alex decided he had never seen anyone quite so debonair. The man was a mannequin, resplendent in a blue suit (Alex was to learn Jimmy had no less than twelve suits in his baggage), pale blue silk shirt, dark blue silk tie. On his cuffs were matching sapphire links, and a sapphire glinted on his tiepin. The only items of clothing that were not a shade of blue, were his pearl-grey fedora and matching spats.

"Welcome aboard, sir. I'm Alex, and I'll be looking after you on your cruise."

"Pleased to meet you, Alex, I'm Jimmy Walker, Mayor Jimmy Walker of the great city of New York. And this is my fiancée, Miss Betty Compton."

While shaking Alex's hand, Walker slid a $50 bill into his breast pocket. "I'm sure you'll look after us very well, Alex. Show us the way."

When he had settled the first two guests, Alex returned to the gangway to await the arrival of his next charges.

"Wilbur Fredericks, and this here is mother, Joanne, and this angel is our daughter, Christina. This is her first trip overseas, she's mighty excited."

Wilbur Fredericks was a large, jovial man. Although Wilbur carried a little too much weight, Alex could see the echo of a once-powerful figure under the slightly tight three-piece suit. Mrs Fredericks was six inches shorter than her husband, but probably weighed almost as much. She had a pleasant round face and an ample bosom that parted the way before her. Standing beside her parents, Christina was a total contrast. She was a beautiful waif with large cornflower blue eyes and a trim figure. She was an only child and cherished by her doting parents.

Alex's fourth suite would be empty until they picked up the European passengers at Monte Carlo, so he had only one more American couple to greet, a Mr and Mrs Campbell, and it looked as if the Campbells were going to miss their departure. The gangways for tourist class had been withdrawn, and the dock team were approaching the first-class ramp, when a stream of a dozen cars and limousines hurtled onto the dock, squealing to a halt at the foot of the gangway.

Five or six people tumbled out of each car, blowing horns, throwing streamers and generally making as much noise as possible. A group of porters worked swiftly to lift heavy baggage out of two of the cars and manhandle it aboard. The Captain was observing the scene from on the bridge high above and at his signal, the ship's great horn sounded, drowning out the farewells and making it clear it was time to go.

As Alex watched, two figures emerged from the mobile party; a tall, elegant man with a fine, almost feminine face, and a petite woman, clearly older, but dressed impeccably and stylishly. The couple teetered up the incline, the woman holding her husband's arm tightly.

"Mr and Mrs Campbell, welcome aboard the *Empress of the Oceans*. You had us worried for a while. I'm Alex, and I'll be looking after you on your trip."

As Alex spoke, he recognised the woman; this was Dorothy Parker, the famous writer and wit, and her husband, Alan Campbell. Since taking up his duties in first class, Alex had become a student of the society pages in the glossy magazines in the ship's library.

A smile spread over Dorothy's lips as she saw recognition dawn.

"If it's all the same to you, Alex, you can certainly look after Alan if he trips, but I'd rather you catch me if I do. Now, lead us to a bar forthwith, it is essential we do not stop drinking, the consequences are simply too dreadful to contemplate."

On the second morning at sea, Alex took a breakfast tray into Jimmy Walker's stateroom suite. Mr Mayor was still in a silk robe, but Miss Compton was dressed and looking sensational. Betty Compton had been a successful actress and showgirl and she turned heads wherever she went. So far, she and Walker had been undemanding guests and unfailingly polite.

"What's the weather forecast for today, Alex?"

"Good, Miss: fine weather and a calm sea. We should make good time and have a comfortable day's passage."

"Excellent, just what I wanted to hear. We would like to host a small cocktail party before dinner tonight. Is that something you could organise for us?"

"Absolutely, Miss Compton, no trouble whatsoever. How many guests do you anticipate?"

"Not too many. Here, I've written out invitations, twelve guests in total, if they all come that is. Can you see these are delivered this morning, please?"

Alex glanced at the names on the invitations. At the top of the list were two of his other passengers, Dorothy Parker and her husband. He delivered their invitation first, along with a pot of coffee; dry toast, slightly burned, and a pitcher of Bloody Marys.

Dorothy opened the envelope and extracted the invitation.

"Well, well, Little Boy Blue. How droll. Steward Alex, do you know why our former Mayor is on board? I only learned because we were a trifle tardy in boarding, although I dare say some telegrams have been received by now."

Dorothy had taken to calling Alex, 'Steward Alex', every time she saw him, which was often. First thing in the morning, last thing at night and every time one or both of the Campbells came back to their suite to change or lie down, Alex would be summoned and asked to provide cocktails, or whisky with water on the side; water which he always removed untouched when he returned to clear up.

"I see you're intrigued. Hizzonner was tipped off he was about to be arrested, so he packed his baggage, and his luggage too; and booked last-minute tickets on a *very* long trip. The morning of our departure he cabled his resignation to the Governor: Mr Roosevelt was pleased to accept it. Word has it our former mayor and the baggage will be wed soon; perhaps your Captain will be asked to do the needful."

Whether or not any or all of the invited guests had heard of Jimmy Walker's fall from grace, Alex wasn't sure. In any event they all accepted his invitations. Alex had recruited a cocktail waitress to help him with the party. Stephanie was an attractive young woman with whom he had worked before, and always successfully.

It was understood that staff should be handsomely tipped when assisting with private functions and Stephanie knew how to ensure everyone had sufficient drinks to enjoy themselves, but not so much that they would embarrass themselves or their host. Alex and Stephanie had been friends since their first trip; she was married to Johnny, one of the ship's chefs and a friend of Ian's from their restaurant days in Glasgow.

Alex was careful to inform his fellow stewards which of their respective guests had been invited and was in turn briefed on any quirks he would have to deal with.

The party was a great success. Alex or Stephanie offered each new arrival a pre-emptive glass of champagne, which meant they only had to mix time-consuming cocktails for the few guests who insisted on an alternative. This allowed Alex time to make introductions and steer his hosts from one group to another, so ensuring they spent some time with everyone and avoided being monopolised by any one guest. Stephanie made sure all the glasses were regularly refreshed.

As the drinks flowed, the noise level in the stateroom increased along with the temperature. A group formed around Dorothy Parker and Jimmy Walker, who seemed to be enjoying each other, with Jimmy ostentatiously flattering Dorothy, while she gently teased him about being a dandy. Changing tack, Jimmy decided to test Dorothy's ego by bringing the conversation around to Clare Boothe Luce, Dorothy's only rival for the title of the wittiest woman in New York. Both women had come from fairly modest backgrounds and both had worked for *Vogue* and *Vanity Fair*. But unlike Dorothy, Clare Boothe had married serious money, and was now extremely wealthy.

Someone offered that, "Since she married Henry Luce, Clare has become a complete snob."

"Not at all," Jimmy defended her, "she is always kind to her inferiors."

Dorothy's riposte was immediate, "And where, pray, does she find them?"

Jimmy laughed and raised his glass to Dorothy; now the party would be remembered; his guests would dine out on having witnessed Dorothy Parker at her waspish best.

Soon after, the party broke up and the group made its way to the dining room where Alex had arranged for them to sit at one large table. As Jimmy turned to follow his guests out, he slipped $20 to Alex, "Thanks Alex, I saw how well you worked this evening, great job. You'll take care of the girl?"

"Of course, Mr Walker, and thank you."

After brief port visits to Madeira, Gibraltar and Algiers, *Empress* would make her first extended stop at Monaco. She was far too large for the simple port facilities, so the enormous liner would sit at anchor, while her tenders, and some locally hired launches, transported her passengers back and forth to the harbour. Although a new passenger list had not yet been distributed, word had spread that Noël Coward would be joining the ship at Monte Carlo. There was considerable excitement among the first-class passengers and crew as they awaited the arrival of the popular playwright, actor and songwriter.

A few years ago, Alex had seen Coward in his play *Private Lives* at the Liverpool Playhouse, and he was looking forward to meeting the author.

Noël Coward's morning arrival on the *Empress* was suitably theatrical. As his tender was tied carefully alongside the open entry hatch, a young crew member leaned forward to offer an assisting hand across the narrow gap between the tender and the platform.

"Thank you, young man. Oh dear, how unfortunate!"

Overcome by the moment, the deck hand had managed to lean over too far, toppling into the cool waters of the Mediterranean. He was quickly helped back on board, where he was further embarrassed when Coward swept a camel coat off his shoulders and wrapped it around the sodden seaman.

"You'll catch your death; it's a warm bath and a hot toddy for you, I think."

Alex stepped forward, "Welcome aboard, Master. I am your steward, Alex. If you would please follow me, I'll try to get you to your stateroom without further mishap."

"Well, Alex, you look reassuringly dry, so I feel safe in your hands."

When they arrived at Coward's suite, the songwriter immediately noticed the piano in the corner of his sitting room.

"I'm quite sure this does not form part of the standard furnishings on this wonderful vessel, does it, my dear?"

"I thought you might enjoy a piano, you'll be with us a while, I'm happy to say."

"One month. How resourceful of you."

There was a change in his tone as, for just a moment, he stepped out of playing the role of Noël Coward, performer–'Master' to friends and fans.

"And your thoughtfulness is very much appreciated. Thank you, Alex."

Moment over, he reverted to character, "Geoffrey, let us get these trunks opened then perhaps Alex here will show you to your hovel in the bowels of this old hulk. Alex, I believe you have some of my chums incarcerated aboard; Miss Dorothy Parker and Sir Roderick Broadchurch. Would you be kind enough to seek them out and enquire whether they and their respective cellmates might join me in a crust of bread and a cup of tepid water this evening? A gentle introduction to on board living is called for, I think. Geoffrey here will be happy to assist with the chopsticks and so forth, won't you, Geoffrey?"

Geoffrey and Alex settled Noël Coward in his suite and oversaw the unpacking of his trunks. That task completed, Alex escorted Geoffrey further along the corridor to one of the cabins designed for the personal staff of first-class passengers, far from a hovel.

"He's nice, isn't he?" Alex observed.

"He's lovely. He's incredibly generous, even to total strangers, and he hates being cruel to people, even when they are being terrifically difficult. We're here on doctor's orders. He has been overworking dreadfully–a month at sea will do him a power of good. Then we have two weeks in Ceylon before heading back to England."

"Tiffin time, Geoffrey. Let us amble forth and see what rations are available to the inmates."

The two men walked slowly down the corridor until a door opened, and a chambermaid came out of one of the suites, carrying a large pile of used towels. They stopped to allow the girl to pass and, to give her more room, Coward stepped back a pace—and trod on the instep of Joanne Fredericks, who had been following them along the passageway.

He whirled round, "My dear lady, please excuse me. How dreadfully clumsy of me. I fear I have hurt you; I am so very sorry."

"Not at all; it was painful for only a second, and I'm fully recovered. I was daydreaming and should have paid more attention to where I was going. I'm joining my husband and daughter for lunch, and I was lost in my thoughts."

"You are exceedingly kind to forgive me. Please, let us escort you to lunch, in case there are yet more uncoordinated boors waiting to wreak further assaults on your person. Come, Geoffrey, we must form a protective cordon around … I'm sorry, we have not been introduced. Noël Coward at your belated service."

He held out a perfectly manicured hand.

"Joanne Fredericks, from Pasadena, California. Mr Noël Coward, the playwright?"

"The very same, madam. And this is Mr Geoffrey Brown, my assistant."

"Last year, June, I think it was, we saw *Cavalcade* at the Roxy. It was swell, absolutely swell. It is a pleasure to meet you, Mr Coward, a real pleasure."

The three of them made their way to the promenade restaurant where they found Wilbur and Christina Fredericks already at their table.

"Mr Coward, Mr Brown, this is my daughter, Christina, and my first husband, Wilbur. This is Mr Noël Coward and Mr Geoffrey Brown."

Noël was laughing as he shook Wilbur's hand.

"You are her *first* husband?"

"She keeps telling me that if standards slip, she'll just have to find another one."

"Geoffrey, write that down, I shall steal that for my next play."

Wilbur spoke again, "Would you gentlemen care to join us for lunch?"

"I think that would be delightful; thank you, Wilbur."

Chairs were produced, and two more settings swiftly laid out. During the initial exchanges, young Christina was entirely silent, staring intently at her hands clasped firmly on her lap.

"Chrissie, I do think you might at least look at these two gentlemen, I don't think they bite."

Christina looked at her father and blushed.

"You could tell Mr Coward about the play; come on now, I'm sure he'd be delighted to hear all about it."

Wilbur turned to Noël, "Christina, Chrissie, had a part in one of your plays last fall, didn't you, darling?"

"One of *my* plays? Indeed I *am* delighted to hear that. Which play and what part did you have, young lady?"

Noël leaned in to hear Christina as she whispered, "I was Amanda in *Private Lives*."

"A very difficult part, a long part to learn."

Noël looked closely at the young woman, who was clearly discomfited by the attention. He decided to play a hunch. He stood up, ostentatiously fixed a cigarette into his extravagantly long holder, all the while sidling closer to Christina.

"What are you doing here?"

Immediately the young woman sat up straight in her chair and looked up to stare directly at him.

"I'm on my honeymoon," she said, dismissing him with the slightest toss of her head.

"Hope you're enjoying it."

With considerable deliberation, Christina picked up a bread roll and tore it roughly in half; sighing, *"It hasn't started yet."*

"Neither has mine." Noël responded with a huge smile. "Bravo, bravo. I loved the business with the bread roll, excellent improvisation."

Noël returned to his place and addressed Joanne.

"At this point, Joanne, I should say, *'Don't put your daughter on the stage'*."

To everyone's astonishment, Christina interrupted, *"She's a bit of an ugly duckling, you must honestly confess."*

Noël continued, *"And the width of her seat would surely defeat"*

Noël beamed and clapped as Chrissie rounded off his lyric.

"Her chances of success."

"I had been about to say, 'but on this occasion I would made an exception'. A young woman with such exquisite taste surely has a bright future ahead of her on Broadway."

He continued, "Wilbur and Joanne, and Christina of course, I am giving a small dinner tonight, I would be delighted if you would care to join us. And, Christina, you will meet Miss Dorothy Parker, a friend and something of a dramatist herself."

When the Fredericks family appeared at Noël's stateroom that evening, they read the note pinned to the door:

Cell 666: One month penal servitude for crimes against Dionysus and Melpomene.

"Who is Melpomene, Mr Coward?"

"Dionysus and Melpomene are respectively the god and goddess of theatre. As is invariably the case however, the male takes all of the glory and publicity and so poor old Melpomene is largely unknown. I shall start a society to redress the balance."

"Come here, child, and be introduced. This is the effervescent Mrs Dorothy Campbell and her husband, Alan. Mrs Campbell is so famous she uses a nom-de-plume, Miss Dorothy Parker, so she can travel incognito and mingle with the hoi polloi. And this is an old and dear friend, Sir Roderick Broadchurch and his adorable wife, Helena. I am delighted to introduce the Fredericks, Wilbur and Joanne and their talented daughter with impeccable taste, Christina."

Christina blushed once again, but under Noël's gentle banter she gradually lost her shyness and absorbed the conversations going on around her. After much negotiation with her father, they had agreed she could have one very small glass of sherry before dinner and a small glass of wine with dinner.

Noël and the *Empress* were well matched. Noël believed dinner parties should be amusing but should be framed in a formal setting–dinner party as theatre. The *Empress* was stocked with everything required. The table was set with silver and fine crystal, sparkling in the light of the candles set in the centrepiece. Fresh flowers graced each end of the table. While everyone stood around chatting, Christina nervously counted the silverware on the table–she had never seen so many utensils and was certain she would choose the wrong one. Alex spotted her confusion.

On the pretext of topping up her glass, which she politely declined, he whispered to her, "When each plate is served, take a sip of water and wait to see what knife or fork or spoon Lady Helena picks up. Those on the sides, work from the outside in."

She gave him an appreciative nod and began to properly relax.

Finally, Noël announced, "Let's eat, shall we? Thin gruel and slops I expect, but one can't complain. If we hadn't been so wicked, we shouldn't have been incarcerated here."

Christina found herself seated between Alan Campbell and Sir Roderick, who immediately put her at ease, "You must call me Roderick, my dear; and how do you like to be addressed–Christina, Chrissie, Chris?"

"My friends call me Chrissie."

"Well, I shall call you Chrissie, if I may. Now tell me more about your interest in acting and singing, I'm afraid I'm useless at both."

The first course was a light consommé. Christina was engrossed in one of Sir Roderick's tales of his service in India when they started to eat and was able to see which spoon he selected. When the prawn cocktail was served however, she decided to follow Alex' advice.

She had thought it odd when a silver bowl of water appeared by her hand. It had a slice of lemon floating in it, and Chrissie assumed this was yet another touch of European sophistication that hadn't make it to California; after all, there was already a glass of water in front of her. Presumably the lemon water was an accompaniment for the prawns. Carefully watching to see which cutlery Lady Helen picked up, she slowly sipped from her silver bowl.

Dorothy Parker opened her mouth, a cutting comment on her lips, only to change it to *'Ouch!'* as Noël kicked her under the table.

"Sorry, Dottie darling, something just slipped. One can't be too careful about little slips, can one?"

And he too picked up his finger bowl and took a sip, followed in time by everyone else.

The rest of the dinner proceeded without incident. The conversation was light and varied, skipping over the *Empress* and her luxuries, the various ports of call they had visited and could look forward to. Alan Campbell entertained Chrissie with stories from Hollywood and the various movie stars he and Dorothy had met. She decided he was a nice man who was solicitous of his famous wife and seemed not to mind that her profile was so much higher than his own.

Joanne Fredericks was fascinated by Dorothy and Noël's playwriting.

"You both write popular, light-hearted pieces, but then you produce serious, thoughtful works. How do you decide which to do next?"

Noël replied first. "An interesting question. For myself, I admit I do on occasion write with the bank manager in mind. My songs and revues are frothy and popular and I usually know I'm giving the public what they want."

Dorothy spoke up, "But Noël, people don't know what they want until you give it to them!"

"Well, that is sometimes true, I confess. There have been plays of mine, serious ones that the public have embraced; often to my, and my bank manager's, complete surprise and delight. But sometimes, light and frothy is what's required. Like right now, I think."

Dinner was by now finished and Noël led everyone to the piano where he sat down and entertained them with some of his 'light and frothy' comedy songs. While everyone was focussed on Noël, Chrissie approached Dorothy Parker and gently touched her arm. When Dorothy turned around, she was surprised to see Christina holding out a pen and a dog-eared copy of 'Enough Rope', her first book of poetry.

"I wondered, Miss Parker, if you might sign this for me; I admire your work very much."

For once, Dorothy was momentarily speechless, consumed by guilt at the cruel gibe she had been about to launch at this winsome young girl with her *faux pas* over the finger bowl. Thank God Noël had stopped her.

"Of course, darling, but you must call me Dorothy, I'm not so old, really."

She smiled and inscribed the well-thumbed book, *'To my new friend, Christina—a Princess for an Empress. Affectionately, Dorothy Parker'*.

She finished signing just as Noël ended his rendition of *'Mad Dogs and Englishmen Go Out in the Midday Sun'*.

"Noël," she called over the applause, "won't you sing something with Christina?"

"An excellent idea, Dottie. Come and join me, young lady."

Christina was hesitant, but her father nodded in approval and urged her forward.

"You'll kick yourself in the morning if you don't, sweetheart."

Noël shuffled along the piano stool to make room, and began singing, *'Don't Put Your Daughter On the Stage Mrs Worthington'*, gently prompting Christina to sing alternate lines. The applause was warm and heartfelt.

When she lay in bed later that evening, too excited to sleep, Christina thought it had been the most impossibly glamorous night of her life. Would anyone back home believe her stories? Her last thought before sleep finally claimed her, was that she didn't care if they believed her or not.

The last words of the evening came from Dorothy. As she and Alan took their leave, remarkably sober, Dorothy leaned in and kissed Noël on the cheek.

"Thank you, Noël darling, for stopping me from saying something wicked to that sweet young girl. But don't make a habit of kicking me, buster!"

***

The days rolled agreeably on. They stopped at Rome and Athens and marveled at the forlorn ruins of once splendid civilizations. They sailed on to Haifa in Palestine, where they disembarked into a fleet of buses—limousines for the first-class passengers. They spent a week ashore, driving to Jerusalem, enjoying Christmas in Bethlehem and finally leaving Palestine for Cairo and the Pyramids, where they rejoined the *Empress*, for their passage through the Suez Canal.

This year, Alex had been assigned to travel with his passengers on the overland section of their trip; on previous cruises he had remained on board for the short sail from Haifa to Suez where the ship waited for everyone to return.

Alex wasn't a particularly religious man, but he found Jerusalem an incredibly moving experience. To walk the same streets as Jesus! Of course, he knew everything had changed in 2000 years, but superficially the city seemed unaltered since biblical times. Beneath the grime and the hawkers he sensed the immense age of the stones forming the paths and walls and the ancient buildings. He found it easy to lose himself in the history all around him.

He also appreciated how much Hughie would have loved the Pyramids. The guides had led them deep inside to the empty tombs where they stood, awed, before the 4500-year-old hieroglyphics illuminated by flickering torches, looking just as they must have when the Egyptian artists worked on them. In the tight, claustrophobic spaces, the strange figures of men-gods with their attendant cats seemed to shimmer and move in the ever-changing shadows.

It was all completely surreal and brought home once again how far he was from home–in miles and in, he didn't know what exactly, but he could sense the growing gulf between the man he was now and the shop steward who had climbed the scaffolding wrapped around the *Empress* when she was still Hull 384.

It wasn't the first time he had felt the dislocation.

On his final cruise working in tourist class, Alex had been asked to help out at one of the formal dances in the first-class dining room. A section of carpet had been removed to reveal a dance floor, featuring as a centrepiece, an ornate marquetry compass rose inlaid in the polished wood. Late in the evening, not long before his shift was due to end, Alex was swept by a wave of emotion when the band played *'Always'*.

He was completely transported, imagining Annie dancing in his arms, not in her red spotted dress, but in a long flowing backless silver gown draped in soft folds from her lovely shoulders. He was in tails and Annie's eyes shone as she took in the wonderful scene; the music, the candles and champagne and the elegant dancers pirouetting around them. God, how his Annie would have loved this! And how beautiful she would have looked!

His reverie was shattered when a nasal voice nearby finally penetrated his consciousness.

"I say, waiter! How many times must one ask for service? Champagne, man, at the double!"

"Of course, sir, my apologies."

"Do you know, waiter? I've been wondering who you remind me of; and I've just remembered–father's undergardener. He was a bit slow on the uptake as well. No relation, I don't suppose? Probably not, you don't sound like a Devon man. Anyway, run along now and bring us some bubbly, the good stuff mind; there's a good chap."

Alex had long ago developed a thick skin, so the passenger's condescension rolled right off his back. No, what he resented, was being interrupted while dancing with his wife.

Meanwhile, Christina's familiarity with Noël and Dorothy gave her considerable cachet among the other young people travelling in first class. She found herself invited to parties and participating in deck games; and in the evening she went dancing with the group. They were mostly from New York, Philadelphia and Boston, and they were much more sophisticated and worldly-wise than her friends in Pasadena. Her parents weren't entirely happy with this development, but felt they had no choice but to allow their daughter some freedom. The group were the only first-class passengers of her age.

"We trust you, sweetheart, but be careful, not all of these kids will be as kind as they may appear. And remember, one glass of wine at the most."

"Yes, mother. Don't worry, I'll be careful."

And she was careful. But her interactions with Dorothy, together with the attention she was receiving from the young men, gave Christina a new air of confidence that only encouraged the boys even more.

The leg of the cruise from Suez to Bombay was a long one, six days at sea. The entertainment director and his team organised a series of activities, with a feature event each evening, all previewed in the ship's daily newspaper slipped under every cabin door each night while the passengers slept.

The ship had a costume library for fancy dress balls and themed dances; like the book dance, where guests had to go as a character from a famous book. There was a series of lectures, where they were given slide talks on the sights they would be seeing in India and Ceylon.

On some mornings, Alex would seek out Christina with an invitation to join Dorothy for breakfast. Christina eventually learned these were the days when Dorothy didn't have a 'rag', as she termed her hangovers. These visits became the highlight of her days. Dorothy would regale her with stories of New York and Hollywood and, on especially memorable mornings, they would collaborate on limericks and comic poems about their fellow passengers and the crew. For the rest of her life, Christina would treasure the album where she carefully pasted up the silly poems she had helped the great Dorothy Parker to write.

Dorothy's favourite pastime was parlour games; so when she was in the mood, she and Christina would round up eight or nine people and play Alphabet Minute, Charades, What Am I Thinking About?, What's My Job? or some of the many other games Dorothy knew. On these nights, Dorothy would be so involved in the games that she quite forgot to drink. When the fun was over, she would ask Christina; Chrissie, as she now called her, 'and you must call me Dottie' to take a walk around the ship with her.

When they arrived in Bombay, they were transferred onto a private train. First class passengers had suites with showers, a servant to attend to each family and a dedicated dining room. They visited Delhi and Agra and, of course, the Taj Mahal.

Soon after breakfast on the morning of their visit to the Taj Mahal, a young man knocked on the door to the Fredericks' compartment. As the train swayed along the tracks, Francis Fitzgerald asked the servant if he might have a word with Miss Fredericks.

"Miss Fredericks, Chrissie, some of the chaps have arranged a dinner this evening, overlooking the Taj

Mahal. I was hoping you would consent to be my guest?"

Frank Fitzgerald was on the fringes of the group that Christina mixed with. He was a diffident boy, no older than herself, and she realised that it had taken a great deal for him to extend this invitation.

"Thank you, Frank, that would be lovely. Yes, I would be delighted to be your date."

The day after the passengers set off on their overland trip, Alex went ashore and called into the company office to pick up his mail. There was a letter from Kate and one from each of the four older children. Kate sent updates about the children, all entirely inconsequential, but enough to provoke a wave of homesickness. There was also a letter from Ian - less intimate, but welcome nonetheless.

Dear Alex,

It still seems strange to be addressing letters to you in Bombay; letters that will catch up and pass you by somewhere on the seas. Agnes and I visited Clydebank on Sunday. Hughie has copied out a big map of the world onto a huge sheet of paper Jim got from the drafting office. He traces out where you've been from your postcards and the notices in the newspapers and he told me all about the places you visit from reading in the library. He's a clever boy; he must get it from Annie, certainly not from you. Your family are all fit and healthy, and Kate and Jim are wonderful with them. You can see how proud they are of the two boys. Kate realised that Agnes and I had never seen them dressed for school, so she made them put on their Academy uniforms for our benefit. I thought Jim was going to burst with pride.

One piece of bad news, John MacLeish died suddenly. He was a good man. There was a terrific turnout at his funeral. Apart from the Lodge, there were dozens of your old mates from the yard. On of the union men spoke and told everyone how, although they had fought all the time in the yard, MacLeish was an honourable man who treated everyone with respect. Did you know he had the Military Cross?

The turncoat Ramsey MacDonald retired as Prime Minister last week …'

Ian went on about the perfidy of politicians and the never-ending struggle of the working classes to better themselves. Alex missed his chats with his brother, and in a reversal from the usual pattern, it was thinking about Ian that made him reach for his watch chain.

Ian had been right; people had noticed his watch and he caught the occasional glance of surprise and re-assessment in their eyes.

When they left Bombay, they had three days at sea before their next stop, Colombo, where Noël and Geoffrey would disembark. On their first night back at sea, Dorothy and Christina had one of their talks, as they meandered around the deck of the *Empress*.

"Well, how was it? What happened? Did he kiss you?"

"Oh Dottie, it was lovely. He had a corsage for me, he asked me a million questions–he wanted to hear all about you by the way, he's a great admirer. And yes, he did ask if he could kiss me."

"And?"

"And I said yes. It was the Taj Mahal after all."

"And?"

"And that was it. He kissed me. It was very nice of him, quite delightful."

"Mmm. Well, it's a start I suppose. Now, Chrissie, tell me what you know about birth control," commanded Dorothy.

"I, well, I know, well I know it's immoral. And… well, that's it, I guess."

"Nonsense; listen to me, a woman who has had an abortion. Oh now, don't make such a fuss. It happens every day. Listen."

And Dorothy proceeded to give Christina a crash course on the facts of life, as understood by a self-described libertine.

"I would *not* recommend you follow my example, but trust me, honey, as long as God makes little green apples, guys will chase you, and woo you, and tempt you. Best you know the score."

"I don't know if there'll be too much wooing…Dottie, what's that?"

Chrissie's sharp young eyes had spotted something glinting on the deck. They walked closer until she could pick up whatever it was.

"Why, it's an earring; it might be a diamond."

"Let me see. You know what, Chrissie? I believe it *is* a diamond."

"I'll give it to Alex, he'll know what to do."

Alex made discrete enquiries: The earring belonged to Betty Compton that was, until she and Jimmy had been married in Cannes during the *Empress's* stop in Monaco. The new Mrs Walker was suitably appreciative when she sought Christina out to thank her.

"I can't tell you how grateful I am, Christina, really grateful. Jimmy gave me these earrings in Rome, just days after we were married. I'd hate for him to learn … oh Christina, could you keep this a secret, I mean, between you and me? I'd be ever so grateful."

"Of course, Miss Compton, I mean Mrs Walker, your secret's safe with me."

Betty examined the young woman before her. "You know what, honey, I believe it is. Come on, let's take a walk; and it's Betty, please. You already make me feel ancient with that lovely skin of yours; hearing you call me Mrs only makes it worse."

And so Chrissie added another celebrity to her circle of *Empress* friends.

Betty had been born in England but had moved to New York as a child. She had been a member of the Ziegfeld Follies and had danced on stage with Fred Astaire. Betty was poised and beautiful and devoted to Jimmy Walker.

"Jimmy has become a target for all sorts of do-gooders and so-called reformers. He thinks we need to stay out of the newspapers for a while, so that's why we're on this cruise. We'll leave the ship in Australia and sail directly back to England in a couple of weeks. I'll see my grandparents for the first time since I was four years old!"

The following evening was Noël's last night on board. He and Geoffrey would disembark at Colombo for their Ceylon sojourn. Noël was hosting a cocktail party to say goodbye to his friends and admirers, including, of course, the Fredericks family. The party in Cell 666, as it was still labelled, was in full swing when Dorothy and Alan turned up, obviously extremely drunk.

Dorothy was a mess. She looked as if she had slept in her clothes, her hair and makeup were awry and her eyes were unfocused. Initially, Alan gave the appearance of being in somewhat better shape; until he tried to speak, when it became clear he couldn't construct a sentence without tripping over his words. Dorothy, however, was having no trouble with her words. She was maintaining an unbroken monologue on the subject of Noël and his very, very, very good friend, Geoffrey. She couldn't imagine exactly how extensive was the range of services Geoffrey provided for Noël and matters were about to degenerate completely, when Alex gently explained to Dorothy that the party had run out of whisky and perhaps the Campbells would be better off in their own cabin, where Alex had deposited a fresh bottle.

"Just like the tightwad Limeys to run out of whisky. Come on, Alan, let's leave this trash."

If Alex hadn't been holding her, Dorothy would have fallen on her face before she made the door. As it was, in the shocked silence that followed their departure, everyone heard the sound of Alan sliding down the wall onto the passageway floor, as Alex used his free hand to unlock their stateroom door.

"Time, I think, for music!" announced Noël as he strode to the piano and began to sing. Within two minutes Dorothy had been forgotten and the atmosphere was once again jovial, as Noël went through his repertoire of songs. Betty could see the one person not back in the party mood was Christina, who was still visibly upset by the embarrassing scene. Betty approached her.

"Don't let it bother you, Chrissie. She won't remember a thing in the morning."

"Perhaps not, but I will. I don't think I can face her after this."

"Of course you can. Dorothy can't handle drink and she doesn't realise it. Some people are like that. One drink is never enough unless they're distracted. Dorothy's problem is she can't stand being on her own, and the company she keeps in New York are all professional drinkers. Dorothy thinks it's normal to have a Scotch at breakfast; after all, pretty much everyone she socialises with does."

"Shouldn't someone tell her? I mean, no one would want to be like that, surely?"

"Don't try to be that someone, honey, not if you want to stay her friend. You just have to accept her the way she is or drop her. Don't go trying to reform her, she'll only hate you for it."

"I'm *never* going to get drunk! Never!"

Betty laughed, "Good plan, honey."

Next morning Christina was up and dressed early. She had asked Alex to tell her when Noël had finished his breakfast, and as soon as he gave her the word, she crossed the passageway and knocked on his door.

"Enter!" he called.

"Ah! Young Christina. I thought it was my jailer, Geoffrey. You are a much more pleasant sight first thing in the morning."

"I wanted to see you before you left, to thank you for being so kind to me."

"Not at all, my dear, it is I who must thank you for flattering my dreadful ego; a performer never tires of a receptive audience."

"I have a small gift for you, Master, and I didn't steal it, I bought it from the ship's store."

She handed Noël a small box, carefully tied with a ribbon.

"I do love gifts," he said, "but there really is no need."

He carefully unwrapped the box, opened it and lifted out a solid silver finger bowl with an enamelled *Empress* crest. He looked at her and smiled.

"Alex explained about the finger bowl; he knew I wouldn't want to make the same mistake again. But you were so gracious and kind." Her voice tailed off.

"What a sweet gift, from a sweet girl. Come over here."

He led her to his desk where he kept a pile of writing pads. The top pad was clearly in use; page after page was covered in scribbled writing and musical notation, with many crossings out and changes.

"I never travel without good writing pads. Here we go. I'm working on a new show; well, I'm always working on a new show, or a play, or a song, can't help it. Ah yes, here it is."

While he had been talking, he had been searching through the pad. Now he carefully tore out a page. Then he opened a drawer to find yet another used pad, this one much less cluttered. More quickly this time, he turned to a particular page. However, instead of tearing it out as before, he laid the pad on his desk and wrote something near the top of the open page.

"Come and see. That first one is my working pad. I jot down ideas as they come to me and work on them when the spirit moves. This other pad here is for finished works. See, here is the completed version of a song, *'I'll Remember Her'*. And now there is a dedication—when it is published later this year, and for evermore, it will be dedicated, *'For Christina'*. And this is for you, my dear, the working sheet of the song with all my scribbles and alterations."

Christina could think of nothing to say that wasn't completely inadequate. She turned and threw her arms around him and hugged him tight.

"Thank you, Master, thank you so very much, for this and for everything."

"Nothing at all, my dear. I shall keep my finger bowl on the piano at home, so people will ask me about it, and when you are a world-famous actress, I shall tell them I taught you everything you know."

***

For several days, Noël's departure somewhat deflated the atmosphere among his friends in first class. He had been the source of much merriment and entertainment, both formal and informal. The five-day passage to Java was in any case, the dreariest segment of the trip so far. The climate didn't help. It was unusually warm and humid, and with no air-conditioning on board, a variety of air scoops were deployed in a vain effort to make the cabins remotely bearable at night.

Young Frank Fitzgerald continued his fruitless pursuit of Chrissie.

As she had explained to Betty, who had taken on the role of chief confidante, Chrissie thought Frank was perfectly nice, but she felt absolutely no attraction to him. However, his niceness prevented her from coming right out with a straightforward rejection; and so he continued to hover around.

For days after Noël's final cocktail party, Chrissie's relationship with Dorothy was strained. The young woman found it impossible to forget the image of Dorothy, drunk and cruel and oblivious to the effect she was having on those around her. She still accepted Dorothy's invitations to breakfast, and after a couple of poetry writing sessions and late-night promenades, they resumed their earlier familiarity. But things were not quite the same.

She confided in Betty, in their final conversation before she and Jimmy disembarked in Australia before sailing back to England.

"I'm sorry, honey, but it's called growing up. The older we get, the more our mistakes catch up with us, not least because we've made more of them. When you're friends with someone like Dorothy, you have to take the whole package. The very thing making her witty and sharp is the same thing making her cruel and unfeeling. Throw in her attitude to drink, and you've got yourself quite the explosive mix."

Frank was nothing if not persistent in his dogged attentiveness towards Christina.

Unfortunately for his prospects, their kiss at the Taj Mahal had convinced Christina he was a perfectly nice young man, but not someone she was in any danger of falling in love with. She admitted to herself she was using him as a shield, giving her some protection from one or two older fellows who seemed interested in her, but who intimidated her. The problem was exacerbated by the claustrophobic group of young people left aboard. Even though they had long since dropped the barrier between First and tourist class as far as dances and games were concerned, the demarcation line was still rigid when it came to meals and shore excursions. There were in total, only twenty-two single passengers between the ages of sixteen and thirty still on board *Empress*; twelve young women and ten men.

One of the group, George Wetherburn, 'the Third', as he invariably introduced himself, was especially persistent. At twenty-three, he was five years older than Christina and had graduated from Yale five months before the *Empress* had sailed. He was cruising with his mother, whose husband had died when George was only four, leaving her immensely rich and with endless hours to dote on her only child. George grew up indulged, self-confident and with an easy charm from having been part of adult company from an early age. He was also handsome, and aware of it.

"Why won't you take a stroll around the ship with me, Chrissie?" George asked for the umpteenth time, "It's a lovely night, the Milky Way is right above our heads. What could be more perfect?"

Christina decided it was time for the truth.

"I won't come with you because I don't trust you. And I don't trust you, because I know about your bet with Charles. There; now you can save yourself any more wasted efforts. If it is any consolation, I won't walk out with Charles either, so I won't affect your wager."

"Oh! You've heard about that, have you?"

"Yes, and all the sordid details–a point for each base you manage with each girl, and an extra three points for, well, I don't need to tell you what for. It would be disgusting and demeaning for a couple of sixteen-year-olds, but for you and Charles, it's plain pathetic."

Later, Christina reflected that it was her conversations with Betty, and more especially with Dorothy, that had given her the confidence to talk to George the way she did. And at that moment, her feelings about Dorothy changed and she accepted her friend for what she was, a flawed person yes, but a strong woman who had made her own way in a hostile world–and moreover, someone from whom Christina had learned a great deal. When the ship stopped for three days in Hong Kong, Christina bought Dorothy a pretty silk fan and presented it to her.

"I just wanted to thank you for all the time you've spent with me on this trip, it has meant a great deal to me."

"Why thank you, darling. But don't be too nice to me, will you? Somehow I seem to be horrid to the nicest people—I'd say you were in grave danger."

The leg of the cruise from Japan to Hawaii was one of the longest of the entire adventure. In recognition of the *Empress's* Scottish heritage, the ship celebrated Robert Burns' Day on January 25th. Scotland's national poet was honoured with a traditional Burns Supper.

Joanne Fredericks was dubious.

"We don't have to eat haggis, do we?"

Chrissie was more enthusiastic.

"I'm looking forward to it. We studied some of his poems in school; my favourite is *'My Love is Like a Red, Red, Rose'*. I may give the haggis a miss though."

"That's a nice song; I didn't know it was a poem."

"Yes, mother, it was originally a poem someone put to music. Helena Broadchurch is going to sing it tonight; she's Scottish. It's very romantic. And our steward, Alex, is going to recite the *Address to the Haggis*, another Burns' poem. He told me about it this morning. I think he's nervous about it all."

The day after the Burns Supper, which, despite Alex's misgivings, was a huge success, they encountered moderately heavy seas, but the majestic liner was not much troubled. There was some pitching, but the Captain reduced speed and the ship's motion became less pronounced. It seemed that lunch service would proceed as normal, so the tables were set and the kitchen staff moved into high gear to prepare the huge tables of hot and cold food for the buffet and finish preparation for the full-service restaurant at the same time. Flowers were retrieved from the cold store to be cut and arranged for the various displays. Two private functions had been scheduled and these placed yet more demands on the teams of chefs, sous-chefs and assistants.

On the bridge, the Captain was preparing to hand over command to his First Officer before he went down to host his table for lunch.

"Everything is on schedule Mr Rostron, the next course alteration is due in one hour and twenty minutes. If you need me, please don't hesit …"

At that moment, the lookout on the port wing bridge yelled out, "Motion on port horizon!"

"What on earth is he saying?" queried the Captain. 'Motion' meant nothing at all.

Nonetheless, the Captain heard the concern in the lookout's voice and hurried out to the wing where he took the binoculars from the man's hand. A dark line spread across the entire horizon. With no sense of scale, it was impossible to accurately judge the distance.

"What in God's name is that?"

Seconds passed.

"My God, it's a huge wave! Hard to starboard!"

The rogue wave was over 90 feet high. There had just been time to turn the Empress to meet it head on before a huge wall of green water smashed over the ship, fortunately after all the passengers had been rushed unceremoniously off the decks.

***

The *Empress* spent an extra two days in Hawaii while the most essential repairs were carried out and vital breakages replaced. A new tender was ordered, to replace the one torn from its davits and hurled against a crane, destroying both. During the passage to California, comprehensive lists of what else had to be provided were drawn up and cabled ahead to meet them in San Francisco.

Alex told the family about the damage the wave caused in a letter posted from Hawaii.

'... *You've no idea of the extent of the damage. The tables had just been set for lunch, so when we went to help clear up, there was just a huge pile of broken plates, glasses, tables, chairs, everything; all piled against one wall. Every light was broken, every mirror on every wall. It was unbelievable. Four crew were killed in the galleys. Boiling water flew everywhere and two small fires broke out. Some of the kitchen equipment broke loose and crushed people. It was terrible to see. Fifteen crew in total were killed, most in the engine room, but four were washed overboard and never found. Amazingly enough, no passengers died and the crew deaths were more or less hushed up. Mind you, the doctors are being kept busy with cuts and burns and broken bones. We're only half full now, so there was enough crockery to serve a cold dinner that night. ...*'

As the *Empress* pulled away from Honolulu, the passengers standing at the rails on the port side of the ship waved and, for many of them, there was a real sense of ending. Roughly one-third of the remaining voyagers would leave the *Empress* at her next port, San Francisco; including the Fredericks family and Dorothy and Alan. For some, California was home, or at least close to home, while many of the East Coast guests preferred a train journey of three nights to a further two and a half weeks on board ship, with only a couple of interesting stops en route through the Panama Canal.

They would have five more nights on board crossing the Pacific; but at Chrissie's suggestion, the Fredericks would host a farewell lunch rather than a dinner, in the hope that all of the guests would arrive and depart sober.

Rather than use their stateroom, Wilbur made arrangements with Alex to reserve a section of the Empire Restaurant, which was duly partitioned off with plants and wooden screens. In addition to the Campbells, they invited Sir Roderick and Helena Broadchurch, who would stay on board all the way to New York. As an act of contrition, Christina invited Frank Fitzgerald and his parents, while Wilbur and Joanne added several couples they had befriended during the voyage. Wilbur had also engaged a band from the ship's orchestra to play for them during and after lunch.

Naturally, Frank asked Chrissie to dance as soon as the music started.

"I will, Frank, but you must understand I have to dance with our other guests as well."

When the music ended and the musicians had departed, and much to Dorothy's delight, Chrissie suggested they play some of Dorothy's favourite parlour games and the company spent the rest of a beautiful afternoon enjoying themselves, while the great liner cut through the once again calm waters of the Pacific Ocean.

Apart from the rogue wave, they had been incredibly lucky with the weather throughout their trip. They had experienced some rain, but only one tropical storm, when for two days they had faced rough waves, high winds and heavy rain.

On the last night at sea before they reached San Francisco, there was a grand costume ball. The younger guests congregated around the dance floor and enjoyed themselves. Just after midnight, a clearly nervous Francis Fitzgerald sought out Wilbur Fredericks just as he and Joanne were preparing to find Chrissie and retire to their suite.

"Mr Fredericks, sir, I, well I'm a bit worried about Chrissie. She disappeared a little while ago with George, and I don't think she looked too great. I'm not sure if I should even mention it; I mean, maybe she's quite well, but, I …"

"You did the right thing, son." Wilbur reassured the boy, taking Joanne by the hand and marching her swiftly to their stateroom, which was empty. Having no idea where to look for his daughter, he called for Alex, who appeared within minutes.

"I tell you, Alex, I don't care much for that George character; far too smooth, if you know what I mean. And Chrissie's no match for him, I suspect."

"Don't worry, Mr Fredericks, I'll get some of the other stewards to help; we'll find her. Just stay here with Mrs Fredericks, so I know where to find you."

Wasting no time, Alex rounded up three of his colleagues, including Edwards, the steward responsible for Mrs Wetherburn and her son, George.

Edwards confirmed Wilbur's view of George Wetherburn.

"He's a nasty piece of work, Alex. The girl's father is right to be concerned. Have you met the new nurse, the one who replaced Gertie in Singapore? I saw Wetherburn talking with her this morning, he was very animated. I thought at the time something fishy was going on. Let's go and see her."

Alex and Edwards hurried to the nurses' quarters, located next to the ship's infirmary. The *Empress* had two doctors, four nurses, a dentist and a fully equipped four-bed infirmary where minor operations could be carried out, broken limbs set and most illnesses treated; although sunstroke, sunburn and various stomach ailments had made up most of their caseload before the injuries caused by the enormous wave. The new nurse, Marjory Robinson, had been a last-minute replacement when Gertie had received a cable instructing her to take the first available ship back to England, where her father was desperately ill.

"Nurse Robinson, I saw you talking this morning with one of my passengers, George Wetherburn. I'd like to know what you were discussing."

Instantly the nurse became defensive.

"I'm not sure that's any of your business, Mr Edwards; it was medical matter and therefore entirely confidential."

Alex had no time for a protracted argument.

"Listen to me. Wetherburn has gone off with a young girl, one of my passengers. Now you're going to tell me what he said or we're going to the Captain right now."

Alex's native accent, which he had learned to disguise, came to the fore.

"Ah'm dead serious. We're no' wastin' another damn minute. Speak, woman! Now."

The nurse was clearly scared.

"He said his mother was suffering from chronic back pain and needed something to make her more comfortable. He asked for some chloral hydrate."

"He asked for chloral hydrate? An' you gave it tae him? You bitch; you knew damn well what he wanted it for. Pack your bags, you'll be off this ship in the mornin'"

Now Alex was seriously worried. Apart from his professional responsibilities, he had grown fond of

Chrissie, who was charming, unfailingly polite and always considerate of him and all of the crew. In fact, the young woman was the favourite of the entire first-class crew department. He turned to his colleague.

"They could be anywhere, there are dozens of empty cabins now. Can you get everyone up and searching? Everyone: chambermaids, servers, porters, everyone. We need to look everywhere. We'll start in first class."

In less than five minutes, more than a dozen crew members were discretely searching every room and space on the *Empress*.

In the event, logic was the key, not numbers. As Alex sped back to the first-class passageway, he reasoned Christina would begin to feel sleepy, perhaps unsteady. If Wetherburn wanted to get her out of the ballroom, he would pretend to escort her back to her own suite.

Although there were over 150 first class staterooms, there were only ten different key patterns. As Wetherburn had obviously planned his abduction, he may have been able to work out that suites sharing the same final number also shared the same key pattern. By this point in the cruise, everyone knew pretty well who had left the ship, and so which cabins were unoccupied. The Wetherburns were in stateroom 156.

When Alex reached the passageway containing the Fredericks' cabin, he used his master key to enter 316— empty. 326 was empty at the moment, but still occupied. 336 was also empty; but as soon as Alex let himself into suite 346 he could hear sounds coming from the forward bedroom. He knew the guests from 346 had disembarked in Australia. In five strides he was at the bedroom door and threw it open with a crash. In the light spilling into the bedroom he could see Christina lying on top of the cover, naked down to her waist. Wetherburn was standing at the foot of the bed, easing her dress over her hips.

"What are you doing here, steward? Can't you see we're busy?"

Alex stepped over to Wetherburn and smashed his fist hard into the sneering face, breaking Wetherburn's nose and sending a gusher of blood down his front. The young man screamed his pain and disbelief and crumpled to the floor, clutching his face. Alex stepped over to Christina, who was barely conscious, completely unaware of what was happening. He gently covered her with a sheet, just as he heard someone enter the outer room. He moved to intercept whoever it was, determined to keep this matter quiet, for the sake of Christina and her family. However, it was Edwards, who had come to the exact same realisation as Alex about Christina's likely whereabouts, but a few minutes later.

"She's fine, we got here just in time. Can you step along to the Fredericks' cabin and ask Mrs Fredericks to come here, and could you take this piece of shite to the infirmary? Oh, and spread the word Chrissie's been found, safe and unhurt. We'll say she fell asleep in the library and had no idea we were looking for her.

In seconds, Joanne appeared, beside herself with worry.

"Don't worry, Mrs Fredericks, She's fine. Nothing happened, I mean, she's still your little girl. And I've called the doctor, he'll be here directly."

"Thanks to you, Alex, thanks to you. Is she drunk?"

"Not exactly, it wasn't her fault."

Alex explained about the drug.

"It's called a Mickey Finn; Wetherburn will have slipped it into her drink without her notice. She's blameless, Mrs Fredericks; he's an evil person who tried to take advantage of her–but he failed. And no one will know what happened, the crew all adore your daughter and will keep this completely quiet."

"Thank you, Alex. Where is he, Wetherburn, I mean? Wilbur will want a word with that young man."

"I should think he'll be in the infirmary by now."

Alex looked at her as innocently as he could.

"It seems I have to thank you yet again, Alex. Who's that?"

Joanne had heard someone open the outer door.

"I expect that'll be the doctor."

It was indeed the ship's senior doctor.

Alex explained the whole story once more while the doctor examined Chrissie.

"I'm so sorry, ma'am, one of my staff is in part responsible for this appalling situation. I assure you she will be dealt with most severely. And am I to assume you are responsible for the broken nose my colleague is dealing with, Alex?"

"That would be correct, doctor."

"Well, well."

He turned to Joanne, "Your daughter will be absolutely fine, Mrs Fredericks. Her breathing is completely normal. I suspect she had only a small dose; her attacker would have wanted her sleepy, not entirely comatose. She'll be right as rain in the morning and will almost certainly have no memory of what happened. We can carry her to her room, or you can sleep here beside her, whichever you prefer."

"We'll leave her to rest here. If I can ask you to wait with her a moment, I'll get some night things and tell Wilbur what's happened. We'll go back to our own suite when she wakes up and can walk by herself."

"I'll wait with her. You can go, Alex, if you have things to do."

"Thanks doctor, I'll go help stand down the crew; we've got everyone looking for Christina. Good night, Mrs Fredericks. I'll see you in the morning, I'm sure."

But at seven o'clock in the morning, Alex was summoned to the Captain's office. When he arrived, he was surprised to see Mrs Wetherburn sitting in a chair in front of the Captain's imposing desk.

The Captain dispensed with any pretence at pleasantries.

"Steward, I was summoned fifteen minutes ago at the urgent request of this lady, Mrs Wetherburn, who tells me you assaulted her son yesterday evening, breaking his nose. Can this be true?"

Mrs Wetherburn interrupted. "Of course it is true, I went to the infirmary myself, and the nurse told me what happened. My son is still asleep as we speak."

At that moment, there was a commotion outside the Captain's office and George Wetherburn wrestled open the door and stepped in, a robe thrown over hospital issue pyjamas. He looked terrible. A large bandage covered much of his face and both eyes were deeply blackened.

His mother let out a scream. "Look! Look at his face. My son, my poor son."

"Mother, what are you doing here? We need to leave immediately, come on."

Wetherburn's voice was muffled and barely comprehensible.

"Do not be silly, George, this man hit you. One must stand up to bullies. I came to see the Captain first thing, I suppose the nurse told you I was coming here, but you shouldn't worry about me, you should be resting."

Alex decided to bring matters to a head. He indicated the other empty seat before the Captain's desk.

In a voice dripping with sarcasm, Alex addressed Wetherburn.

"Please, Mr Wetherburn, you shouldn't be standing; sit down, sir, and we'll get this cleared up."

He turned to the Captain, "Sir, I suspect that as we are a full hour before the watch changeover, and in the rush to assure Mrs Wetherburn that I would be confronted immediately, you may not yet have had the opportunity to read last night's reports. If I could direct you, sir, to the reports from myself and the two doctors, I think the situation may be made clearer."

The Captain had known Alex for three years and knew his exemplary record, so he pulled his tray to himself and saw that the reports Alex mentioned were at the top of the overnight paperwork. There was silence for a minute or so as he reviewed the documents, which were terse and to the point.

When he had finished reading, the Captain set the reports down and slowly returned the tray to its customary position in the far corner of his desk. He thought for a moment then addressed George Wetherburn, who was squirming in his seat.

"I am going to leave this room; there is an urgent matter requiring my attention: I have a young woman and her parents to attend to. You will explain to your sadly deluded mother *exactly* what happened last night. Mr Campbell will remain in the room to ensure the accuracy of your report. You will then pack your possessions and remove yourself from this vessel. No steward will help you; no porter will assist in carrying your trunks. Anything you cannot carry yourself, will be thrown off my ship. Madam, I bid you good day. If you wish to proceed with us to New York, you are, of course, most welcome. If not, I will take my leave of you now. You have my sympathy."

***

Six weeks later, the children welcomed Alex home then noisily moved across to the Craig's flat to examine their new souvenirs. Kate turned to Alex with a strange look on her face, "You've got two letters. One is from a woman."

"What letters? What woman?"

She handed him two envelopes, both with American stamps.

He opened the first envelope.

Dear Alex,

I am so very sorry we didn't see you before we left the Empress. I had cabled my brother from Japan, promising him we would make his sixtieth birthday party—then we had the wave and the delay in Hawaii, so I'm afraid we had to catch that train.

Between Joanne and the Captain, I understand just how much you did for my daughter and my family. I will never be able to repay you, to thank you enough. Some good deeds are easy and deserve no particular commendation; but your actions displayed real care for our daughter, a sense of honor, and a concern for my family going well beyond what one could demand or expect.

In a way, I hate to send you money; it is an inadequate token of how much you mean to us — and will always mean to the

Fredericks family. But, what else can I do? I hope it may provide some benefit to your children that in some small way encompasses the enormous debt my child owes you.

We will remember you always in our prayers. I wish you a long and happy life. And if, by chance, you are ever close to our home, I hope you will visit and let us tell you, in person, how much we appreciate your care and thoughtfulness.

Yours ever,

Wilbur Fredericks'

Inside the envelope was a cheque, drawn on a British bank, for £1,000. Even with tips and overtime, this was four or five years' income for Alex. It was vastly more money than any Campbell had ever seen at one time. Without a word he handed the letter, and the cheque, to Kate; then he opened the other envelope.

'Dear, dear Alex,

How can I find the words to express what I want to say to you? I need Noël and Dorothy beside me now to help, but sadly, they are not here.

Even before that terrible evening I was a little infatuated with you. You were always so kind, so dignified, so thoughtful. Do you remember the finger bowl? Somehow, when you had finished explaining everything to me, I felt wiser, more sophisticated; I had quite forgotten to be humiliated by the episode, thanks to you.

I hope your family is pleased to have you home, especially the children. I'm sure they are as clever and wonderful as you told me—is it too much to ask that one day I will meet them?

Who knows?
I remember nothing of that night, but I have learned everything.
You are forever my protector, my knight in shining armor.
I send you my love and eternal affection.
Yours ever,
Chrissie'

Alex handed the second letter to his sister-in-law.

When Kate had finished reading both letters, she handed them to her husband.

It took Alex two cups of tea to explain the Fredericks, Noël, Dorothy and the eventful last night of the Fredericks' *Empress* cruise. At the end of his story Jim looked at him,

"So you went and found that poor lassie, and saved her, and walloped the boy, and kept it all quiet?"

Alex nodded. "You should have been there; it was amazing to see. It must have taken ten minutes for the sorry creature to tell his story. He kept trying to skip over the worst parts, but of course, I was there to jog his memory. By the end, his mother's lips were two white lines, stretched taut across her face. It was priceless. '*George*', she said at the end, '*I see I have been wrong about you all these years. I will accept the Captain's offer and continue my cruise alone. You will be left here, by yourself. I will provide you with $100. That is the last money you will see from me or from your father's estate. You are a liar and a bounder and I am ashamed of you.*' And then she very graciously apologised to me and left the room. I followed immediately behind her. I felt sorry for her. The Captain had ordered two crewmen to escort Wetherburn off the ship."

Then Alex's voice dropped.

"All of this meant I never saw the Fredericks family again. By the time it was all over, they had left the ship. Wilbur left a scribbled note saying that they had to leave to catch their train, but that he would be in touch. That's why they sent the letters."

Kate smiled. "Oh well! I saw the return name and address on the envelope and I thought…well I thought something else. It's been a long time since, since Annie left us and…" her voiced drifted away.

"I don't think there will ever be anyone else for me, Kate. I know Annie would be fine with me meeting someone else, but I have everything I need here with you and Jim and the children."

After a moment Jim spoke again. "Your world seems so far away; it's good to have you back for a while. And we're very proud of you."

"Ah, never mind. What's for tea?"

But Kate had something else to say.

"You'll get your tea in a minute. I need to get Robbie first; we had another letter while you were away."

Alex looked over at his brother-in-law, but Jim ignored the question in his look. After a minute, Kate returned with her son.

Robbie was almost eighteen now, and he blushed as he handed Alex an opened envelope, carefully pulled from his back pocket.

"This is for you, Uncle Alex. Well it's for me, but really, it's for you."

Alex slid the letter from its envelope. It was a letter accepting Robbie as an undergraduate in Glasgow University, starting in the autumn.

Alex read the letter twice and looked up at his nephew, the first person from any family he knew to go to university. He was finding it hard to breathe. Eventually, he managed to collect himself. He reached out his hand.

"I couldn't be more proud of you, son. This means everything to me. And Robbie, from now on, call me Alex."

As they stood, hands clasped, Robbie said to his uncle.

"Hughie will be right behind me; everyone says he's the cleverest boy the Academy has ever seen."

Alex was home for a month. His children seemed to have doubled in size. They were thrilled to have their father home again and pestered him endlessly for stories of exotic places, only a little exaggerated to give larger roles to tigers, elephants and monkeys. Then there were dozens of souvenirs—mostly more picture postcards, but also little trinkets from some of his shore trips. For Kate, there was a pearl from Japan and for his other sister-in-law, Agnes, a bright silk scarf from China.

As a special treat, Alex took everyone on a trip down the Clyde to Rothesay, on the Isle of Bute. Ian managed to get time off work so he and his family could come along. They all spent the night in a nice hotel.

After lunch the children were sent into the garden to play. Much to Hughie's disgust, Robbie was invited to stay with the adults as they found seats in the lounge, which was otherwise empty.

Alex got right to the point.

"I've been thinking about what to do with all that money from America."

No one had mentioned the money for nearly two weeks, but he felt that now was the time to raise it.

"First of all, you need to know I think of this as family money, not just mine. I'm not sure we should do anything with it right now. The *Empress* is not much more than half full most trips, and most of the other liners are doing even worse. And Cunard will bring the *Queen Mary* into service next year; that'll add even more capacity. Jim's back in the yards, at least until *Queen Mary* sails and probably after that, working on her sister ship. It would be nice to know the money's here if we ever really needed it. Also, I'm thinking that if I can stick it out another five or six years, that'll be ten years I'll have done, and we would have had a fair wee bit stashed away. If we add this money, maybe we could think of having a hotel ourselves, one like this. I have an idea that a small luxury hotel in Troon, or Prestwick, near one of the golf courses, could be very successful. I've learned a lot about the rich and what they like, and Ian understands the restaurant business backwards."

There was a stunned silence for a few minutes until Ian spoke. "You never cease to surprise us, Alex. I like the sound of your plan. And talking of sounds, you sound different these days–I think you're losing your accent, you're sounding quite posh."

"I hav'nae lost it." Alex said in his broadest Glaswegian accent, "it's just easier for folk to understand me if I speak different."

Ian laughed, "I'm not complaining, it sounds nice."

Ian looked around at the others. "You're the head of the family, Alex. Now you've given us a new dream."

Alex spoke again.

"One more thing though, about the money. Robbie here is going to university and he tells me Hughie will be following him in due course."

He turned to Ian and Agnes, sitting together on a small couch. "I think your two boys should go to the Academy as well. And I'll put £50 aside for each of the girls for when they get married."

Agnes fumbled for her husband's hand and squeezed it hard as she looked at her brother-in-law, her eyes bright. "Thank you, Alex, for everything."

"That's alright, Agnes, we're family."

He paused before adding, "Just six more years. 1941 will be a great year for the Campbells and the Craigs!"

1940

SOMEWHERE IN THE NORTH ATLANTIC

The *Empress* had been transformed once again, and not for the better. Her gleaming white paint was long gone. For the past twelve months she had worn a dirty coat of grey, becoming rustier and more disheveled with every trip. There was no longer the manpower or the paint or the desire to keep up appearances. Her outline was the same as it had always been, except at her bow and stern, where anti-aircraft guns had been mounted.

At the outbreak of the war, the *Empress*, along with all of the other great liners, had been requisitioned by the government and converted into a troopship.

Her once glorious interior was splendid no more. Her stained glass, paintings and sculptures, her crystal glasses and silver services had all been taken off to be stored in a New York warehouse. Her beautiful wooden panelling and stunning murals were now hidden behind cheap, unpainted plywood walls. Even the carpets in her grand rooms had been lifted, replaced by coarse hessian coverings.

Luxury suites that once held a family, now held beds for ten. The first-class dining room had been furnished with three hundred metal bunks.

All of the cocktail waiters and most of the chefs were long gone, replaced by cooks who served up an unwavering diet of soups, stews and bread-based puddings.

But for all that, the remaining crew of the *Empress* could still hold their heads high. They were performing a vital role, bringing thousands of troops from Canada, Australia, New Zealand, India and South Africa to North Africa or to training bases in England.

The liners were the swiftest vessels on the seas and needed no escorts or convoys. They relied on speed to outrun any U-boats or surface warships. Only in as they approached England did they need protection, from enemy aircraft.

On this particular trip, the *Empress* was steaming east at full speed through a heaving Atlantic Ocean. The steel-grey sky merged seamlessly into the ocean. The Canadian troops on board were not enjoying the motion of the ship, and in these conditions in peacetime, the skipper would have slowed his speed to ease everyone's discomfort. But for now, the comfort of his passengers was the least of his concerns; keeping everyone alive was his only priority.

The passengers in the single remaining first-class corridor, the sole corner of the *Empress* retaining its old splendor, were also seriously out of sorts; but at least they could be sick in the privacy of their own bathrooms.

1941 Clydebank
SCOTLAND

Alex forced himself to remain calm; Hughie was behaving as Alex himself had twenty-five years earlier. Losing his temper might mean losing his son.

"Son, there's nothing dishonourable about being in university. The country needs new weapons, better warships, faster fighter planes—somebody has to design them. Anyone can be a soldier, not everyone can do what you can do."

"But I'll not be designing anything, not for years. I'll be a useless student. If I join the army, or the navy, I'd be useful, I'd be fighting. Like Robbie, and even you. You're old, and you're still in danger on the *Empress*. Don't deny it!"

In two months, Hughie would be seventeen and eligible to be called up. But he had already been accepted by the University. He would be the youngest undergraduate for many years, but then he had the best school exam record for many years.

"Look, there's a reason why students are exempt. This war will be won by brains, not like the last one, thank God. It's your duty to study hard, get qualified then use your talents to win this bloody war and save as many lives as you can by bringing it to an end. It's your duty, Hughie. Your duty to the country and the family."

Hughie couldn't think of an answer to that, but Alex could see the boy was still unhappy.

Alex was on an increasingly rare leave back to Clydebank. Alone among the *Empress's* senior stewards, he had been ordered to remain in his pre-war station, in charge of the only section of the ship that would be recognisable to a pre-war passenger. Senior politicians, flag rank officers, diplomats and occasional celebrities on propaganda or morale-raising visits were still housed in splendour and had Alex to look after them.

On trips out of England, the guests on the rest of the *Empress* varied enormously. Unless she was heading to Egypt carrying troops, she was usually more or less a ghost ship, often with fewer than 100 passengers. On some sad voyages, she would be taking wounded men home, men too damaged to fight again. Usually they would be missing one or more limbs or be blinded. Occasionally, and saddest of all, they had lost their minds and would wander around the ship looking for long dead colleagues.

In two days, Alex would head back to Liverpool to rejoin his ship, but this evening he was enjoying a rare glass of whisky with Jim and Kate after their supper.

"Alex, you know how you told me about having all your personal things ruined when the porthole blew in?" Jim prompted.

Kate obviously had no idea what her husband was talking about. Alex saw her blank look and explained.

"Oh, it wasn't a big deal, Kate. A near miss exploded in the water, and it blew in the porthole in my cabin. It wasn't dangerous, but it meant the waves could batter in until it was sorted. Of course, I wasn't in the cabin. When I did get back, two hours later, everything was soaked through. I could dry my clothes, but my writing paper and my pen were ruined, and the last lot of letters I had from all of you. It was a miracle my watch wasn't damaged too, we were at Action Stations, so I wasn't wearing it. Thank God it was in a drawer and protected from the water."

Jim crossed the room and reached down beside the coal bin.

"This'll maybe keep your stuff safe in future."

He handed his brother-in-law a gleaming brass tube. It had been made from an empty naval gun shell.

"I persuaded a friend in the machine shop to turn a thread in it and to make a lid to fit. He promised me it would be completely waterproof."

Alex studied the cut-down shell casing. It was maybe a foot long and around six inches across—perfect for storing writing materials and his watch and chain and the foreign coins and souvenirs he still collected to bring back for the children. He could barely make out where the lid joined the body. The lid had been mill edged to provide a grip to open and close the casing. And in the middle of the body of the shell was engraved the Masonic Square and Compasses symbol and below that, Alex's name.

"This is great, Jim, thank you, thank you very much. And tell your mate thanks from me."

Alex reached across to shake the hand of his brother-in-law, and his friend.

***

Robbie had joined the University Air Squadron in the final year of his course and was commissioned into the RAF one month after graduation. He was in constant peril, flying a Hurricane over Kent as the Battle of Britain continued to rage. At 22 he was already a veteran and had been promoted to Flight Lieutenant.

His sister Jenny had joined the WAAF and had been posted to an operations centre in southwest England, near to Bath. She saved up her travel vouchers so that once a month she could travel across southern England to visit her brother.

However this month, she would be headed north, to Liverpool, to have lunch with her uncle. If their luck held and the recent spell of atrocious weather continued to keep the Luftwaffe grounded, Robbie would try to join them.

Jenny met Alex's train from Glasgow and they made their way to the Adelphi Hotel where they found a quiet corner to chat and drink tea, and wait for Robbie. An hour after they sat down, Robbie arrived, looking extremely dashing in his RAF uniform. Jenny smiled as she saw the stir her brother caused among the young and not-so-young women scattered around the lounge. Although Jenny was unaware of it, the three of them made a very attractive group as they sat absorbed in each other's company and conversation. Like his nephew and niece, Alex was in uniform and now, aged 41, he was a striking man, tall and well built, and with a more polished presence than when he worked in the shipyard. Jenny had the eye-catching red hair that ran in her mother's family and she was as slim and tall as her Aunt Annie had been, and even more beautiful.

After their lunch, Alex showed them the gift their father had given him.

"We're lucky you know," he said, looking fondly at his niece and nephew, "not all families are as close as we are. It's a precious thing, to be looked after and passed on one day to your children."

Jenny replied, "I don't think luck has much to do with it Uncle Alex; you and Mum and Dad, you've made us as close as we are. And don't worry, we'll always stay close, won't we, Robbie?"

"You know we will, although we'll have to work even harder to make sure. I have a feeling our generation will move about more; I don't think Clydebank is big enough to hold Hughie, for example. He's going to do great things, I just know it."

Robbie looked at his watch and continued. "I'm sorry, but I need to go. I borrowed a motorbike and need to get back to Broughton to catch a ride in the back of a Wellington."

Alex knew that Jenny had arrived in a car borrowed from an officer in her operations centre.

"Do you know, I've never been in a plane, or on a motorbike, or driven a car, and here you two are whizzing around the country. Sometimes it's hard to take it all in."

Robbie answered him as he stood to leave, "But we've never seen New York or the Pyramids, or India or Japan or a hundred other amazing places you've seen, Alex. Anyway, safe travels both of you."

He shook his uncle's hand and turned to give his sister a hug.

"Hold on, Robbie, I'll walk out with you, I need to head back as well. Thanks for the tea, Uncle Alex, I'll see you again soon I hope."

She stepped forward to hug him and receive a kiss on her cheek.

Alex watched proudly as the two young people walked through the grand room together, animated and full of life. He had a moment of doubt, wondering if he should have focussed on the girls' education as much as on the boys'; but he dismissed the thought–Jenny was a beautiful young woman who would make a wonderful wife for some lucky man. Maybe he should have asked about the officer who trusted her with his car?

***

Very late the following evening, the *Empress* slipped out of the Mersey estuary and made her way at full speed around the northern coast of Ireland. The stormy weather that had grounded the Luftwaffe had moved north so they sailed through driving rain–welcome cover from enemy bombers and obscuring visibility for any German ship or submarine looking for a target.

As Alex settled down for the night, his final waking thoughts were of his niece and nephew, and of how proud he was of them.

For their parts, both Jenny and Robbie were already asleep after long, tiring journeys back to their respective quarters at opposite ends of southern England.

An hour after Alex fell asleep, his 15-year-old daughter Jean, and Jenny and Robbie's father Jim, were both dead, victims of the first night of the Clydebank Blitz.

Young Jean Campbell and her Uncle Jim died with four of their neighbours, huddled under the stairs of their tenement. The six fatalities happened when a German bomb crashed through the skylight over the stairwell and exploded half way down the building, causing an entire section of the stone staircase to collapse, killing them all instantly.

Jim and Hughie had been taking turns volunteering as firewatchers in the shipyard across the street, so Hughie saw the billowing cloud of dust burst from the entrance of his close. Heedless of the bombs falling everywhere, except, ironically, on the shipyard itself,

Hughie raced across the street; only to be in time to help pull out the lifeless bodies of his sister and uncle.

Now in a blind panic, Hughie tore the skin off his hands digging through the rubble, frantically seeking Betty and Alan and his Aunt Kate. He kept calling their names, his fear mounting with every second he wasn't finding them, when through the bedlam of the sirens and bombs and explosions, he heard his aunt calling his name.

"Hughie, Hughie! Over here. It's OK, we're safe, we're fine!"

It was Kate, holding tight to her niece and nephew.

"There wisnae room for everyone under the stairs, so I took these two out the back to the shelter. Hughie, where are Jim and Jean?"

Their terrible grief over Jean's death was exacerbated by the fact that the three youngsters had come home only four weeks earlier.

Like most of Bankie families with school-aged children, they had obeyed the prominent 'Evacuate Forthwith' notice in the newspapers on the first day of the war. Jean, Betty and Alan were taken to the local school with their tiny cardboard suitcases. A string was placed around each of their necks, bearing a brown label with their name, age and destination address.

Kate knelt in front of them, while Hughie stood behind, his arms embracing all three of his siblings.

"Now, remember what I said, you've to hold hands and *never* be separated."

"What if Alan has to go to the toilet, Auntie Kate?"

"You two go with him. You don't have to go inside, but you wait for him at the door. Same for you Alan, never leave your sisters. Right? And what else Betty and Alan? What is the other thing?"

"Do we have to?" pleaded Alan.

"Tell me what the other thing is!"

Alan gave a huge sigh, "We have to do whatever Jean tells us."

"Promise?"

"Promise."

Hughie came around so he too could squat down before them.

"There's one more thing. You're going to the seaside, to Girvan. And there's lots of your friends going to the same place, so you'll have a great time. But if you're ever sad or scared, just remember, stick together and you'll be fine. And don't forget we love you; Dad loves you and Mum is watching over you from heaven. And I'll come and see you soon, and so will Auntie Kate and Uncle Jim."

But the expected bombing raids failed to materialize. Some families had brought their children home by Christmas, but Kate was adamant that their weans had to stay safe. But as 1940 arrived, and still with no air raids, even she wondered if it was worth the misery of being separated.

Finally, Betty's birthday came around and Kate and Hughie decided enough was enough. Their local school was operating again; most of the children's classmates were back home and so, one weekend near the end of February, Kate and Hughie took the train down to Girvan, and brought the three youngsters home.

And now Jean was dead.

Robbie and Jenny would learn of the death of their father in less than 24 hours. In the Atlantic however, Alex attended to his duties, completely oblivious of the disaster that had ripped his family apart.

1941 At Sea

On her first full day out of port, the *Empress* steamed past the west coast of Ireland, and on into the Atlantic. The principal passengers under Alex's care were Robert Menzies, Prime Minister of Australia, and his party. They were returning to Australia after four months in England, where Menzies had been attending the War Cabinet.

On the first morning at sea, Alex knocked on the door of the Prime Minister's stateroom suite. To his surprise, the door was opened by a young woman, of around thirty he supposed. Instantly, he was struck by her vivid green eyes. Alex was discomfited, even more so as a knowing smile appeared on her face–she was well aware of the effect she was having on him.

"Can I help you?" she asked in a pleasant Australian accent.

Alex had recovered his poise, but couldn't suppress a smile; he could see she was amused rather than annoyed by his reaction, and he found he was amused at himself.

"Alex Campbell, ma'am, Senior Steward; here to introduce myself and offer an introduction to life on board the *Empress of the Oceans*."

"Well, you had better come in then."

She led Alex into the sitting room and introduced him to the Prime Minister and to a captain of the Royal Australian Navy who had been briefing the Prime Minister.

"It's an honour to be serving you, sir. My job is to see that everything possible is done to provide for your comfort and safety during our voyage. I am on duty 24 hours a day; please do not hesitate to call if there is anything you require. In particular, I would like to know your preferences regarding breakfast and other meals, when and where you would prefer to eat and any loves or hates I should be aware of."

"Well, it is a comfort to know we'll be so well looked after, Mr Campbell. Tell me, have you served on the *Empress* for long?"

"I think it fair to say, sir, that I have been with this ship longer than anyone else aboard. I was on her launch crew, but more than that, well, may I show you something?"

At the Prime Minister's nod, Alex walked over to the corner of the cabin and rapped hard on the wall.

"Right here, behind this wood, there's a steel beam running all the way down through the ship."

Alex pointed at a spot about three feet off the floor.

"Right about here, welded to the beam, there's a tiny metal plate. There's a name on it, Fraser McIver. He's a friend of mine, and this is where he put his name, so he'd be part of the *Empress* as long as she sails."

"You see, sir, I was one of the men who built the *Empress*. I drove in my share of rivets and walked every inch of her hull. She's the finest vessel to ever sail the seas, and the best built."

"I'm delighted to hear it. And where is your name, Mr Campbell?"

"My plate is on the bridge, sir. I wanted to be high up, near the command. Of course, when I welded on my plate, I had no idea that one day I would sail on the ship I helped to build."

"Well, I see you've met Miss Murray. I imagine you can get all the information you require from her, but if I could perhaps trouble you for a pot of tea and some toast at your earliest convenience, I would be most grateful."

Alex made his way to his tiny galley where he could prepare simple snacks for his passengers. His thoughts were in turmoil. Since the day Alex had met Annie, he had never given another woman a second thought. Even now, more than twelve years after Annie's death, he was surprised to recognise he had formed an instant and strong attraction to Miss Murray and was already looking forward to talking with her.

Over the next two and a half weeks, Alex fell deeply in love. He had plenty of time to do so. The *Empress's* Captain had assigned an assistant steward to work alongside him and had made it clear that Alex's only responsibility was the Australian Prime Minister. Alex would supervise the assistant, who would take care of the remaining dozen or so passengers in first class.

For his part, Robert Menzie's requirements were slight. He took a light breakfast in his suite; otherwise he was content to join the Captain and some of the other senior officers for lunch and dinner. Apart from organising an occasional bridge evening in his suite, his demands on Alex were few and far between.

This left Alex free to spend many hours every day with Alice Murray. They exchanged their life stories and bonded over a shared love of books. Alex showed her every part of his ship and tried to convey the splendour and glamour of life on the *Empress* before the war.

"If only you could have seen it, Alice. These walls shone in the candlelight. And the silver and crystal! And the women twirling in their beautiful gowns. Well, it was magnificent. I may not have agreed with how they came about their money, but my goodness, it made for an amazing spectacle."

"What an interesting life you've led, Alex. From soldier to steelworker to confidante of celebrities. Could you ever give it up, do you think? I mean, after the war?"

"The very day this war ends, I'll set foot on dry land and never leave it. I want to fix myself to a place and never travel again. I can't tell you how sick I am of flitting from one place to another."

He told her of his idea for a small luxury hotel in Scotland, catering to wealthy golfers and run by his family.

"To have a place that's mine, that I own. Not just own by purchase, but really own. By sweat and effort and pouring something of myself into it. And not only mine, but the family's too. A place we belong to, and that belongs to us. Where we'll be safe and secure for generations to come. That's my dream."

"So you couldn't imagine living somewhere other than Scotland then?"

"Never. Well …" He looked at her and understood her question fully.

"Well," he stammered, "I always imagined–I mean I never imagined."

He blushed.

"It's OK, Alex, I understand. I didn't mean to pry."

Each startled by their emotions, they turned to look over the rail as the ship's wake trailed a narrow foaming line to the horizon. After a minute, Alex moved his hand to cover Alice's as it lay on the warm teak rail.

"I never imagined I would meet someone like you, Alice." Alex strove for the words to express his feelings. "I never imagined I would have these feelings again. I had closed myself off, and I was happy to do so."

After a moment, Alice replied.

"I understand, I do. Because I think we're feeling the same things."

They would have been appalled to overhear the conversation happening high above them, on the command deck.

"Are you concerned about this situation, Prime Minister?"

"Should I be, Captain?"

"I don't believe so, sir. Steward Campbell is an honourable and steady man. There are men who have a natural dignity and integrity; men you know you can always rely on. Steward Campbell is one of those men. I would trust him with my life."

"Well then, there is nothing to say. Love is hard to find in these dark days; who am I to forbid it? But I fear they will have hard decisions to make when we reach Australia."

The statesman gave a little laugh.

"Do you suppose they are the only people on this ship unaware that everyone on board is watching them fall in love?"

Alice was pouting a little. "I wish you could show me around Cape Town; on our one day here on the way out, I wasn't permitted to go ashore; I had to assist the P.M. in hosting a day-long meeting onboard with some South African politicians. And now I discover this time we're to fly immediately to Pretoria for two days while we're in port. It's so frustrating."

"Yes, it is; but you can tell me all about Pretoria when we're back on board. I mostly only ever see port cities in my travels, I don't imagine I'll ever see Pretoria or Johannesburg." Alex replied, trying to be the voice of reason, although he was as disappointed himself.

As soon as the ship was safely docked and the passengers had disembarked, Alex went ashore with his friend Johnny Fraser, one of the *Empress's* chefs. Johnny and his lovely wife Stephanie had been the only husband and wife on the *Empress's* crew until Stephanie had left the ship at the outbreak of war. She had been Alex's partner at many cocktail parties over the years. Together they had made a formidable team looking after the ship's most important guests at a never-ending series of cocktail parties and private dinners.

Alex and Johnny's first stop would be the shipping office, to drop off mail for home. There would be no incoming mail to collect until the return trip, as no letters could have travelled to Cape Town faster than the *Empress*–a situation that wouldn't change even when they reached Australia, and a depressing thought for men already desperate for news from home.

It was a surprise then to see both of their names on the 'Mail to Collect' board. Briefly they supposed it must be old items held up somewhere in the company postal system for months on end. Then they noticed several other *Empress* names on the board, many of them long-serving crew from Scotland.

With a sinking feeling in his stomach, Alex stepped over to the counter and was handed a telegram. Johnny watched as his friend opened the message with shaking hands; wartime telegrams never brought good news.

JIM AND YOUR JEAN KILLED IN AIR RAID STOP EVERYONE ELSE SAFE STOP KATE

Johnny watched the colour drain from Alex's face as he summoned the courage to ask for his own telegram. His younger sister had been killed, also in an air raid.

He turned and looked for Alex, in time to see his back disappear though the door of the shipping office. He ran after his friend, registering as he passed, a few *Empress* colleagues sobbing as they too read messages of death and despair.

"Alex, Alex, wait up!"

But Alex didn't wait or didn't hear him. Eventually Johnny caught up with him and saw the anguish in his friend's face. He was about to say something, actually to ask something, but wisely he stopped himself and simply walked alongside his friend in silence as he strode through the city with no apparent goal in mind.

Eventually, after more than two hours, Alex's pace slackened and Johnny was able to steer him back to the port area, to familiar streets and bars.

"Come on, Alex, let's go in here."

Johnny bought them a half bottle of whisky and poured two large glasses. Gently, he reached out and took the telegram from Alex's hand and read it, while passing over his own dire message.

Johnny finished his glass in three or four mouthfuls; but even in his grief, Alex wouldn't surrender to drink. He sipped at his whisky, but after half a glass he announced, "I'm not getting drunk, Johnny, I'm going back to the ship. Don't get into trouble."

Just as Alex stood up, four Royal Navy sailors came into the bar and walked past their table, passing immediately behind Johnny.

"Look, fuckin' cruise ship wasters. Don't know the meaning of fighting."

Faster than anyone else could move, Johnny was at the sailor's throat and had smashed his fist into the man's face. Before the other three sailors could exact retribution, two South African policemen appeared, seemingly from nowhere, and pulled Johnny off the Royal Navy man, subduing him with a well-placed crack of a baton on the back of Johnny's head.

In the seconds before matters could escalate further, Alex whipped Johnny's telegram off the table and jammed it into the hand of the Navy man who had been assaulted.

"Read this, arsehole, before you say another word."

The sailor read the telegram and looked quizzically at Alex.

"His sister. She was twenty-three and has two wee girls. Her husband was killed at Dunkirk. Now get out of my fucking sight, before I kill you myself."

He turned to the policemen.

"Can you let it go? He's a bit drunk and we've had a terrible, terrible day. Let me take him back to the ship. He'll be no more trouble, I guarantee."

The older policeman had heard Alex's summary of the telegram. "OK, Jock, we'll let him go this time. But if I see him causing trouble again, I'm taking him in, I guarantee *that*."

The two friends trudged slowly back to their ship. Johnny retreated to his cabin and drank whisky. Alex lay on his bed and stared at the ceiling for two days, getting up only to use the head and drink some water.

But, at last, the passengers reboarded and the *Empress* set sail for Australia.

Alice had looked for Alex the moment she set foot on board and was disappointed, and a little hurt, when he wasn't there to meet her; and didn't come looking for her that evening.

The following morning, Alice was with Robert Menzies when they heard Alex let himself in with the Prime Minister's breakfast tray. She couldn't suppress a gasp when she saw Alex. His eyes were dull and his face a hollowed out, lifeless shadow of his normally intelligent expression.

Menzies too, was shocked by Alex's appearance.

"Is everything in order, Mr Campbell?"

"Quite in order, sir. Will there be anything else?"

"No, thank you."

Alice caught the eye of the Prime Minister and he gave her the tiniest of nods. She scurried after Alex as he left the suite.

"Alex, Alex, what is it? What happened to you?"

He didn't answer her. She saw his eyes begin to water and she grasped his hand and pulled him down the corridor, into her cabin.

"What happened, darling?"

She had never called him darling, or used any other term of endearment, and it broke something in him.

To Alice's horror, Alex folded at the knees and collapsed kneeling before her, with his head in his hands, sobbing his heart out, shoulders heaving. He cried properly for the first time since he was a child. He cried for Annie, for Jean and Willie, for Jim, for his dream, for his family. He cried for Johnny's sister and for all the others who had died in this God-awful war. He cried for the men who had fallen around him in the last war—the war to end all wars.

Alice knelt down and held him as he rocked back and forth. Gradually, between heaves, he was able to tell her his wretched news. When she judged the time was right, she gently led him to her bed and made him lie on it. She covered him with a blanket and, when she was sure he was asleep, she crept from the room and quietly closed the door.

"What is the problem? Has he been drinking?" asked the P.M. when Alice finally reported back for duty.

"Not at all, sir," Alice replied sharply, and went on to explain what had transpired in her cabin.

"Sorry, I shouldn't have jumped to conclusions. Take as much time as you need to help him. But remember, we will arrive in Australia sooner than you might think."

That night, Alex finally woke up in nearly total darkness. For a moment he was confused, trying to work out where he was. Then, in the pale light cast by the moon, he saw Alice lying beside him, looking at him. She reached out and gently pulled him to her. As she kissed him, he wrapped his arms around her and felt her naked body. They made love and he fell asleep once again, with Alice beside him.

***

The days passed slowly, tenderly, each pouring its balm into Alex's heart. Alice's love helped him to absorb, drop by painful drop, the anguish of the death of his daughter and Jim, who had been much more than simply his brother-in-law.

Robert Menzies and his officials had done all of their talking, and so few demands were made on Alice's time. By virtue of some strange wartime alchemy, no one seemed shocked or scandalised by the relationship between the two lovers. They took care to be discreet; but in time, even they understood that everyone knew of their relationship and probably of how many nights Alex spent in Alice's cabin.

When they had come to terms with the fact that their relationship was no longer a secret, they were free to devote themselves to each other, finding sheltered spots on one of the decks from where they could watch the sun rise or set, or laugh at the dolphins playing in the ship's wake, or look up at the dazzling display of the southern sky.

However, each gentle day brought them closer to Australia and the time for decisions.

"I know you have to go back, Alex, but I want you to know that, if you ask me, I'll come with you."

"Even if there wasn't a war on, I'd have to go back. Hughie and the two wee ones will need me, and I need to see how Kate is coping on her own."

He tilted her face so she would be looking directly into his eyes, it was important she saw the truth in what he was about to say.

"I can't ask you to come with me, not just now. Britain is no place for you while this war is on. I'm away most of the time and, the truth is, I don't want to introduce you to my children when my return will re-open all the wounds of Jean's death. I don't want them associating you with that sadness. And the wee ones are certainly too young to understand how I could fall in love with someone while Jean was barely in her coffin. They know nothing of the weeks before I learned, when I fell in love with you."

They sat in silence for many minutes before Alex spoke again.

"I expect to be on the *Empress* for the duration. But the day we win the war, I'll quit. If you still feel the same then, I'll send for you and we can look for that wee hotel together. I'm sure Ian and Agnes and Kate will still be up for it. But I'd do it if it was only the two of us."

Now it was Alice's turn to feel the need to communicate the depth of her feeling. She locked her eyes on his and told him, "No matter how long it takes, I'll be waiting."

The *Empress* would be berthed in Melbourne for three days. As soon as she could disembark, Alice took a taxi to the railway station to catch the train to Geelong. She wanted to have an hour with her widowed father before she introduced him to Alex.

"He'll be thrilled, but I don't think it's fair to suddenly turn up with a man on my arm after six months away, and no mention of you in my letters from London."

"Don't worry, I'll go with Johnny to the shipping office and pick up any messages and some money. And I've got your detailed instructions right here—although I have been on a train before, you know; dozens, all over the world," he teased.

This time neither Alex's nor Johnny's names were on the mail list, so they visited the cashier and found the nearest bar. There was no point in dropping off any mail for home—theirs would be the fastest transport to the UK. Alex had sent Hughie a letter from Cape Town, confirming he had received Kate's telegram. He had been too distraught to say much else beyond sending his love to everyone and some inadequate words of consolation for his sons and remaining daughter.

"I'm sorry to be leaving you by yourself for the next two days, Johnny, but I'm on an overnight pass, and I need to meet Alice's father. I may never have another chance, which is a strange thought."

"Of course you have to go. And don't worry; I'll keep out of trouble. See you tomorrow."

The truth was that Alex was extremely anxious about his friend. Since Cape Town, Johnny had been a changed man. His position gave him ready access to the wine stores on board ship and he had been drunk on several occasions. His friends in the kitchen had been able to cover for him so far, but with hundreds of soldiers to be fed every day on their way home, it was inevitable that sooner or later he would be in serious trouble.

Joseph Murray was indeed delighted to meet Alex and thrilled his daughter had at last found someone she wanted to spend her life with. She had had a few romances over the years, but Joseph was coming to believe his daughter had decided to devote herself to his own welfare, at the expense of finding her own happiness. She still lived with him, sleeping in her childhood bedroom, rather than enjoying a social life in the city. This was not what he wanted for his only child.

"It's a pleasure to meet you, Alex. And I'm very sorry for your loss; you must be desperate to get home to your children. You're going to need some time with them when you do get back."

"I'll miss Alice of course, every day; but I'm sure she's explained things to you."

"Yes, she has. Now we must enjoy the hours we have together."

Joseph decided to lighten the atmosphere. "You know, Alex, you're almost midway in age between Alice and me. I think you've given me hope; maybe I'll start looking around myself. What do you think Alice, could I still catch one?"

She laughed. "Don't think you're fooling anyone, Dad. You've had a dozen widows from the bowling club baking cakes for you for years. I don't suppose they've stopped in the time I've been away?"

"Oh, I don't want a dried-up old stick. If I was to step out with anyone, she'd have to be lively and fun."

Now Joseph was looking slightly bashful.

"There is someone I wouldn't mind seeing, not new exactly. Do you remember Roy and Doreen Henderson?"

"The bookie? With the glamorous wife? What about them?"

"In the throes of a divorce. He ran off with a lot of money and a twenty-something cashier. The tax people were after him apparently. They're in Ceylon, living the plantation life. It's been a huge scandal, and no one's speaking to Doreen. I don't think the wives want her around their husbands."

Alice was grinning as she explained.

"You should see this one, Alex, a real knock out. Why her husband would trade her for a younger model, I've no idea. Doreen has curves on curves and isn't afraid to show them off, if you know what I mean? So you're interested are you, Dad?"

"Well, maybe not to marry, but ..."

"Daddy, I'm shocked, shocked!" But as Alice couldn't stop laughing, neither of the men believed her.

Eventually she was able to ask her father, "Does everyone still go to dinner at the golf club on Saturdays?"

"I suppose so; I haven't been since you and I were there, months and months ago."

"Well, let's see how brave you really are, Joseph Murray. I dare you to call Doreen and invite her to have dinner with us at the club. That should give Geelong something to talk about for a few months!"

They had a wonderful evening. Doreen was as striking as Alice had indicated, and without her overbearing husband dominating the conversation, she was a funny and charming dinner companion.

Inevitably the conversation turned to events in the war and the tragedies in Alex's family, and Doreen was solicitous and sympathetic. But after a while, she steered the conversation back to safer territory, encouraging Alex to tell stories about the celebrities he had met in happier times.

At the end of the evening, as the men helped the ladies into their wraps, Alice couldn't resist a look around the room, nodding to familiar faces. She leaned into the others and murmured, "I'm afraid the Murray family will be kicked off the Geelong social register now."

"Why's that?" asked Alex.

But it was Doreen who answered, with an impish smile, "Because one is obviously madly in love with a pommie sailor and the other is stepping out with a soon-to-be-divorcee. You *are* taking me dancing next week, aren't you, Joseph?"

For a second Alice saw the vulnerability and fear below Doreen's bravado, but also her relief and delight with her father's answer.

"And the week after," he replied, beaming at Doreen and holding himself a little straighter than before.

***

For once Alex was pleased he had a full complement of passengers to keep him busy on the long voyage back to England.

He had a mixed bag of civil servants - British and Australian, and a cross-section of Army and Navy staff officers from both countries and a couple from New Zealand. Alex soon realised that none of them would have been able to afford first class travel before the war.

A few of them reacted to their newfound elevated situation by playing lord of the manor. By and large, Alex indulged them, preferring to be busy.

Gossip soon reached the stewards' wardroom that a new Second Engineering Officer had joined the ship in Melbourne and was proving to be unpopular with the men who served under him.

***

Philip Armstrong was the middle son of a Bradford pharmacist. His older brother, Peter, had excelled at the prestigious Leeds Grammar School. But just when Philip had been due to follow his brother into the school, their father's abuse of the pharmacy's drugs came to light. It also emerged he had been steadily extracting the life savings from an elderly patient.

Within months, Philip's father had committed suicide, the family's income dried up and they fell into a financial abyss. His mother's brothers stepped in to provide her with a basic income. As Peter had only one more year before he would go to university, the uncles agreed to finance his final year at school, especially as he had already won a cadetship to the military academy at Sandhurst. However, they refused to pay for private education for Philip or his baby brother, Jeremy.

For some people, these events would be seen as challenges to be overcome. And indeed, Philip did well at the local school; but with no financial support forthcoming from the family, university was out of the question—he would have to find a job.

Philip's resentment at what he always saw as a massive injustice smouldered for the rest of his life. As he watched his contemporaries head off to university, boys he had easily outperformed in primary school, his bitterness only grew and festered.

Then, to his surprise and chagrin, finding a half-decent job proved more difficult than he had anticipated. His good school results got him plenty of interviews, but somehow he failed to shine in face-to-face encounters. Just when he was becoming desperate, he found himself in the office of the head of recruitment for a mid-sized shipping line.

"It's a three-year training programme. During that time, you'll spend around eighteen months at sea, learning on the job. There's no pay, but we give you a small allowance and you'll get three meals a day and your own bed. If you pass your exams, you'll be an engineering officer, and after that, it's up to you. What do you think?"

Philip had learned his lesson.

"I think it sounds wonderful, sir. When can I start?"

Three years later, Armstrong passed his exams and joined his first ship as a serving officer, the *Pride of Dover*, a small freighter carrying bulk cargoes between England and the Baltic ports. He was issued with a smart new Third Engineer's uniform. However, this achievement did nothing to alleviate his bitterness over the humiliation he had suffered at the hands of his mother's family.

***

Soon after the outbreak of war, Armstrong had joined the *Empress of New Zealand* as Second Engineer, where he proved to be a capable, if unimaginative engine room officer. In the spring of 1941, three days from landfall, a major fire broke out in the ship's engine room and tugs had to be despatched to bring her to safety. The *Empress of New Zealand* was towed into Melbourne harbour and it soon became clear the ship would be in dry dock for many months. So when the Second Engineer of the *Empress of the Oceans* was taken to hospital with a compound fracture of his left leg, arrangements were made to transfer Philip Armstrong to his new ship without delay.

Armstrong was something of a martinet who took every opportunity to exercise his authority over the engine room hands. Men were routinely reprimanded for the most insignificant departures from textbook procedures, even when these variations had developed from years of dealing with the peculiarities of the *Empress'* particular design. Engine room hands who had been tending equipment successfully for years, were now instructed by Armstrong that they should revert to the 'correct' way of doing things—according to Armstrong. Although the Merchant Navy was less rigid than the Royal Navy, there was nonetheless a well-defined hierarchy, and no one wanted to get on the wrong side of an officer. His instructions were followed, but the men grumbled among themselves, and his reputation spread throughout the ship's crew.

***

On their fourth day at sea, Alex requested a meeting with the Captain.

"I requested an interview, sir, to express my appreciation for your understanding on the last leg of our voyage. I also wished to advise you that Miss Murray and I have come to an understanding, and her father is fully in agreement with our intentions."

"I am pleased to hear of it, Mr Campbell, and I wish you every happiness. But for the moment, please do whatever you can to keep those Royal Navy men out of my sight and off my table!"

The trip passed uneventfully, and soon enough Alex was standing against the rail as the sky lightened and the first rays of the sun picked out the tops of the African mountains. They had sailed around the Cape and in an hour or so they would be tied up, but this time in Simon's Town, the navy base south of Cape Town proper. They would be here for two nights before heading for home at last. The crew had to take a train to get to the shipping office, situated close to the civilian harbour in the city. There were letters waiting for both Alex and Johnny, follow up communications to the dreadful telegrams they had picked up weeks ago on the outbound trip. Before they opened their mail, they first visited the cashier's office. Alex collected a few pounds to buy a couple of beers and at least one good steak dinner ashore. He could see however, that Johnny was collecting a substantial sum.

"Why do you need all that money, Johnny?"

"I need to pay back Armstrong; I owe him thirty-six pounds."

"Why in God's name do you owe Armstrong money?"

Johnny looked embarrassed.

"I borrowed thirty quid two weeks ago, to get back into the poker game."

"You lost thirty quid at poker? My God, Johnny, that's a lot of money!"

"It's worse than that, Alex. I borrowed the thirty because I had already lost fifteen I picked up in Melbourne. Forty-five pounds I've lost. But I'm done. No more poker for me."

"And Armstrong, is he one of the poker players?"

"Oh no, no. He lends money; ten per cent a week. That's why I need to meet him at the hotel bar to give him his thirty-six quid. Come on, let's go."

Alex watched as Johnny handed over the money. He saw Armstrong hand something to Johnny in return.

Afterwards, Johnny explained.

"My wedding ring and my watch. Armstrong always insists on holding something against the loan. Come on, let's go. I don't want to stay here, and I don't want to talk about it."

They walked until they found a bar that wasn't full of sailors, where they could read their letters in peace. Alex opened his envelope nervously; it turned out to contain letters from Kate and Hughie. He learned little more about the deaths of Jim Craig and his daughter, but he understood how difficult it would have been for Kate or Hughie to commit details to paper. Instead they told him about the two funerals and about the other people who had died or been hurt in the raids. Even in the depths of his grief at his sister's death, Hughie's letter managed to be more lyrical than his aunt's. As Alex read it for the second time, he could feel the cold spring rain running down the necks of the mourners and smell the freshly turned earth at the cemetery. He was powerfully aware of the vast gulf between his home in Scotland, and where he sat now, in Africa.

The roll call of other casualties listed in the letters gave him some understanding of how devastating the attacks had been. Of 12,000 homes in Clydebank, only seven were undamaged after two nights of continuous bombing. Over 500 people were dead. And yet, in the out-of-date copies of the London newspapers and in the South African papers they looked at, the Clydebank Blitz rated barely a mention. He knew it wasn't that the writers didn't care; simply that this was but one among a never-ending torrent of stories of death and destruction.

Reading the letters again, Alex realised once more how desperate he was to get home and hold his children. But he also recognised how much more resilient he was as a result of his relationship with Alice and the hope she represented. He was overcome by the strongest need to write to her again. He had already dropped a letter to her in the post box in the shipping office, but he wanted to write another letter and get it posted before they left Cape Town. He turned to his friend, who was staring at the wall.

"How's Stephanie?" he asked.

"She's coping as well as she can. My mother is helping her look after my sister's two girls, but Mum wants to get back to her own house down south and Stephanie has her work. Steph's not sure what to do. It's a bit of a mess, I think. But she's waiting till I get home before deciding anything. Oh, and she said to tell you how sorry she is about Jean and Jim. She heard about it from Agnes."

"I appreciate that. Listen, I'm going back to the ship. I want to write to Alice before we leave. Are you coming back?"

"No. I've always had a notion to go up the cableway to Table Mountain. I think I'll do it today. I'll see you tomorrow."

But the following day, Saturday, Alex couldn't find Johnny. He hadn't come back to the ship to sleep, which most of the crew did to avoid the cost of sleeping ashore. Alex spent the afternoon writing to Alice yet again, but by five o'clock he was worried. He decided to go into the city to find his friend. The crew tended to use the same bars, restaurants and brothels year after year, so looking for someone in a large city wasn't as crazy as it seemed. He jogged to Simon's Town station, posting his letters to Alice on the way. When his train arrived at the port area of Cape Town, he began a methodical search of the bars and restaurants—he was pretty sure Johnny wouldn't be in a brothel any more than he would himself.

As he left the third bar, still with no sign of his friend, he saw a couple of policemen keeping an eye on the groups of sailors moving from one bar to another, some already worse for the wear, even this early in the evening. He approached the policemen and had started talking before he recognised the older of the two men.

"I'm looking for a crew member off the *Empress of the Oceans*. Oh, hello again, Sergeant, I just recognised you."

The big South African looked at him.

"Good evening, Jock. Are you looking for the same friend who got in trouble a few weeks ago?"

"Well, yes as it happens."

"He's in jail."

The sergeant saw the look on Alex's face.

"Don't worry, he's not too bad. Picked another fight though, another Royal Navy man. He'll be in front of the judge Monday morning; he'll likely get off with a fine."

"But we're leaving tomorrow, at three o'clock. He needs to be on board before we sail or he'll be in all kinds of trouble."

"Sorry, Jock. He's been charged and all the paperwork's been done. Can't unwind the clock."

"Is there nothing I can do? I've got to get him home; he's got to be on that boat tomorrow."

"There's a bail hearing at ten in the morning. If he hands over fifty pounds bail money, they'll let him out."

The problem was that Alex didn't have fifty pounds in cash and he knew Johnny wouldn't either. The coming of war and the *Empress's* transformation from luxury liner to utilitarian troopship had led to many changes, not least a complete drying up of tips–a considerable portion of Alex's pre-war income. And now the shipping office was shut and wouldn't open again until Monday–there was no way to draw any money before then. *'Armstrong,'* he thought, he would borrow the money from him.

"OK steward, I can loan you fifty pounds, usual terms, ten per cent a week until you pay me back."

"But that's ridiculous. We'll be at sea. I can't pay you back until we get to England, so that's at least another two weeks, ten more pounds."

"It's not my fault your friend got into trouble. Do you want the money or not?"

Alex had found Armstrong as soon as he returned to the *Empress*. He hated dealing with him, but could see no other way of getting Johnny back on board before the ship sailed.

"OK, I'll take it," he said through clenched teeth.

"Not so fast. What about collateral?"

"Collateral?"

"You need to give something worth sixty pounds. You'll get it back when you pay back your loan."

"I know what collateral is, Armstrong. My word is my collateral. I've been on this ship since before it sailed. Everyone knows my word is good. Don't worry, you'll get your money and your interest."

"It's 'sir' to you, steward. And I don't give a damn about you and your word. You'll hand over the security or it's no deal."

Alex tried to stay calm as he thought things through. Slowly, he reached into his waistcoat pocket and pulled out his grandfather's watch.

Before he handed it over, Alex stared at Armstrong, "Listen to me, Armstrong, this has nothing to do with you being an officer, so don't fuck with me. If I told the Captain about this, you'd be out of a job in a second, and let's not pretend otherwise. Here take this; it's worth a lot more than sixty pounds. And if you step off the dock at Liverpool before I hand you your money and get this back, I'll come for you. There's nowhere, on land or sea, I won't find you. And when I do, I'll beat you senseless. Do you understand?"

Alex stepped forward until their chests were touching, and looked Armstrong in the eye.

"Sir?" he spat.

Armstrong was about the same size as Alex, but at that moment he felt nothing but fear. He knew Alex would indeed find him if he tried to cheat him. He took a half step backwards.

"Take it easy, steward. I'll go get your money. Wait here."

"I'm sorry, Alex, I really am. Sorry I cost you £50. I'll get it back to you."

The two men were walking briskly away from the shabby prison to catch a train back to their ship before it sailed without them.

"Don't be sorry to me, Johnny. It isn't about the £50. Be sorry to your family. Be sorry for drinking and gambling the money they need. It's time to stop, Johnny. You've got two weeks to pull yourself together or the rest of your life will be nothing but a disaster for you, for Stephanie and for those two wee girls. Grow up, and be a man, for God's sake."

As they walked up the crew gangplank to board the *Empress*, there was a loud crash to their left, and they instinctively swivelled towards the bow of the ship. The chains from the forward crane were swinging madly to and fro and a deck crew was scrambling to pick up whatever had fallen as they had been lifting it aboard.

Within five minutes, everyone on the ship knew the *Empress* was carrying a cargo of gold.

***

They were almost home at last. To avoid the mines and U-boats in the approaches to the English Channel, the *Empress* had, as usual, steamed all the way around Ireland so as to approach Liverpool from the north. Alex stood against the port rail and stared into the darkness. He knew that, if the clear skies persisted until dawn, Scotland would be visible from this vantage point. But for now, sky and sea blended together in the inky darkness. He looked up. The Milky Way was amazingly bright tonight.

A peculiar side-effect of the wartime blackout was that once again the inhabitants of Britain, even the city-dwellers, lived under completely dark skies. Even by wartime standards however, this night, was special, magical. From one horizon to the other, high across the sky, the stars formed an arch of shimmering lights. With a son as curious as Hughie, and so many nights at sea to learn from experts, Alex had become something of an authority on the stars and constellations. One of his earliest thrills on the *Empress* had been to see the southern skies, with completely new stars, completely new patterns. The sight immediately took his thoughts to Alice. Was she looking at her southern stars right now?

'You fool!' he thought. Of course she wasn't. Alice would be arriving at work on an autumn morning. The sounds of kookaburras and spoonbills and parrots would have accompanied her walk to the station. She was half a world away; where it was morning, not evening; autumn, not spring. There were so many miles between them.

Alex went below. He would write her a quick letter to post tomorrow in Liverpool.

When he finished writing his letter, Alex realised he had run out of envelopes, so he folded the sheets and slid them into his brass cartridge case container and tightened the lid, as always with a fond thought of Jim, his late brother-in-law. At the precise moment when he had properly sealed the container, *'All Stations'* was sounded.

It wasn't uncommon for *'All Stations'* to be sounded in Home Waters. Generally, it was in response to a message from one of their destroyer escorts that a U-boat or enemy warplane had been detected in the vicinity. On this final leg of her journey, two Royal Navy destroyers had escorted the *Empress* since she had turned east to round the island of Ireland.

However, by the time Alex had pulled on his lifejacket and reached his fire station, he could hear the dull thump-thump-thump of an anti-aircraft gun and he realised they were under attack this time.

This was only the fourth or fifth time the guns had been fired in anger. The first occasion had been when they tried to shoot down an unsuspecting RAF plane coming for a closer look at the famous liner. Fortunately, the pilot had turned away before any damage was done.

Alex's station was on 'D' deck, in the lobby in front of what had been the first-class dining room, now an enormous dormitory. The lobby was the intersection of the two principal passages through the ship, passages that would have to be kept free of flames in the event of a fire to prevent passengers being trapped inside their cabins. He was also expected to help control the flow of people and ensure everyone was wearing a life jacket.

He arrived on station as the first soldiers appeared. Two things worked in favour of an orderly alert—there were fewer than 400 passengers aboard, and they were almost all servicemen who could be expected to remain calm and to follow orders.

Alex spotted the first issue needing his attention.

"You two, run back to your cabins and get your lifejackets."

As Alex finished speaking to the two Aussie soldiers, there was a crash and huge explosion behind him and he was thrown across the lobby to smash into the wall of the boarded up purser's office. He blacked out for a few seconds before coming to on the floor, with his back to the wall and his left arm at an odd angle.

Gingerly he used his good arm to investigate and with one touch realised he had a broken arm. However, the skin wasn't broken and he assumed it wasn't too serious. He pulled himself to his feet and looked around. The wall to the dining room where he had been standing was more or less entirely gone. Flames licked through the empty space where the grand double doors once stood. The lobby floor was strewn with bodies, some moving weakly; some, like Alex, pulling themselves to their feet, and some obviously dead. He started to make his way through the crowd to find his fire hose. As he started to move, his damaged arm twisted and he gasped with the searing pain that brought him to a halt. Using his good hand he managed to get his trouser belt off. He yelled above the increasing roar of the fire.

"Hey, can you buckle this for me?"

The soldier looked blank for a moment, then understood. He tightened Alex's belt, securing his broken arm firmly against his lifejacket.

"Thanks. Find some other men who can walk and start getting the wounded out of here, onto the deck."

The Australian nodded and went to work.

Alex turned again to find his hose and understood why he had survived the explosion. The thick water pipes serving the fire station had largely protected him from the blast, but with a shock he saw that although both pipes were now fractured, no water was gushing from them. Either there was another rupture on a lower deck, or the pumps were not functioning. He ran over to the Australian who had helped him a moment ago, who was now supporting a man with a bloody leg, slowly assisting him to the door leading to the deck.

"I'm going to the other side to see if the other fire hose is working. Take charge here and keep everyone moving. If any more come up without lifejackets, tell them to take them off the dead bodies."

By now the lobby was filling with smoke and the heat of the flames from below was rapidly increasing. Already, Alex could see the wooden floor smoking in the areas nearest the dining room. He pushed his way through the milling soldiers, but when he arrived at the starboard station, it too was out of action. The hose had been unwound, but it was clear no water was available to fight the flames. The pumps must be out. This probably meant the engine room had been hit.

Quickly putting his working arm around the waist of a civilian struggling to walk, he pulled the man though the door onto the promenade deck and settled him on a bench. He trotted over to the rail and looked down. Even though it had only been a few minutes, he could sense the ship was slowing down. With all of the uproar around him, it was hard to be sure, but he thought he could no longer feel the ever-present vibration of the ship's engines and propellers.

More and more men were now gathering on the promenade deck. Alex spotted one of the ship's officers.

"Do we know how badly we're damaged, sir?"

"A direct hit in the engine room. We've no power to drive the ship or run the pumps, but one generator is still functioning, so we've got electricity. Engineering is trying to get the pumps working. At this point ..."

"Take cover!" someone shouted.

The German plane was back, this time raking the *Empress* with cannon fire. With no hydraulic power, neither of her guns could be turned to train their fire anywhere but dead ahead and dead astern. Alex crouched and looked forward to see the bomber roar down the side of the ship. He could hear the sounds of the cannon shells striking—thuds as they tore through the wooden decking, crashes when they blew out glass doors and portholes and screams as they struck steel and shattered into hundreds of shards of red-hot metal that tore through the bodies of the men on the deck. Alex turned back, just in time to hear a muted cough, as the officer who had been talking to him died, blood pouring from his open mouth. The man looked surprised rather than hurt.

Amidst all of this bedlam, the fire was raging unchecked. With no means of fighting the flames, it was only a question of time before fire consumed the ship.

Word came from the stern that the German bomber had flown away, so Alex decided the best course of action was to get everyone mustered close to the lifeboats, ready for the order to abandon ship, which must come soon, he thought.

The boat deck was one level above where he was, so he moved along the deck, urging the troops to hurry up the companionways, first ensuring that each uninjured soldier took responsibility for one of the many injured or in need of assistance. By now, flames were rising high over the ship and, with the danger from the air now gone, the two escorting destroyers approached closer to the *Empress* to pick up her lifeboats.

Alex's attention was caught by what seemed to be the last soldier on his deck. He was standing at the furthest forward section, apparently uninjured, but showing no signs of moving. Alex hurried towards him and saw he was young, probably only eighteen or so. He was frozen to the spot, unable to move or to think clearly.

"Come on, soldier. This way now."

Midnight 25th May

As Alex grasped the young man's arm, the order to abandon ship was heard all over the *Empress*.

Alex spoke urgently to the immobilised soldier.

"Listen! You'll be in a lifeboat in a minute and look, you can see the destroyer, it's not far to go before you'll be safe. Come on, hold the rail and get on up there."

Alex walked the young man around the corner to the nearest flight of steps, where the soldier finally released Alex's good arm and began to climb up the steep companionway, one careful step at a time. Alex took a last look around and put a foot on the bottom step.

At that instant, the fires roaring below the ammunition store for the forward anti-aircraft gun finally reached a critical temperature, and the entire cache of hundreds of high-explosive shells exploded in an enormous ball of flame and lethal shards of metal.

Another few seconds and he would have been above the blast wave of destruction. As it was, Alex was hit by the force of the explosion and his head slammed into the metal wall beside him. He lost consciousness instantly.

1:00 A.M. 26th May

An hour later, Trevor Henderson, the *Empress's* Captain, stood talking with the Captain and First Officer of HMS *Halifax*, one of the escorting destroyers. Henderson had also broken his arm and had sustained burns to the side of his face. He had crossed temporarily to the escorting vessel to have his arm bandaged and to discuss, in confidence, what had to be done next.

"It's been an hour and she's no lower in the water. I think it's possible she won't sink, even though the fires are still burning. We were pretty low on oil and I think most of what's flammable will have been consumed soon."

The Royal Navy captain replied, "I think you could be right. We'll put out a call for a couple of tugs and, if she hasn't settled any deeper in another hour, we'll put a couple of lines on her and begin a tow ourselves. Commander, would you action that now, thank you."

As soon as they were alone, Captain Henderson turned to his opposite number.

"Captain, in addition to the usual materials, the *Empress* is carrying a large consignment of gold, many tons of gold. For as long as she stays afloat, I need to do everything possible to recover that gold."

"My God! Well, I can put a party aboard in, let's say, thirty minutes. If she is holding on then, I think there's a reasonable chance she'll continue to float."

"Thank you, but if you don't mind, that gold is my responsibility, mine and the *Empress's*. If you can help get us aboard and transfer the gold in your boats, I'd rather use my officers and men to get hold of the stuff. Plus, they know their way around the ship; your people don't."

"Very well."

A plan of action was quickly agreed. When the gold had been loaded on the *Empress* in Cape Town, one of the cranes on 'A' deck had lifted the gold aboard on pallets and the freight cage had been used to lower the pallets through the forward hatch, down to 'D' deck. From there, crew members had used a pallet truck to push the gold thirty yards along a passageway forward to the bullion room, a specially reinforced walk-in safe about fifteen feet on each side and eight feet high.

Now, *Empress* officers would lead two work parties of four seamen. After an initial reconnoitre, the first party would go below to bring the gold to the loading hatch and manoeuvre it onto the freight cage lowered from 'A' deck above. From there the second team would be responsible for hoisting up the gold and transferring the pallets onto the destroyers' tenders which would shuttle back and forth between the stricken liner and the *Halifax* and the Canadian destroyer, *HMCS St. Joseph*, 'St. Joe'.

While this was going on, the two destroyers would tow the *Empress* at around four knots; a slow speed that would allow the launches to easily hold station alongside the burning ship.

1:30 A.M. 26th May

Captain Henderson's next stop was the *Halifax's* sick bay. The *Empress's* doctor was trying, vainly as it transpired, to sew a finger back on one of the soldiers who had been brought over from the stricken liner. Both medical teams had worked through the most serious injuries by now and were tackling the less severe problems.

"Will I be able to play the trumpet do you think, Doc?" the Aussie corporal wanted to know.

"I don't see why not, it's only a pinkie."

"Bonzer! I've always wanted to play a musical instrument."

The doctor pulled a face.

"I think that's only the thirty-second time I've heard that one, no wait, thirty-third."

The Captain had checked the three beds in the destroyer's tiny sickroom, much smaller than the one on his own ship.

"What's wrong with Steward Campbell, doctor? I didn't see any major injuries, even the head wound doesn't look too bad to me."

"The fact is, we don't know. Doctor Carrington here was a neurologist in civilian life; he thinks there must be a brain injury, but we daren't open him up here."

The doctor from the *Halifax* turned from his own patient.

"We'll make sure he's a priority when we get to Liverpool. I'll write him up for the receiving team. Now, Captain, let me take a look at that arm."

3:00 A.M. 26th May

Since her conversion to war duties, the *Empress* had operated with only seven officers in addition to her Captain. Following the attack, only four were fully fit and available for duty. Captain Henderson assigned command of the recovery job to Chief Engineer MacDonald, assisted by Second Officer Everett. However, nearly two hours passed from when the *'Abandon Ship'* signal had been given before the *Halifax's* launch came gently alongside the still burning liner. The emergency nets used to speed the evacuation were still in place and the recovery teams scrambled up them onto the forward deck, where the two officers assessed the situation. The flames amidships were lower than when they had abandoned the *Empress*, but the deck plates themselves were, if anything, hotter than two hours ago, evidence that fires continued to rage below.

The explosion of the ammunition store, one deck above, had destroyed one of the 'A' deck cranes. Their first task was to make the remaining crane useable manually, since they had no hydraulic or electrical power. As soon as this was accomplished, the men worked together to rotate the crane until the jib was positioned so the hook was set immediately alongside the hatch.

Now came the first really dangerous manoeuvre. Chief Engineer MacDonald had to wedge a foot into the hook and hold tight to the crane's wire then be lowered down to verify that access to 'D' Deck was still free. Then he had to be dropped further, all the way to the deepest hold, seven decks below. This is where the freight cage was stored, the cage that would be used to lift the gold.

While MacDonald donned his engineer's hat and heavy gloves and prepared himself for the ordeal, the other men looked around nervously. There was no sign the fires were growing. In fact, in the minutes they had spent on board, the height of the flames seemed to have diminished slightly. Nevertheless, they constantly shuffled their feet and swivelled their heads as they listened to the roar of the fires and heard faint crashes as pieces of the ship were consumed somewhere below them.

Finally, MacDonald was ready. He switched on his hard hat lamp and gave a wave to the men operating the crane, signalling them to slowly position him directly over the gaping hatch. Fortunately, the sea was calm and there was barely any sway in the cable. Everett and MacDonald tested their walkie-talkie reception and the signal was given to slowly lower the hook.

"Beer deck clear." MacDonald's voice could be heard clearly over the ever-present background static.

"Charlie deck clear. Don clear. Edward clear. Freddie deck clear, but heat increasing. George deck clear, but very hot now. Slow down. Five feet, three, STOP. Down in hold. All clear and maybe not so hot. I think the nearest fire must be on George deck."

There was silence for several minutes, as MacDonald worked below to secure the hook through the shackles of the chains secured to each corner of the cargo cage. The cage was of course smaller than the hatch itself. Any of the three-foot high sidewalls could be dropped to create a bridge from the cage to the relevant deck for loading and unloading. After a while, MacDonald's voice came over the radio once again.

"OK, lift me up, easy."

There were coloured markers woven into the lifting wire to show the crane operators when the cage was level with each deck. As the marker for 'D' deck touched the jib, MacDonald's voice could be heard again.

"STOP!"

The men on deck peered over the open hatch. Four decks below, they could just make out the dancing beam from MacDonald's helmet and hear the clang as he dropped the side wall facing forward, and after a pause, the fainter sounds as he closed it up again.

"Proceeding into the passageway. Looks OK so far. Six feet in; twelve feet. Bloody hell!"

Everett pressed his transmit key. "What's up, Chief?"

"The floor's badly buckled here. I can step over it, but we'll never be able to push anything on wheels over this mess. We're going to have to carry everything out box by box. Going on."

There was another pause.

"OK, I've reached the room. Only that buckled floor back there, otherwise, no problems. You can come down now."

Quickly the cage was lifted and the Second Officer climbed in to be lowered so he could join Chief MacDonald. The design of the safe locking mechanism meant both safe keys had to be used simultaneously in order to open the door. MacDonald had been given the Captain's key, while Everett used the key handed over reluctantly by the Bank of England official responsible for the gold.

"Right, Mr Everett, let's get this opened."

The men turned their respective keys and MacDonald turned the heavy brass handle all the way back around to the unlocked position and opened the door, which despite its obvious weight, swung easily on its brass hinges. They secured the open door against the bulkhead, using the brass dog catches installed for that purpose. A quick glance inside showed the boxes of gold piled six high, almost filling the space.

"We'll take one with us to show the others," suggested MacDonald.

Ten minutes later, the two officers were standing beside the rest of the group.

MacDonald spoke. "It's going to be fine as long as the fires don't get any worse. That buckled floor is the only problem, but it's a big one. We'll have to carry everything out one box at a time. It will take two men to carry one box, so this is going to take a long time. Let's get started. Mr Everett, will you tell the launch what's happening and have them signal *Halifax*. Two men in the cage at a time, four boxes of gold each load. Simkins, you and me first, then Adams and Masters. We'll load and the rest of you get the gold on board the launch. Let's go."

The men worked steadily. Whatever the fires were doing on the *Empress*, they weren't getting any worse around the foredeck. However, the buckled floor was a major problem, and the task went much slower than they had planned. After an hour of hard work, forty boxes of gold had been loaded onto the *Halifax's* launch. The Chief Engineer appeared at the hatch, having come up in the cage with two boxes.

"Mr Everett, would you take over below. I'm going over to the *Halifax* to talk with the skipper. We need more men on this, we'll have to work through the night."

With MacDonald aboard, the *Halifax's* launch motored back to her mother ship, and the launch from *St Joe* took up station alongside the *Empress*.

Captain Henderson was waiting for his Chief Engineer.

"We need more men, sir. The buckled floor is holding us up, but the biggest chokepoint is the manual hoist. It takes an age to lift the cage, lower it over the side onto the launch, unload and reposition. I don't know what will happen if the sea cuts up. And we need to relieve the men on the hoist frequently - they have the hardest job."

3 P.M. 26th May

The work was slow, but by relieving the men regularly, a steady pace was maintained. At three p.m. a signal was received from Naval Operations, advising that two tugs from Greenock would be on station by seven p.m. to take the *Empress* in tow. Judging by the pace of recoveries, Captain Henderson estimated they would have finished extracting the gold well before the arrival of the tugs.

However, just before four p.m. an R.A.F. submarine hunter reported a probable U-boat sighting about 20 miles away. The decision was made to send the *St. Joe* on a wide sweep pattern, although her launch would continue to operate the shuttle service to and from *Halifax*. This news was soon passed on to the men working on the recovery and they picked up the pace, more nervous now about the danger they were in.

5:50 P.M. 26th May

At 5:50 p.m., the *Halifax's* launch relieved that of the *St. Joe,* and six fresh deckhands clambered up onto the *Empress*. The men being relieved wished their replacements luck as they lowered the cage with four more boxes over the side then clambered down the netting. They didn't know exactly how many boxes of gold were left, but they knew the job was almost complete and they would not be required to come aboard the stricken liner again.

The new shift worked to reposition and lower the cage into the darkness of the shaft. Below, Adams and John Brownlish dropped off two boxes beside the hatchway. They took a breather for a moment as Nigel Murdoch and Second Engineer Armstrong lifted the first box of gold into the cage.

When it became clear that more work crews would be required, Armstrong had been ordered to take charge of a work party. He had never been on board a fighting ship and had no idea where things were. However, his first thought had been his money belt, he didn't think he could get away with wearing it while he clambered about the *Empress* alongside the rest of the work party.

Like Alex, Armstrong had been off-duty when '*All Stations*' had been sounded. He had grabbed his money belt, which also held Alex's watch and chain, and quickly tightened it around his waist under his shirt. Now he searched frantically for a secure hiding place. Fortunately, there was something approaching chaos on the *Halifax*, with hundreds of men looking for somewhere to sit or lie down, sheltered from the wind; so no one paid attention as he moved around the ship.

Finally, he spotted a shadowy void behind a duct feeding cold air to the engine room. He wedged the belt tight behind the pipe and made his way back to where the launches were being loaded with a new team for the *Empress*.

Armstrong was on his fourth turn below the Empress's decks. He had become progressively more nervous as the night wore on. When they received the intelligence about the approaching U-boat, he reached the limits of his courage. As they bent down to lower another box of gold, there was an enormous bang and the ship shuddered. The cage swung away from the passageway and Murdoch lost his balance, let go of the rope handle of the box of gold and barely managed to catch hold of the edge of the cage before he would have fallen sixty feet into the hold.

"What the hell was that?" Armstrong screamed into the radio.

A calm voice answered from above. "It's OK, sir; it was a torpedo attack, but one missed and one was a dud. The Canadians are after the bugger. He won't fire on us again."

The deckhand looked at his mate with a smirk. The men had heard the fear in Armstrong's voice.

"He's probably worried some of his precious 'collateral' is about to sink!"

The two of them laughed.

Down below, Armstrong had had enough. He turned back towards the passageway and yelled,

"You two, back here, right now. We're going up until we get a better picture of what's happening. Come on Murdoch, let's get these two loaded."

They swiftly loaded the two boxes.

"Murdoch, Adams, get in the cage. Send the cage back down before it's used to transfer this lot onto the launch."

As Murdoch and Adams slowly disappeared up though the hatchway, Brownlish turned to Armstrong.

"We could probably pick up at least one more box before the cage comes back down, sir."

"To hell with that. We've done enough."

After what seemed an eternity, the cage returned, the two men clambered in and Armstrong signalled for them to be lifted out of the depths of the ship. As soon as the hoist stopped, they climbed out and the two boxes of gold waiting on deck were once again loaded into the cage and swung over to be lowered to the launch. Armstrong sent Adams, Murdoch, Brownlish and two more of the deck crew down the netting and, as soon as the launch confirmed the cage had been emptied, he directed the pair on the crane to drop the cage on the *Empress's* deck and follow him over the side.

As soon as they were safely on board, Armstrong went forward to join the *Halifax's* bosun who was piloting the launch.

"Cast off and let's go, bosun, fast as you like."

6:30 P.M. 26th May

The R.A.F. spotter had been accurate in his estimate of the U-boat's distance. However, the submarine that had attacked them, and was now being pursued by the *St. Joe*, was a different boat. As boatswain Henry Brown closed with the *Halifax*, the first U-boat finally came within range of the *Empress* and immediately launched two torpedoes.

The U-boat's first torpedo hit the *Empress* about 110 feet from her bow, bursting directly into a fuel tank. Although there was not much fuel left, the tank was full of combustible vapours. The resulting huge explosion tore the entire bow section away. This enormous part of the ship sank immediately, while the main body of the ship began to take on water and to settle lower.

Meanwhile, in a cruel twist of fate, the second torpedo missed the *Empress* completely, but struck a glancing blow against the *Halifax*, and exploded twenty feet away. Although the impact was not enough to penetrate the destroyer's hull, the launch, which had just arrived alongside, was lifted completely out of the water, stern first, and smashed violently against her mother ship's steel sides, disintegrating into four sections, which immediately sank. Everyone on board was killed instantly, except Armstrong and bosun Brown who had been up front, protected by the fore cabin.

There were multiple injuries on board the *Halifax* and some superficial damage, but nothing that threatened the safety of the ship. Order was quickly restored, and a tender launched to picked up the two men who had survived the destruction of the shattered launch. The bodies of two of the fatalities were also recovered. It was almost twenty minutes after the explosion before they were able to lift the tender back onto the ship.

6:45 P.M. 26th May

While the operation proceeded to save the survivors of the launch, Captain Henderson watched helplessly as his command of over ten years gradually drifted further away, slowing rapidly as it did. The fires on board, now augmented by fresh flames from the torpedo explosion, provided hellish illumination to the scene.

Finally, almost gracefully, the *Empress of the Oceans* turned on her side and slipped into the cold embrace of the dark waters, carrying with her the memories of hundreds of voyages and thousands of passengers. She had known years of gaiety and luxury, joyous years—all terminated by the call to arms.

Now the *Empress* lay at the bottom of the ocean, the ocean she had once crossed in peerless elegance and style.

And in her undamaged bullion room lay thirty gold ingots, each weighing twenty-five pounds.

Armstrong knew he had panicked. He should have recovered more of the gold—after all, he had no inkling the second attack was coming. But the near miss had unnerved him completely.

But now it didn't matter.

He sat before his Captain in the wardroom of the *Halifax*, a sling supporting his dislocated shoulder and a bandage covering a cut on his forehead. Henderson was dog-tired and operating under more stress than he realised following the loss of his command.

"Thank you for agreeing to this interview, Mr Armstrong. There will be an official enquiry when we get back to Liverpool, but for my own benefit, I'd like to clear up a few matters. I should tell you that this interview will form part of my own formal report."

"Yes, sir."

"You told me you sent up the two final boxes, that is correct?"

"Yes, sir. I ordered Murdoch and Adams into the cage with the last consignment. I know I was exceeding the agreed weight limit, but in the circumstances…"

"Quite. You did the right thing, and you showed the behaviour I would expect by remaining below until everyone else was safe."

"Well, not quite, sir; Brownlish was still with me. He and I were the final lift."

"And you are certain the strongroom was empty?"

"Quite certain, sir. I was the last person to look, and I made sure."

"And how many boxes were on board the launch for the final return trip?"

"Seven, sir."

"Seven. I see. Well, Mr Armstrong, that gold is now scattered at the bottom of the ocean, but at least we recovered the bulk of the consignment. A tragedy that we came so close to recovering all of it without loss of life."

"Yes, sir, a tragedy, as you say. May I ask how many boxes we did recover in total?"

"Over five hundred boxes. That will buy a lot of food and weapons and will help win this ghastly war."

"Indeed, sir."

1941 Aftermath

CLYDEBANK, SCOTLAND

The sinking of the *Empress* provoked an outpouring of grief in every corner of the United Kingdom, and further afield. For ten years she had been the pride of the nation. Even when larger, faster ships came along, in particular Cunard's two *Queens*, the *Empress* continued to exert a powerful hold on the nation's imagination. The combination of her uniquely graceful design and the widely published images of the great white ship in exotic ports of call bestowed on her an unsurpassed aura of luxury and glamour.

Even before the terrible news was announced to the press, cables had gone out to British ambassadors, to heads of governments in Allied states and, of course, to the dominions and colonies of the British Empire. And so it was that Alice Murray was called to the Australian Prime Minister's office to be told of the sinking before she could read about it in the newspapers.

"I am terribly sorry to be the bearer of such dreadful news, Miss Murray; but you must keep your hopes up. I gather the vast majority of the passengers and crew were rescued and are even now on their way home. A casualty list will no doubt be issued in a few days."

The rest of her week passed in a daze. Alice was unable to focus on her work as she waited to be relieved of the overpowering feeling of dread that was wearing her down. Finally, the morning came when the Geelong Advertiser carried the *Empress of the Oceans* casualty list. One of the first names listed was Alex Campbell.

The fog of war takes many forms. The well-intentioned efforts of the medical team on the *Halifax* had ensured that Alex was rushed off the destroyer and into a waiting ambulance to be delivered post haste to the emergency team at Royal Liverpool Infirmary. Unfortunately, this urgency meant he wasn't recorded as leaving the *Halifax* and consequently he was listed as 'Missing, presumed dead'.

Lacking contacts in high places to give them advance warning, Kate and Hugh learned the fate of the *Empress* from the two-inch headlines in every newspaper in the country. Like Alice, they too had tense days of dreadful anticipation until the morning came when they read the news they had feared, and later received the telegram confirming Alex's probable death.

However, unlike Alice, the family had to endure their loss for only three days, before the mistaken report of Alex's condition was discovered and a new telegram received, advising that Alex was alive, but in a critical condition.

Less than three months after she had lost her husband and niece, Kate now had to deal with the emotional torment of the apparent loss of her brother-in-law and head of her family, and subsequently the news of his survival, but with serious injuries.

The family was living in scruffy temporary accommodation several streets away from their own flats–no one knew how long it would take to rebuild the staircase of their close. It made everything even worse.

"I'm going down to Liverpool, to see Dad." Hugh told Kate as soon as the second telegram arrived, late in the afternoon.

"I think that's a good idea, son. Why don't you pack a bag and go through to Glasgow now, you can go to the restaurant and tell your Uncle Ian the good news. You can stay the night with them, and get the early train in the morning."

At eight o'clock the following morning, Hugh took his seat in the compartment of the train heading for Liverpool. His journey would take four hours.

Eight minutes later, seconds before the train was due to depart, the compartment door slid open and a man in uniform stepped in, giving Hugh a friendly nod as he did. Hugh had hoped to have the compartment to himself, but at first glance, his fellow passenger appeared nice enough.

"Are you going to London too?" asked the stranger.

"No, only to Preston. I change there for Liverpool," Hugh replied.

The man reached out his hand, "Rabbi Louis Rabinowitz. Padre," he added seeing Hugh's glance at his sleeve. "Technically, Captain, but all chaplains are addressed as Padre, even the kosher ones."

"Hugh Campbell; pleased to meet you, Padre."

"Unlike me, you sound like you belong in this part of the world. Are you going to join your unit?"

At that moment, the train jerked as the engine pulled them away from platform one of Glasgow Central station.

"No, I'm not in the Forces, although…Actually, I'm only a student. My dad has been injured. I'm going to see him in Liverpool, in hospital."

The rabbi had noted the hesitation but ignored it for the moment.

"What happened to your father?"

"We don't know. Four days ago, we were told he was probably dead; then yesterday we were told he's unconscious in hospital. That's all we know."

"It must have been a terrible shock for your family. I mean to hear of his death and then that he's alive."

Hugh found himself telling the rabbi about Jean and his uncle Jim, mentioning his mother, as he explained how his aunt and uncle had basically raised them while Alex was at sea.

There was a silence for a while as the rabbi digested Hugh's story. Finally, he had another question.

"When I asked about joining your unit, you were uncomfortable."

"I wanted to join up, but my dad made me promise I'd go to university. He said it was my duty to become an engineer. It was during his leave before he sailed last time. But I hate it, not being in uniform, I mean. I'm going to ask him again if I can leave uni and volunteer."

"Why did your father say it was your duty to become an engineer?"

"You need to understand, Padre, my father is crazy about education, completely crazy about it."

And now Hugh once more opened up to this complete stranger, telling him his story, his family's story.

"Then he insisted that winning the war needed engineers more than soldiers or sailors."

"Your father is a remarkable man, Hugh. I'm sure you know that, but I wonder if you understand how rare he is? We have a teaching in Judaism, *'It is not your responsibility to finish the work of perfecting the world, but neither are you free to desist from it'*. It seems to me your father has never desisted from trying to perfect the part of the world he has taken responsibility for, his workmates, his passengers and especially his family, his entire family. I would like to meet him."

"He is a great dad; I wish we could have seen more of him. He wanted us to have a family business by now, one that he and my aunts and uncles could all be part of."

"I think you are allowing yourself to feel a little sorry for yourself: You wish you had seen more of your dad, you wish you could join the Forces, no doubt you wish you had not lost your mother all those years ago. Now you've lost your sister, and your father is injured, maybe badly."

Rabbi Rabinowitz sat back in his seat as he continued.

"You're maybe thinking I'm being hard on you? You have had things to bear, of course you have. But your father has set you an example. It is your duty to follow it. Decide your priorities; absorb the blows and the pain; make the sacrifices. You're going to university because your father instructed you to do so. There is another quote in the Talmud, *'Greater is he who performs an action because he is commanded than he who performs the same action without being commanded.'* We Jews do love to quote, don't we?" he smiled.

"From what you've told me; many years ago, your father decided what his life's work would be; to ensure his sons and nephews had the best education money could buy. To build a secure business to provide for the well-being of his entire family–brother, in-laws, nieces and nephews, as well as his own children. And until this war came around and added a new duty, one to his country, your father had sacrificed everything, devoted everything to achieving these goals. That is truly a life well lived!"

They talked on. Rabbi Rabinowitz told Hugh about what was happening to the Jews in Europe, what had happened in the years before the war. But all the time they talked, a part of Hugh's brain was mulling over the rabbi's words about his father. Alex had been set on his goals for years. Now he was older, Hugh understood that his father had determined his priorities years before he received the miraculous cheque from America. All those visits to the Art Gallery, all the overtime, the decision to go to sea, everything geared to bring his family to a better, safer, more secure harbour.

At last the train approached Preston, where Hugh had to change for Liverpool. He stood up and, before picking up his bag, he held out his hand.

"Thank you, Rabbi. You've given me a lot to think about. It's been a pleasure talking with you."

"And you too. Please give your father my wishes for a speedy recovery and please forgive one more Jewish saying, *'If you save just one life, you save the whole world.'* Your life as a student may not seem important right now, but one day your work may save that one life. Shalom aleichem, Hugh. Peace be upon you."

Hugh spent the rest of his journey thinking about his conversation with the rabbi, and about his father's life. Where before he had admired his father's actions as a series of discrete, unconnected events, now he saw Alex had been implementing a grand plan. And he knew he didn't have an equivalent vision for his own life. His father had set an example; now Hugh had to decide whether to follow it.

According to the porter at Liverpool's Lime Street Station, the hospital was less than a fifteen-minute walk. Hugh set off, anxious now to see his father and to reassure him that his son would fulfil his ambition and graduate. Hugh hadn't worked out the rest of his plan, but he knew the first step was to complete his education. Although he was worried about his father, he felt strangely elated as he bounded up the steps leading to the main entrance.

After a ten-minute wait, he was told his father was in Ward Eight, on the second floor. It wasn't visiting time, but in view of Hugh's long journey to get here, he was allowed to go up to the ward.

"But you'll need to ask permission from Matron to visit your father," he was warned.

He pushed open the heavy swing door to the ward and immediately saw the Matron's office to his left. He politely knocked on the open door and the nurse turned to him.

"What are you doing up here? It isn't visiting time; you'll have to come back later I'm afraid. I can't think why you were allowed in at all."

"Sister, my name is Hugh Campbell, I've just arrived from Glasgow to see my father, Alex Campbell, who is a patient here I believe. Can I please see him, for a moment? Then I'll leave and come back later."

She looked at him oddly then gestured to the chair beside her.

"Take a seat, Hugh."

He sat down, nervous now.

"I'm dreadfully sorry; but your father passed away not twenty minutes ago. He never regained consciousness. I'm afraid there was nothing we could do for him. I'm so very sorry."

***

Alex's death provoked a strange reaction in Kate. Over the following weeks, the idea grew in her imagination that her late sister's family, which by now she thought of as her own, was in some way jinxed. Annie herself had died young; before that, their first baby, Willie, died when only a two-year-old and then there was the death of lovely Jean. And now Alex. Hugh was at university and essentially an adult now, but what was to become of Alan and Betty, just thirteen and fourteen? Kate loved them dearly, and she now developed an all-consuming fear that the youngest children would die if they stayed in Clydebank. She was constantly aware that, although there had not been a repeat of the horrendous nights in March, the Germans were still mounting raids targeting the shipyards, and people were still being killed.

Finally, one Saturday morning, she sat down with Hugh and explained her fears.

For his part, Hugh was trying to come to terms with the loss of his father, coming on top of the death of his young sister.

Hugh felt guilt about Jean's death; if she had still been safe in the evacuation house in Girvan; or if he had been at home that night, taking care of her, then she wouldn't have been under those bloody stairs. Of course he knew this was ridiculous, but they had grown so close since Annie's death.

And his dad had died doing his duty. He was quite old and still he had given his life, while Hugh remained a useless student. He had joined the Officer Training Corps, which would at least mean he would go into action immediately on graduation. But for now, his exempt status only added to his feelings of guilt, despite his determination to fulfil his father's ambition by graduating.

Alex's death also brought back Hugh's memories of his mother, which were fading with every passing year. It was a bit like waking from a particularly vivid dream. One moment, he was immersed in the sense of his mother; she was right there, singing to him, cuddling him, tucking him in at night. But then she was gone, slipping away. Was that a real memory, or a remembrance of an imagined memory? Did she really sing *Bobby Shafto* to him when he was little, or did his dad tell him she did? He wasn't absolutely sure one way or another.

Now, he was keenly aware of being an orphan, even though he had come to view Kate as his surrogate mother. What were Betty and Alan going through?

But, through all of this, Hugh took strength from his conversation with the rabbi on the train. Their chat and Hugh's subsequent determination to follow his father's example, kept him focused. In his methodical way, he had spent the journey home dealing with his grief over Alex's death by trying to work out the goals he should set for himself. He wasn't altogether there yet, but he knew one of his most important tasks was to accept responsibility for his younger siblings, Betty and Alan. He would work to give them the advantages his father would have sought for them.

"I think I understand what you're feeling, Aunt Kate; but what can we do? Do you want to move, away from Clydebank? Or we could have them evacuated again, but this time until the war ends. Most of the local weans have gone somewhere else."

"No, not that. I've been thinking, Hugh. You know your dad exchanged Christmas cards every year with an American couple? Do you remember the first letters he got from them, about helping the young girl? I don't know how much you understood, you were young."

"I remember; and a couple of years ago, Uncle Jim explained what Dad did for them, Dad would always brush it off when I asked him about it."

"Aye, he would. But did you know they gave your father £1000? That's what helped pay for you and Robbie to go to university, and Gerry and Leckie's schooling too. Oh dear, what will happen now to those two when the schools go back next month? I never thought."

"I did, and I already told Aunt Agnes the boys will be staying on at the Academy. When I saw the lawyer about Dad's will, I told him, too."

Kate looked admiringly at her nephew, always wise beyond his years.

"You're so like your father, Hughie, Hugh. He was so proud of you and for good reason."

Kate paused for a moment before continuing, "But listen; there are lots of children from England being sent to Canada 'til the war's over. I've been thinking of writing to that American and asking if he'll take Betty and Alan and keep them safe. But you're, well you're head of your family now, so I think you need to decide."

This was not an option that Hugh had considered.

"I'm not sure. Will they want to go? It means leaving their friends, and Alan is well settled at the Academy."

"I know, but if they go to Girvan or wherever, they'll only be marking time. I mean, their schooling will be interrupted anyway, and who knows how long this will go on for? And you know how much I thought of your father, but I must tell you; I didn't agree with him about the girls, about their education I mean. Look at how things are changing. Women doing men's work, women in uniform, flying planes even. Americans don't think like we do. I've been reading in magazines; American girls go to university just like boys. Betty should have the same chances as Alan. There, I've said it, but please don't think I'm speaking against your father's memory, please. But of course, the main reason I want them to go is to be safe. I worry about them every night. If anything happened to any of you, I'm not sure I could take it. I'm at the end of my strength, Hugh."

Hugh was well aware that some girls went to university in Scotland; he studied alongside some of them. But he knew there were very few, and none from working class homes. And Hugh paid attention to everything. He was aware that living standards in America had raced way ahead of Britain, and evacuation in Scotland was indeed merely a way of parking children and keeping them as safe as possible. Plus, some young ones had come back from the earlier evacuation with terrible stories about their treatment. Maybe his brother and sister *would* be better off in America.

"Alright, Aunt Kate, here's what I'll do. I'll talk to Alan and Betty at the weekend and we'll see how they feel."

Hugh did talk with Alan and Betty and after a great deal of conversation they decided that, yes, they would like to go to live in America. Hugh suspected American films had more influence over their decision than fears about air raids.

And so Kate sent off a letter.

Dear Mr and Mrs Fredericks,

My name is Kate Craig. My late sister Annie was the wife of Alex Campbell. You will, I'm sure, have heard that the Empress of the Oceans was sunk recently by the Germans. I'm sorry to tell you that Alex was killed in that action. We miss him every day.

I read the letters you sent Alex some years ago, to thank him for coming to the aid of your daughter, and I know he enjoyed receiving your Christmas cards over the years. Your generosity helped enable Alex's sons and nephews to have a wonderful education. His oldest, Hugh is now attending Glasgow University, following in the footsteps of my own son, Robbie. We are very proud of them both, and very grateful for your kindness.

Now I am asking you for another favour on Alex's behalf, although if he had lived, he would never have asked you himself.

Alex's two youngest, Alan and Betty, are thirteen and fourteen and live with me, as they have since my sister died twelve years ago. My own husband and Jean, Alex's oldest daughter, were both killed in an air raid three months ago and I am terrified something will happen to Alan and Betty. So, I am writing to ask if they can both come to you in America to be kept safe until this awful war is over. Hugh wants to stay on at university, until he graduates and then can help fight the Nazis. I pray the war will be over long before Alan is old enough to want to do the same.

*Hugh has decided that his father's money should continue to pay
for the education of his other cousins, Alex's brother's family,
but even with this, there will still be quite a bit of your gift left,
enough, Hugh is sure, to pay the fares for the two children.
Hugh has talked with them and they are happy to come to the
United States.*

*I know this is a lot to ask, but I am desperate. Our family has
suffered so much these past few months; I can't bear the thought
of anyone else dying. My Robbie is a fighter pilot in the RAF
and my daughter is a WAAF, I worry about them every day.*
Yours sincerely,
Kate Craig'

The reply arrived four weeks later.

'Dear Kate,

*We were so very, very sorry to hear of Alex's death and for all
the other terrible losses you have suffered. Indeed, we are sorry
for all of the trials the British are experiencing. You are all in
our prayers every night.*

*Your brother-in-law was a remarkable man and his memory
remains dear to our family. We would be delighted and honored
to welcome Betty and Alan into our home. Our daughter
Chrissie left for college five years ago and Joanne is already
looking forward to having youngsters in the house once again.*

*If you contact the Cunard office in Glasgow, you will find that
tickets have been arranged for the children to travel next month
on the Queen Mary, leaving from Liverpool. There is a
children's evacuation program that will look out for them during*

their voyage. Other than perhaps a little pocket money to spend on the journey, please send no money with the children. Please.

Chrissie lives in New York now, building a career on Broadway. This means she can meet the children on their arrival and accompany them to our home here in California.

Please do not think of this as a favor, but rather an opportunity for us to do a small thing in memory of a brave man and to make a tiny contribution to helping Britain in these dreadful times.

If there is anything else we can do for you or your family, please write immediately. Meanwhile we look forward to welcoming Betty and Alan into our home. When you contact Cunard, we have arranged that they will cable us confirmation, so no need to worry about writing before the children leave.

Yours faithfully,

Wilbur Fredericks.

P.S. We should have thought of this earlier, but you should from now on receive packages of some of the things we understand are hard to come by in Britain these days, like sugar, chocolate and dried fruit.

The postscript was added at the urging of Joanne Fredericks.

Before offering to accept the children, Joanne had gone next door to talk with her neighbour, Lillie, who had come to the United States with her English family when she was a baby. More to the point, Lillie taught in the local high school, and Joanne wanted to be sure there would be no trouble integrating the children into their new school.

"Oh, don't worry about that; they'll be absolutely fine, I'll look out for them. And Joanne, this is a wonderful thing you'll be doing. Take a look at this letter I received two days ago, from my cousin in Cornwall, in England. Look at page two."

'... *All our young people are in the services now. Tom's girl is in the WRENS. David is in the Royal Navy—Peter a lieutenant in the Indian Army & Ethel Mary a nurse in the Royal Navy. Not to mention 'our Joe' who is doing just as good work on the Civilian Army.*

Our next door neighbour invited us in to join their family and we had a merry evening. The Christmas cake was a great success although it was an experiment. We each gave some of our ration of fat. We couldn't get enough dried fruit — not raisins or currants and I had to use dried eggs and dried milk, neither of which we could get fresh.'

Further on in the letter she read,

'I wish you could have seen England before the war. The whole strength of the country is turned on winning the war and non-essentials are not being manufactured—I have no doubt it will be a long time before we shall go back to the variety and quantity of pre-war food as we shall have to help starving Europe for a long time...'

When Joanne finished reading the letter, she looked at her neighbour.

"It makes you want to weep. What those poor people are going through. And I can't believe her generosity about helping starving Europe. Here they are in the middle of fighting a war—being bombed, not enough food to buy—and already she's thinking about helping others afterwards."

1945

NORTH CHANNEL OF THE IRISH SEA

On a particularly sunny day, light penetrated from the surface far above and played across the enormous wreck. Barnacles and anemones were well advanced on their relentless colonisation. Starfish and all manner of tiny crustaceans moved across decks that had once hosted beautifully dressed women on the arms of handsome men, promenading in balmy tropical evenings. Schools of fish moved lazily in and out of open hatches and broken portholes.

From the stern, the wreck was still recognisably the *Empress of the Oceans*. Two of her funnels were still intact, although now lying near to horizontal as the great ship lay on her side.

At the opposite end of the hull, however, the scene was one of utter devastation. Over 100 feet of the ship was simply missing, exposing a jumble of tortured metal. Lengths of fabric waved in the ever-present currents; winding sheets for the corpse of the devastated liner. In one stateroom, ripped obscenely apart, a small octopus had taken up residence in an open wardrobe.

Invisible from outside, the once grand dining rooms hid other predators waiting for curious fish to come within reach. The piles of smashed tables, chairs and other debris provided countless hiding places. In the desert that is the seabed, the wreck of the *Empress* played host to more life than could be found for miles around.

An ominous shadow swept along the length of the hull; but with no prey in sight, the shark moved on in its perpetual journey through its watery domain.

1945/46

CLYDEBANK, SCOTLAND

As 1946 approached, Kate could look forward to the return of her niece and nephew in six months, when Alan would finish high school. In his letters he called it 'graduating', although Kate couldn't shake the idea that only people who finished university, graduated. Folk 'left' school. Six months ago, Hugh had agreed to Betty's request that she stay on in California an extra year, so she and Alan could travel home together via New York and a last holiday with Christina, now a successful Broadway actress.

By now, Kate was used to receiving letters from America. Joanne Fredericks had made sure that Alan and Betty took turns to send a letter every week for four years, although some were little more than a scribbled note. Kate didn't mind. It was enough that the children kept in touch.

She heard the letterbox rattle followed by the swish of the envelope landing on the floor.

Kate looked at the clock on the mantle shelf: 9:30. She would give Hugh another thirty minutes. Aunt and nephew still occupied the two adjacent flats. A year ago they had finally been allowed back into their old homes.

Kate had assumed Hugh would move into Glasgow when he went to university, but he wanted back into his family flat. She suspected he didn't want to break the bond with his younger brother and sister; he wanted them to know their home was still in Clydebank. Still, he had often slept on someone's couch or bed near the University; she didn't know which and she would never ask.

And now Hugh worked in Hillington, a designer at the giant Rolls-Royce aero engine plant, so he could cycle to work in half-an-hour.

Kate still struggled to remember to call her nephew Hugh, and not Hughie, as he had requested when he started university. Aunt and nephew were unusually close and enjoyed each other's company. They shared breakfast most weekend mornings, and occasional weekday suppers when Hugh was home. And despite his protests, Kate insisted on doing her nephew's laundry.

During the war she had kept busy working in the local military hospital and, since the war had ended, and with it her job, she worked there as a volunteer. In her heart, she realised she had to do something with her life, she was not yet fifty after all; but in truth she had put her life on hold until the children came home.

Kate got on with preparing breakfast, first knocking on Hugh's door to give him a fifteen-minute warning.

Twenty minutes later, Hugh appeared in her kitchen, looking only slightly dishevelled.

"Morning, Aunt Kate."

"Look, a letter from America. You open it and read it to me while I finish these sausages. But pour the tea first, please."

Hugh carefully tore open the envelope. Two years ago, Alan had asked him to keep all the stamps, although the subject had never been mentioned again. Hugh suspected it had been a passing fad, but he had formed the habit now. He quickly scanned the card and its accompanying note.

"It's a Christmas card, from Wilbur and Joanne, and a letter. Oh my God! Listen to this!" Hugh read aloud, excitement growing as he read.

Dear Kate and Hugh,

I hope this card finds you both well and looking forward to the holiday season. Alan and Betty are doing just swell. I know they will both be sending you letters with their cards, so I'll let them tell you what they've been up to.

In less than six months, Alan will graduate and your children will be ready to return to Scotland. They're not children now, but wonderful young people, who Joanne and I have come to love as if they were our own. I fear we will miss them terribly. No matter! Here is what I want to suggest to you both.

We want to thank you for allowing us to share your family for the past few years. So, if you call once again at the Cunard office in Glasgow, the same man who arranged everything for the kids, will have tickets for both of you to come to the States, to collect Alan and Betty. You would sail to New York on the

*Queen Elizabeth, then you would fly from New York to LA,
where we'll meet you and you can attend Alan's graduation.*

*After a vacation here, we'll all travel back to New York.
Chrissie and the kids want to spend a little time together before
they are separated by the Atlantic Ocean; they've become close
these past few years. Then you guys can take the Queen
Elizabeth home again.*

*I do hope you'll agree—it would be wonderful to actually meet
after all these years. Please say yes!*

Yours ever,

Wilbur.'

The instant Hugh read out Wilbur's invitation, Kate's
heart leapt. She knew immediately she wanted to go. To
go to America! What an idea! She had never been
further than Arran or maybe Girvan, whichever was
further from Clydebank. She had reconciled herself to
the fact she probably never would travel, and now this
incredible offer from this amazingly generous, and
seemingly astoundingly rich, American.

She looked at Hugh, her heart in her mouth.

"What do you think, Hugh? Do you think we should
go?"

"Are you kidding? To fly across America! I spend my
days working on engines for planes and I've never even
seen one flying up close. I would kill to go! If they don't
give me the time off work, I'll pack it in."

1946

SOUTHAMPTON, ENGLAND

On a damp, grey, April evening, Kate and Hugh boarded the Glasgow to London sleeper train. Ian had finally been demobbed from the Army and was back home; so he, Agnes, and their two youngest children came to wave them off on their adventure.

Ian hugged Kate and turned to shake his nephew's hand.

"I'm jealous; you're going to have a great time, I'm sure. And here's a letter to give to the Fredericks. The envelope's so thick because each of the weans have written them a thank you, and there's some photos too. Make sure they know how much we've appreciated their generosity to the whole family."

"Don't worry, Uncle Jim, I'll make sure."

After an overnight stop in London where they had dinner with Robbie and Jenny, they took a morning train to Southampton, where they presented themselves at the Cunard office at 10:00 a.m.

They tried their best to hide their shabby looking luggage and absently fidgeted with their collars and cuffs as they looked around at their fellow voyagers, who all looked very smart indeed. They were asked to take a seat until their names were called.

When they did make their way to the counter, the elderly clerk studied their tickets and passports, spending a particularly long time examining Hugh's documents.

Eventually he looked up and, still holding the blue passport in his hand, asked Hugh,

"Are you by any chance related to Alex Campbell, of the *Empress of the Oceans*?"

"Alex Campbell was my father. This is my aunt, his sister-in-law. We're going to America to bring home his two youngest children, who were evacuated."

"Would you please take a seat again? Sorry, I'll be right back."

The man vanished through a door behind him and Hugh and Kate took a seat, more bemused than ever. In less than three minutes, the man returned with a colleague, who proceeded to shake their hands enthusiastically.

"Mr Campbell, Mrs Craig, you don't know me. My name is Johnny Fraser. Hugh, I was a friend of your father's. He saved my life. I can't tell you how happy I am to meet you. Can you come through here, please? Don't worry, we'll get you on board in plenty of time."

Johnny led them through the same door used by the clerk. They soon found themselves in his grand office.

"Not too bad, eh? These days, I'm in charge of all the catering supplies for the Cunard Line. We're just gearing up again after the war."

He told them about the terrible day in Cape Town when he and Alex had received news of the tragedies at home; and about the next visit, when Alex bailed him out of prison, and how Alex had shamed him into stopping drinking. Johnny thought it wise not to mention Alex's romance with Alice - he had no idea if they had ever heard of Alice.

"I was fairly badly injured when the *Empress* went down. They sent me to a specialist burn unit in Devon. It was only many weeks later I learned about Alex. I wrote to your Uncle Ian, who I knew before the war. I should have sent this to him of course, but … anyway, now I can give it to you."

Johnny took his wallet from his pocket and took out £50.

"This is the money Alex put up to get me out of jail. I was supposed to give it to him when we docked, but of course, I never did. I'm pleased I can finally do the right thing."

"Thank you, Mr Fraser, but that won't be necessary, it's …"

Johnny interrupted him sharply.

"If you take this money, son, you'll be doing me a favour—you'll be helping me close the circle with your father's memory. I could never pay you the smallest fraction of what I owe that man. Your father was…"

He broke off, clearly overcome with emotion.

After an embarrassed moment, Hugh put the money in his wallet.

"Thank you, Mr Fraser."

"Thank you, Hugh. Oh, I wish Stephanie, my wife, was here. She and your father worked together lots of times before the war. She could tell you stories about your dad!"

He laughed, "Make your hair curl, I can tell you! We used to live in Glasgow, you know, even though I know it doesn't sound like it. For family reasons we moved back down here after I got out of hospital and I'm afraid I lost touch with Ian."

Johnny became serious again.

"Hugh, Kate; Alex wasn't a Cunard man, of course, but he served on the *Empress* for so long and he was so well respected. People in our business mostly move around from ship to ship, like me. There are hundreds of people scattered throughout the service who had cause to thank Alex Campbell at one time or another, for a kindness or a favour and who honour his memory today. Never forget that. Ever. Now, here's what's going to happen today."

And what happened was that Kate and Hugh were re-assigned to a two-bedroom suite in first class. To their intense embarrassment, a stranger arrived with their meagre luggage, which was unpacked and put away for them. Then their steward arrived to introduce himself.

"I'm Keith, Keith Waterstone. I'll be your steward on your trip. It's my job to see you have everything you need to have an enjoyable passage on the *Queen Elizabeth*, the greatest ship to sail the seas. Better even than the *Empress of the Oceans*."

He smiled at their surprise. He explained.

"Alex Campbell was my first boss, the best boss I ever had. When I was told you were coming up here, I asked to be assigned to you. I understand you have £50 burning a hole in your pocket?"

Keith escorted them to the newly opened onboard shopping area. It turned out that a new lightweight suit and tuxedo for Hugh, each with shirts, shoes and ties *and* three dresses for Kate with requisite shoes and handbags, all came to £40. Which was a lucky and surprising coincidence, as nothing they bought had had a price tag. Later Hugh realised that it had nothing to do with coincidence and everything to do with yet more goodwill to his father's memory.

As Keith had left them he whispered to Hugh, "You'll be amazed at the stuff people leave behind when they leave the ship. Don't be surprised at your new luggage when you're being repacked to disembark."

At the final shop, Hugh was taken away to explore more of the ship, while a young female sales assistant helped Kate spend another three pounds of Johnny's money on new underwear and, miracle of miracles, several pairs of nylon stockings.

"There's no rationing on board, Mrs Craig. The government wants the Yanks to spend all their dollars on the ship, and they make up nearly all the passengers. Wait 'til you see the food!"

The days passed in a blur. Keith ensured they were invited to cocktail parties and to sit at the most interesting tables at mealtimes. And after seven years of rationing, the food was beyond anything they could have imagined.

At first Kate was intimidated by their fellow first-class passengers and almost wished she was in tourist class, where she felt she belonged. But then she paid attention to her nephew and saw how he held his own in any company, no matter the subject of conversation. Whether dinner table discussions turned to politics, the new atomic bomb or the latest novel, Hugh was well informed and able to contribute. It was quickly apparent that he was invariably the smartest person in any company. She was overwhelmed with pride in her nephew and decided they did belong here after all.

Finally, early on their last morning on board, Keith knocked on their door.

"Come with me you two, special treat."

He led them along confusing passageways, up several flights of stairs, until finally he knocked politely on a mahogany door.

"Enter!"

They stepped into what they immediately realised was the bridge of the ship, far above the main deck below.

"Ah, Mr Campbell, Mrs Craig, delighted you could join us. Thank you, Keith; perhaps you could come back when we're approaching our dock."

The Captain led them forward to stand before the windows that ran the full width of the enormous liner. Before them was the spectacular panorama of Manhattan.

In the foreground they saw the Statue of Liberty, welcoming them to America. Behind, the ranks of skyscrapers marched into the distance, to where the Empire State Building stood imperiously above everything.

Closer, bright yellow ferries zipped back and forth to Brooklyn and Staten Island. Nearer still, two fireboats sent up huge jets of water to form an archway they sailed right through; New York's salute to the *Queen Elizabeth*. It was a breathtaking scene.

"I never had the pleasure of meeting Mr Alex Campbell, but his Captain, Captain Henderson, is a great chum of mine, and he spoke most highly of him. You must be very proud."

And Hugh realised once again how proud he was of his father. He had learned years ago that Alex had been respected all over Clydebank, but to hear Johnny and Keith talk about him as they had, and now to hear it from the Captain of the greatest ship afloat!

All too soon, Keith returned to guide them through the process of disembarking, and they bade farewell to the Captain. They saw their nearly-new leather luggage closed up with their clothes, old and new, pressed, folded and packed neatly for the next leg of their remarkable journey.

***

With a final, heartfelt thank you to Keith, they stepped onto the gangway and took their first steps in New York.

Being first-class passengers, they glided quickly through customs and immigration and had just returned their passports to Kate's handbag, when Hugh thought he heard his name being called. He looked up, but could see no one who seemed like they might be looking for him. Not that he expected anyone to be meeting them.

The only person looking remotely in their direction was an impossibly beautiful young woman who seemed pre-occupied trying to persuade a gaggle of photographers to give her some space. She stared right at Hugh and called again,

"Hugh! Hugh Campbell!"

With an impatient shrug, she pushed through the photographers and walked confidently towards Hugh and Kate, reaching out her hand as she approached.

"You look a lot like I remember your father. I'm Christina, Chrissie. And you must be Aunt Kate; Alan and Betty have told me so much about you. I'm here to drive you to the airport. I'm sorry it has to be such a rush, but we'll have lots more time together when you pass through Manhattan in a couple of weeks."

Throughout this exchange Hugh was completely dumbstruck. Chrissie was easily the most glamorous woman he had ever seen in real life. Kate saw his reaction and took over with an amused grin.

"It's kind of you to meet us, Chrissie; I must admit I'm glad we don't have to navigate our way to the airport by ourselves."

Chrissie waved over a porter and instructed him to follow them to her car with the suitcases. The car, a brand new Packard Super Eight had a huge trunk that easily swallowed their luggage. As she tipped the porter, Chrissie invited Hugh to sit up front with her.

"You don't mind, do you, Kate? It's just that Hugh might want to see an American car being driven so he won't be surprised by anything when he drives one in California. Betty told me you don't drive, Kate, is that right?"

Hugh finally found his voice.

"Chrissie, Kate doesn't drive and neither do I. I won't be driving in California."

"Of course you will. It's easy; everyone drives in California. My dad'll have you driving in an afternoon, you'll see."

"Yes, we'll see." Hugh laughed, finally at ease. "Why were those photographers bothering you back there?"

Chrissie told a white lie. "Oh, they always look out for first-class passengers; there's usually a few celebrities on board. Did you meet anyone interesting?"

In reality of course, the photographers were curious about who the attractive and newsworthy Broadway actress, Christina Fredericks, was meeting off the ship. Hugh and Kate would be out of town when their pictures appeared in the gossip columns the following day. Chrissie had come a long way from the shy 18-year-old that Alex had rescued eleven years previously. Now she was a sophisticated New Yorker, the latest toast of the town.

The short drive from the Manhattan pier to the new airport in Queens was a revelation for Hugh and Kate. The streets were so busy and colourful; so *lively*. And the cars! Thousands and thousands of cars; some basic and obviously old, but many sleek and new, and almost every one much bigger than British cars. Every street was jammed with people. And no matter where they looked, there were businesses selling every conceivable type of product. Advertisements promoted an Aladdin's cave of clothes, food and drink, cars, cigarettes and a myriad other products. It was an assault on their rationing-constrained senses.

Too soon, they were saying goodbye to Chrissie and boarding their TWA flight to Los Angeles. When Kate nervously dug her hand into Hugh's arm during take-off, he determined right then, that not only would he not show any fear of flying, he would feel no fear.

They were both startled to hear the pilot's voice broadcast in the cabin, advising passengers to look out their windows for a final dramatic view of the Manhattan skyline.

When Kate had recovered her poise, she turned to Hugh, "Chrissie's very pretty, did you notice?"

"Did I notice? You know very well I noticed. She's absolutely stunning, but don't worry, Auntie Kate, I know she's well out of my league. I'll pretend she's my sister."

"I'd like to see that," scoffed Kate. "And Hugh, for the millionth time, but especially now we're in America, would you please stop calling me Auntie. It makes me feel old."

"OK, Kate. There, is that better?"

"Much better!"

When Hugh realised other passengers were going forward to visit the cockpit, he plucked up the courage to ask one of the stewardesses if he too could go up front after their first meal. It turned out the flight crew were as interested in Hugh's experience designing engines for Spitfires as he was in the operation of the Constellation. Almost 45 minutes after he left his seat, he rejoined Kate.

"You know Aun...Kate, I think maybe I could drive after all. It's so much more straightforward than flying, and Robbie managed that no bother."

At last, after a quick refuelling stop, the pilot announced they were approaching Grand Central Airport at Glendale. Hugh and Kate looked out of the window, mesmerised by the endless vista of beautiful houses surrounded by palm trees. It took a few minutes to realise that the blue squares everywhere were private swimming pools; an almost inconceivable luxury. It seemed California would be even more exotic than New York.

***

Joanne Fredericks and Kate had decided between them, that the visit of aunt and brother was to be a complete surprise for Betty and Alan; so only Wilbur was at the airport to welcome the travellers when they emerged, blinking, into the California sun.

"Joanne fixed things so the kids'll be coming home together. She asked Alan to pick Betty up from her job; she claimed she had a headache. They should arrive home about thirty minutes after us; plenty time for you to freshen up."

Kate and Hugh were once again bemused by the instant friendliness and openness of Americans. Wilbur talked to them as if they had been close friends for years. Although at first they both found it odd, they soon warmed to this kind and generous man who had become so important in the lives of their family.

"We met your lovely daughter in New York, she kindly drove us to the airport." Kate offered.

"Swell! Chrissie was worried she might not have been available. If you had docked a couple of hours later, she would have been on set."

Kate's voice betrayed her confusion. "On set? Is that what you call the theatre?"

Wilbur laughed. "No, no. Chrissie is a stage actress, but right now she's making her first movie. She has a part in a film being made in New York. She says she got the part because she's already in the city and the budget won't stretch to flying someone out from California. But I suspect she's just being modest."

The drive from Glendale Airport to Pasadena took only forty minutes, but again Hugh and Kate were mesmerised by everything they saw. The cars were even newer and brighter than in New York, and many were convertibles - a thing they had rarely seen except in films. Wilbur's car wasn't a convertible, but at his suggestion, all three of them were sitting side-by-side on the enormous front bench seat. Hugh couldn't resist winding down his window to lean an arm on the door, just like in the films.

Wilbur drove down Brand Boulevard and they marveled at the broad thoroughfare, lined with shops and restaurants.

America, and in particular California, seemed to be created from a different palette than Britain. Hugh realised how his own world was dominated by greys and browns, black, dark greens and beige. In dramatic contrast, here even the houses were painted in warm pastel colours, and clothes came in vivid yellows and reds and oranges. And the rainbow hues of the cars were so vivid–red, yellow, light blue, purple, even cars with two contrasting colours.

And palm trees! Right on the streets! The unfolding streetscapes were a riot of impressions–and all of them more vital, more engaging, more *alive* than anything he had ever seen. It was a sensory overload.

The Fredericks' home was on a leafy street of large houses three blocks from the charming high street, or as they would learn to call it, 'Main Street' of Pasadena. As they turned into the long driveway, they could see that, like most of their neighbours' houses, the Fredericks' home was a low, Spanish-style construction. They caught a glimpse of a swimming pool around a corner of the house, before Wilbur stopped the car at a wooden post standing half way up the long driveway. He leaned out of his window to tap a series of buttons on a box mounted on the post. Up ahead, one of two garage doors immediately opened.

"My newest toy," he beamed. "I told mother it would mean she never has to get out in the rain to open the garage door."

He paused, "Of course it almost never rains here - but if it did…"

He pulled into the garage and helped Hugh take their suitcases from the huge trunk of the car before leading them to the front door. Hugh noted Wilbur hadn't had to use a key to enter his house, he just turned the handle to usher them into the cool interior, where Joanne was waiting to greet them.

Twenty minutes later, washed and changed into fresh clothes, although wishing they had cooler choices available, Kate and Hugh accepted tall drinks in which ice cubes chinked merrily against frosted glass.

"Iced tea. We drink it all the time," said Joanne, seeing their quizzical looks.

"You mean cold tea, normal tea?" asked Hugh.

"Yes, regular Lipton's tea, but really cold. If you want sugar, I can add some."

Hugh took an exploratory sip.

"It's lovely, not like cold tea at all."

They chatted easily. The Fredericks wanted to know all about their flight. The last time they had crossed America, it had been by train. While Hugh was telling them about his visit to the cockpit, they heard the sound of an approaching car then doors slamming.

Hugh looked quickly at Wilbur.

"When you said Alan would be picking Betty up; did you mean by *car*?"

"Of course," replied Wilbur. "They share an old Dodge."

The front door opened and two voices could be heard bickering as they came in.

"Since I had to pick you up today, I should get your turn on Wednesday."

"No way, squirt. I'm going to…"

Joanne thought that making this a surprise had maybe not been such a great idea when Betty stopped in her tracks, looked at Kate, then at Hugh, back to Kate before bursting into tears then running over to throw herself into the arms of her big brother.

"Oh, Hughie, Hughie! You're here! You're really here! And Auntie Kate! You're both here!"

Kate could see that Alan too was crying, but silently. She rushed across the room and hugged her nephew.

"I'm sorry Alan, we should have told you." Kate stammered. "We thought it would be surprise, I mean, a nice surprise. We're sorry, we really are."

Alan had quickly recovered his equilibrium.

"No, don't be sorry. It's just great you're here, it's amazing. We've talked about it so many times, me and Betty, but we never imagined you'd really be here, both of you."

Alan walked over to his sister and gently turned her face to his own. "Didn't we, Betty, a million times? We so wanted them to come."

Betty disentangled herself from Hugh and ran over to Kate, while Hugh embraced his young brother.

Tissues were produced and eyes dried.

Kate held her niece by the shoulders.

"Here, let me take a look at you. My, Betty, you're so bonnie. You're lovely, pet, just like your mother. Isn't she, Hugh? And Alan, how did you get so tall, so quickly? Both of you, you look, you look like film stars!"

Hugh could only stare, bemused, at his young brother and sister. Now that he could take them in properly, he saw they did indeed look a race apart. They both had wonderful smiles, their teeth white and even. Their hair and skin shone with health; they both had soft, even suntans. Alan was wearing unusual blue trousers, with pale blue turn-ups, a check shirt with an open collar and striking canvas and rubber shoes. Alan followed his brother's gaze.

"These are jeans, Hughie, and these are basketball shoes. Everybody wears them. The shops are different here, really different. Well, everything is different."

Everything *was* different. The Scotland that Kate and Hugh had left behind a week previously was still enduring rationing. No one was starving, but everyone was sick of the wartime restrictions, which showed no signs of expiring. In fact, since the war had ended, bread and potatoes had been rationed for the first time. New clothes were still almost impossible to obtain. Food, clothes, furniture, everything was scarce, bland and boring. Now they were in a country that had barely known rationing—and all restrictions had been lifted months ago. It was hard to take it all in.

They watched Alan play in the end-of-season high school baseball game and attended his graduation, where dozens of smiling people came up to them to congratulate them on having such a wonderful family. Betty insisted she had to drive the four of them to a drive-in movie. The movie was fun, but Hugh still struggled with the idea that his young brother and sister could drive, and apparently owned a car.

Five days after their arrival, Joanne and Wilbur joined them on an outing. The Fredericks had been discretely ensuring that the four family members had time to themselves, but on this day they would all go to a part of town the youngsters had never visited.

From Pasadena, they drove in two cars to Olvera Street, so Wilbur could show them the old Mexican quarter.

"Everything in Los Angeles looks like it was built yesterday, and mostly that's true. But the Spanish and Mexicans were here hundred of years before us. This old mission is one of the oldest buildings in the US."

They wandered around the colourful streets, listening to mariachi bands, watching various craft displays, and buying finger food from street vendors.

From there, they took a short drive to the huge farmer's market where Joanne bought some fruit to take home. Although fruit and vegetables had not been officially rationed in wartime Britain; in reality it had been difficult to get hold of anything but basic foodstuffs, especially in the cities. Even before the war, Kate had never seen such amazing displays of every kind of fresh fruit and vegetable imaginable. Many she couldn't recognise, and those she did were incredibly cheap, compared with prices back home.

Their last stop of the afternoon was at *Ralph's*, a new kind of shop, called a supermarket, where Joanne wanted to buy some soap powder. Alan and Betty elected to wait in the car, listening to music on the car's radio, something else that had bemused Hugh. The four adults went into the enormous store. As they passed through the entrance and stood looking over the endless shelves of products, Kate began to quietly cry and she rushed back out to the parking lot.

Joanne followed her outside and tried to comfort her.

"What's wrong, Kate, what's the matter?"

Kate shook her head for a while as the tears flowed down her cheeks. As she dabbed at her face, she turned to Hugh, who had emerged with Wilbur, both looking very concerned.

"How will they deal with Clydebank?" she asked her nephew.

She turned to Joanne and Wilbur.

"I don't know where to start. You see, I've haven't had an orange for seven years; they were kept for children and pregnant women. I've only ever had a banana once. I only ever had a proper steak when Jim took me to dinner to celebrate my 25th birthday. I'm wearing one of the only new dresses I've had since 1937, all three bought on the boat coming here. And see these? False teeth - like every person my age I know. I don't know what to do."

Kate stood forlorn in the warm California sun. All around her, shoppers were coming and going, wheeling stacked carts of food, drinks, household products, in quantities not seen since…well, never seen in Britain.

"I don't want to sound sorry for myself, but I know I do. It's just that the war was terrible; really, it was. Everyone knows how it was for the soldiers and sailors and the flyers, Americans as well as British. They were shot at; wounded, killed. But for us at home, well, apart of course for losing Jim and Jean, it wasn't usually anything in particular, just the awfulness going on and on and never ending. Terrible letters, or no letters. Six years of fearing the postman every day. Not enough food, or coal, or anything. And it broke something in Britain, I think. It's taken the joy out of things. Too many sons, husbands and wives, brothers and fathers, all gone forever. And the money! We spent everything; we'll never get it back. Oh, one day rationing will be over I suppose; but we'll never be the same again. All the houses destroyed, roads, factories. I thought Clydebank was bad, and, my God, it is; but London! You can't imagine—piles and piles of rubble, huge gaps in the buildings, just *everywhere*. It'll be years and years before it's all cleared up."

Kate had stopped crying now, but she wasn't finished trying to explain herself.

"Do you know what happened, Joanne, when we received the second wonderful box of food from you in the war? Hugh and I weren't comfortable keeping everything for ourselves and Ian and Agnes; so we took some things round to a few of our neigbours. Old Mrs Weir, she used to live next door to Alex and Annie; I took her a bar of chocolate and some dried fruit. She cried her eyes out, she was so excited. It was lovely, but so very sad, do you see? You Americans, you'll be in charge now. No, no, don't get me wrong. It's OK, it really is. We had our time and that's that. But it's still hard sometimes. I'm sorry; that big shop was a bit overwhelming. I'm sorry. I'm fine now, honestly, I am."

Joanne gently linked Kate's arm through her own. "You don't need to apologise, Kate. We've been insensitive; I see that now. After all you've been through. Let's go home and you and I can fix dinner. What do you say?"

Kate smiled and nodded and dried her eyes as they walked around the corner to where Alan and Betty waited, completely oblivious to the little drama. Hugh though, was thoughtful and quiet for the rest of the day.

Early the following morning, Wilbur asked Hugh to come out with him. It was a weekday, so when they drove to Wilbur's church, it was empty; there were no cars in the huge car park.

"Time you got behind the wheel, Hugh. It's easy, come on."

An hour later, Hugh was driving confidently and Wilbur made him drive them slowly home.

"I think your aunt might like a quiet day by the beach, don't you? Just the four of you."

And for the remainder of their time in California, they completely relaxed. Betty took them to Santa Monica beach and to the Chinese Theatre, where they put their palms in the stars' handprints. They drove by the Hollywood studios and walked around Beverly Hills for a while. Under Betty's prompting, Kate bought a swimming costume and they spent a few days simply lounging beside the Fredericks' pool. One morning while drying herself after a shower, another delicious novelty, Kate realised she was developing a suntan. She decided she liked it.

Three days before they were scheduled to fly to New York, Hugh asked Wilbur if he could have another driving lesson. At the first coffee shop he saw, he pulled over and asked Wilbur to join him.

Hugh had planned what he wanted to say, so spoke with his customary calm, but confident, voice.

"I've been thinking a lot about what Kate said the day she was upset at the supermarket. I'm more optimistic than she is; but she's right, the next few years are going to be tough in Scotland. I can't see how Betty and Alan could possibly have the opportunities at home they could have in America."

Hugh paused for a second before continuing, "So, can I ask you, would you be OK with them staying on here in California? If they want to, of course. And I have enough of my father's money, well, your money really, to pay for them to go to college, I'm not asking you to do that, you've been incredibly generous to our family already. But if they could feel that your house was still their home, even if they moved into a flat, an apartment, I think it would be easier on them. And I know it would be easier on Kate and myself."

Wilbur took a drink of his coffee to give himself time to think about his answer.

"In Kate's first letter, she told me you used some of your father's bequest to keep paying for your cousins to go to that fine school of yours. We think about Alan and Betty kinda like you think of your cousins, like our own family. They've become two young people we are bound to now by deep ties of love and affection. I've been lucky in my life; hey, I've worked hard too. But you need luck as well as effort. Chrissie is, well, Chrissie will end up richer than any of us, I think."

"What I'm trying to say, Hugh, is we feel connected with Alan and Betty now, and whatever money we spend on them is well within what we can afford. Don't get me wrong now. It may look like they have everything. But they both have had vacation jobs every year. If they want to move into an apartment, they'll have to earn money for rent. We provide the essentials they need - food, clothes, dentist appointments and so on. And the fact is, in California, you need a car. When they're both in college, they'll need one each. But they buy their own gas; they pay for their own nights at the movies or whatever else they want to do."

"I guess what I'm saying, son, is that if the kids want to stay, we'd be over the moon. We've been dreading New York and saying goodbye. I know it won't be easy on you or Kate, but I think you're doing the right thing. One thing I will indulge them in, they'll always know they can go to Scotland anytime they want."

That evening Hugh and Kate sat up late, examining the issue from every angle. Every discussion brought them to the same conclusion; Betty and Alan were far better off staying in California, at least to finish their education; at which point they would make their own decisions.

Kate had the last word.

"I know we're doing the right thing. I only wish I felt it was what Alex would have wanted. He was so strong on the family keeping together. My two are in London, and now two of his weans will be in California. Not exactly his dream of a wee family hotel is it?"

**

"You understand it isn't because we don't want to take you back with us, don't you?"

Betty answered for them both, "Yes, we understand, Auntie Kate. And ... well, it isn't that ..."

"We know, pet. We know you don't want us to feel you're rejecting us. We all want the same thing. We want to be together, but what we really want is whatever's best for you. One day, you'll have families of your own and you'll understand better."

Anyone could see a weight had been lifted from the young people's shoulders. They had already said their goodbyes to their friends and it was with obvious delight that they announced that, no, they were not leaving after all. They insisted on taking Kate and Hugh to the UCLA campus to show them where they would be studying from September–Betty was already taking a few classes.

It was with lighter hearts that they boarded the flight to New York to see Chrissie and to wish Kate and Hugh bon voyage for their trip home, alone.

Chrissie had her own momentous news for them when they met her in Manhattan.

"Guess what? I've got a part in a musical that's opened in London! Oklahoma! It transferred three months ago and one of the female leads has broken her leg. And they've asked me to take over the part!"

She turned to Hugh and Kate; "I'll be travelling to London with you guys!"

Wilbur gave his daughter a hug. "That's great news, honey. How did you get the part?"

"Noël. He recommended me to the producer, who he knows of course."

Hugh was impressed. "Do you mean Noël Coward?"

"Yes, I met him years ago; on board ship with your father actually. Ever since, I send him my reviews and he writes to me now and then, encouraging me. And, of course, he buys me dinner every time he's in New York, which used to be pretty often."

The thought of assiduously cultivating someone as famous as Noël Coward struck Hugh as incredibly smart–and something he would never have contemplated. He decided to emulate Chrissie in future.

After a week seeing the sights of New York, the group shared two taxis to take them down to the dock to board the *Queen Elizabeth*. There were some tears as they said goodbye–although not from Hugh, who was confident he would see his younger siblings again soon, one way or another. A blast from the ship's horn brought the farewells to an end, abruptly summoning the final passengers aboard. Hugh, Kate and Chrissie boarded quickly and immediately found a spot on the rail from where they waved to the four small figures on the dock until they disappeared from sight.

***

On their first full day at sea, Hugh asked Keith, once again their steward, if he could arrange for a visit to the ship's engine room. It transpired another passenger had made the same request, and so it was that Hugh met Maurice Wilkes, an Englishman eleven years his senior. During their tour, the two men recognised they had similar interests, and some common experience with wartime aircraft, although Wilkes had been more interested in finding them and shooting them down. When they were deposited back in the passenger area, they decided to continue their conversation over a coffee.

Wilkes was full of enthusiasm for a new technology he had encountered on his visit to the US, attending a conference.

"I've been working on computers since the last year of the war, but last week I saw a whole new way of instructing and operating them. I can't wait to get back to the Cambridge lab to try out some new ideas."

Over the next two hours, Hugh received a crash course in computing from one of only a handful of people in the world in a position to share this knowledge. Infected with Wilkes' enthusiasm, Hugh sought him out the following day and explained his own situation. Emboldened by Chrissie's example, he came right out with the idea that had formed in his mind overnight.

"Do you think there might be an opportunity for me to work with you and your team in Cambridge?"

Wilkes was surprised but not uncomfortable with the request. He had recognised Hugh's intellectual gifts the previous day.

"Why don't you come up for a visit and meet the rest of the group and we can talk some more."

Keen to maintain momentum, Hugh proposed that after they docked in Southampton, he would escort Chrissie and Kate to London then come up to Cambridge a couple of days later.

Hugh had no professional ties: He had resigned from Rolls-Royce when they refused his request for an extended unpaid holiday.

When Hugh had graduated with a first-class degree in aeronautical engineering, he was immediately commissioned as a lieutenant in the British Army and ordered to report to Rolls-Royce, where he worked on the next generation of engines for Spitfire fighters.

His friends were appalled when he walked away from a secure job in such a prestigious company. But, as he had explained to Kate, he had come to the realisation that his only motivation for taking the job had been the war, and the chance to work on improving planes that were actually fighting. With the coming of peace, he was looking for a new direction in his life. And passing up the opportunity to see America would have been insane, he reasoned.

Hugh had never forgotten his conversation with the rabbi as he had travelled to Liverpool to see his father. Graduating from university and seeing Alan and Betty off to America had, temporarily at least, discharged the first priorities he owed his father's memory and example. He had also persuaded his Uncle Ian and Aunt

Agnes that their younger daughter, now fourteen, should also benefit from an excellent education. Paying for her schooling made him feel he was embracing his father's responsibilities to his extended family.

However beyond seeing to the immediate needs of the younger members of his family, Hugh was still searching for a bigger ambition for himself.

They had a pleasant, but uneventful crossing. Hugh did come to think of Chrissie in a rather brotherly way, and the two became firm friends. Chrissie had a bottomless reservoir of anecdotes about the theatre, and she was amazingly well read in every literary genre–and able to give dramatic recitations of poems and plays from Shakespeare to Shelley.

For his part, Hugh was able to answer every question put to him about the liner, the war and the stars they admired as the three of them walked around the decks each night.

Soon though, the majestic liner was gently nudged into her berth in Southampton and the three travellers disembarked. They took the boat train to London where Robbie and Jenny would be waiting at Waterloo Station to greet their mother and cousin.

After his release from the RAF, Squadron Leader Robbie Craig had briefly contemplated a career as a commercial pilot but realised there were hundreds of qualified pilots chasing a relative handful of jobs. After a couple of false starts, he found himself working as a journalist then as a columnist in Fleet Street. He soon discovered he thoroughly enjoyed the life of a roving reporter. He also realised he had a talent for writing witty articles on a wide range of subjects. And the loosely defined hours suited him as well. He became a popular figure in London social circles, where a handsome single man with the added glamour of being a highly decorated fighter pilot was much sought after by society hostesses—and by their female guests.

There were thousands of single women in London, many of whom had performed important roles during the war and had experienced freedoms their mothers couldn't have imagined. It was a good environment in which to be an eligible bachelor, and Robbie took full advantage of his opportunities.

"Come on, Jen. Why would I want to stick with just one girl? There are so many lovely ladies to be kissed—I can't see myself settling down for years and years."

This conversation happened the evening before Kate and Hugh returned home from the US—one of the rare evenings when Robbie and Jenny had dinner together in London. Brother and sister shared a flat in Kensington, although Jenny spent more than half her life overseas on flying duties. Through an ex-RAF friend of Robbie's, Jenny had found a job as a stewardess on the BOAC flying boat service to Asia and Australia.

Kate had read enough romance novels to be familiar with the expression 'love at first sight', but she had never before witnessed the phenomenon until she saw the look coming over her son's face as she and Hugh and Chrissie walked towards Robbie and Jenny on platform four of Waterloo Station. Even Hugh realised there was something odd about his cousin's distracted welcome as he waited with ill-disguised impatience to be introduced to the gorgeous young woman who, bafflingly, seemed to be a friend of his mother and cousin.

"Chrissie, these are my cousins, Robbie and Jenny."

Fortunately, it seemed that Chrissie was just as smitten by the handsome Scot who held her hand a beat longer than strictly necessary as they were introduced.

"I've heard a lot about you, Robbie, it's a pleasure to meet you at last. And you too of course, Jenny," she added apologetically.

Jenny turned to her mother and raised her eyes to the glass roof of the station, shaking her head and smiling. She had seen women look at her brother that way before.

Robbie addressed Chrissie directly.

"Are you staying in London?"

Hugh interrupted, "Chrissie's here to appear in a West End musical, Oklahoma!"

"That's wonderful! I've seen it already–but of course I'll be going again," he added quickly.

"I have to go to the theatre right away, to let them know I'm here and run over arrangements for rehearsals."

Robbie looked at his sister.

"Jen, why don't you show Mum and Hugh to the hotel and I'll escort Chrissie to the theatre then come over to meet you for lunch?"

Turning to his mother, he explained, "We've booked you into a nice hotel around the corner from our flat. Well, Jen booked it, she gets airline rates."

Kate smiled at her son, "I don't mind if you miss lunch, but you'd better turn up to take me to dinner. You hear?"

***

Chrissie's run in Oklahoma! lasted four months. Barely a day passed during that entire time when Robbie didn't see her. Every single day he gave thanks that his job's unconventional hours allowed him to spend almost every afternoon showing Chrissie around London, taking her to lunch at all of his favourite places. He came to hate Wednesdays, when Chrissie had to perform in a matinee. They were an extraordinarily attractive couple and, between Robbie's society friends and Chrissie's connection with Noël Coward, they were soon swept up in a busy social whirl.

When Jenny was in town, she often joined them, and the two women became close friends. The third time the three of them went out together, it was two in the morning by the time Robbie and Jenny had dropped Chrissie at her digs and walked to their own flat.

"What happened to there being too many lovely ladies to settle for just one girl?" Jenny teased.

"I'm sure I never said any such thing." Robbie retorted, pinching his sister's arm.

Three months into Chrissie's stay in London, she and Jenny had a Sunday evening to themselves for a change, while Robbie went to track down a story in Wales. They decided to cook a simple supper in Jenny and Robbie's flat, so they could have a proper catch up over a bottle of wine. Jenny had returned that morning from a long trip to Japan.

"So, spill the beans, I want to know all about the dashing pilot. Come on, Jenny, give it up."

"All over, I'm afraid, nothing to tell."

"But I thought…so what happened?"

Jenny had wangled her way onto the UK-Japan service ages ago, after she had been assigned the route by chance, filling in for a sick colleague. She discovered that of all the places she had been able to visit with her job, she enjoyed China and Japan the most. She loved how exotic they were, while being so much more civilised and, in the case of Japan, so much cleaner than most of her ports of call.

She had to get used to being stared at everywhere she went—a tall, redheaded, single woman was an outlandish sight for the local people. But she never felt threatened or intimidated; so, she decided she would simply get used to having curious eyes and gossipy chatter follow her everywhere. She even began to learn Japanese and a few phrases of Cantonese. Her language skills were tested in restaurants and in tiny shops where she bargained for exquisite jade and ivory carvings.

As soon as she became established on the route, Jenny caught the attention of one of the regular pilots, Toby Purcell. The trip from Southampton to Japan took six days in their Empire Flying Boat, longer when they had bad weather or engineering problems; which they did on many trips.

On their flights there would be three flight crew plus a clerk, who mostly managed the mail, and two stewardesses. Between preparing snacks, drinks and meals in the galley; cleaning up at the end of each leg; and dragging down mattresses from the upper deck on overnight segments, they were kept busy. But most nights they would be in a good hotel and would have a few hours for sightseeing or shopping, with pretty regular extra days waiting for fair weather or a spare part to arrive.

Jenny and Toby became an item and she enjoyed being shown the local sights by someone who had been in each of their stops many times before. After a while, Toby started putting subtle pressure on her to sleep with him, and on this trip she had admitted to herself she was inclined to go ahead, maybe in Japan when they would have a three-day break before heading home; she dreaded the thought of a one-night stand.

The last stop before the tiny town of Iwakuni, their terminus in Japan, was Hong Kong. The crew was planning dinner in a specialty fish restaurant, but Jenny had cried off, explaining to Toby,

"There's a little man keeping something special for me. I didn't have enough money with me last time. But I'll see you for a quick drink later and, well, we'll be in Japan tomorrow."

She kissed him and tried to make her kiss convey her intentions for the days ahead. She left him smiling.

Jenny arrived at the ferry terminal, only to be greeted with a notice announcing the service to Kowloon had been suspended due to a minor crash between two of the boats. Sailings would resume at seven o'clock, far too late for her to reach the shop before closing time.

Dejected, Jenny trudged back to the hotel; she didn't even know where the fish restaurant was, so couldn't join the others if they had already left the hotel.

She unlocked the door to the room she shared with Jo, and immediately saw her roommate was in bed.

"I was worried I was going to miss you."

A sudden noise to her right made her turn her head, to see Toby emerge from the bathroom, naked but for a towel wrapped around his waist.

"So, Chrissie; as soon as I turned my back, he was in bed with Jo. The worst thing was I had to fly with both of them the next day—and for the whole of last week. I've just had ten days of being tortured."

"Oh my God! Some men! You poor thing; here, you need more wine."

"It wasn't all bad. I got my perfect jade elephant on the way back through Hong Kong, and I made Jo serve all the meals in the smoking lounge every single day. Apart from the horrible cigar and pipe smoke, there was a fat, ugly, middle-aged guy returning home to England after twenty years. I think he had four hands and would have all of them on you at once. She had him to contend with three or four times every day. I almost felt sorry for her by the time we reached Southampton."

"Anyway, enough about my disastrous love life, tell me all about you and Robbie. I notice you're pretty familiar with where everything is kept around here; I'm guessing you were over a few times while I was away?" she teased.

***

Six months after he had met Chrissie in Waterloo Station, Robbie leaned in and whispered to Hugh, who today was his best man.

"Our fathers will be spinning in their graves right about now."

Although Robbie was smiling, in truth there was a touch of sadness about his comment. Uncle Ian would not be present today at the wedding of Robbie and Chrissie–he couldn't bring himself to attend mass in a Roman Catholic Church.

A month earlier, Robbie had stood in the living room of Ian and Agnes's house in Glasgow. He had come to Scotland to introduce Chrissie to the rest of his family and to invite them to the wedding

"I wish you every happiness, son; and Chrissie seems like a lovely young woman, but I don't approve of mixed marriages and, I'm sorry, but neither would your father, God rest his soul."

"You're probably right about Dad, but don't you think it's time we left all that behind? I fought beside Catholics and Protestants against Catholics and Protestants; so did you. Why on earth would you hold grudges against them now?"

"I don't hold a grudge against Catholics, many are fine people, I just think we should keep to our own, that's all."

"I don't remember you having a problem using Chrissie's family's money to send your boys to school. I don't remember any problem when they took in Betty and Alan—and by the way, saw to it that they attended a Presbyterian church in California, even though it meant driving miles."

"I'm telling you, Robbie, I know they're a fine family, and I appreciate their generosity, but that's got nothing to do with…"

At that point Agnes butted in to interrupt her husband.

"You're just being stubborn, Ian Campbell; stubborn and stupid. I'm accepting Robbie and Chrissie's invitation, even if you won't. Kate and Jenny and Hugh are going as well as Betty and Alan and, I can tell you, so are our four. I won't have them grow up with your bigoted attitude. Chrissie's father has been the saviour of this family and I can't believe you don't see that and understand how ridiculous your attitude is. I've never heard of a more Christian family than the Fredericks. Never."

But Ian would not be moved. He truly didn't hate Catholics, but he had grown up steeped in sectarian divisions. He also believed that if Chrissie's family had been Scottish, they would also have been vehemently opposed to the match.

But now Robbie checked his watch again. Twelve minutes, this was becoming ridiculous. He understood that the bride should be a little late, but twelve minutes?

Among the guests in the pew immediately behind the groom and best man was Robbie's best friend from his RAF days, George Smythe. George leaned forward until his head was between the two cousins.

"You're sure she hasn't changed her mind? I would, if I was as gorgeous as Chrissie. When I think of the other men she could be marrying. Wonderful, rich, charming men like, well, like me, for instance."

"Shut up, George. You're not helping. Go back and see if there's any sign of them. They couldn't have got lost surely?"

Chrissie, her parents and Wilbur's brother and his family were all staying in the Central Hotel in Glasgow. But the drivers of the wedding cars were locals and would have had no trouble finding the church. And indeed, the bride's aunt, uncle, cousins and mother were all in their seats. The only people missing were the bride and her father.

George made his way along the aisle towards the church door, until he was brought to a halt by a glimpse of movement through the glass panels and scurried back to his seat.

"They're here! Stand up, you two."

Robbie and Hugh stood and turned around to see Chrissie make her entrance on the arm of her father. Wilbur looked anything but comfortable in his formal outfit, but Chrissie was absolutely breathtaking, utterly radiant.

Robbie heard George exclaim,

"Wow!"

An audible buzz rippled through the congregation as the bride made her way up the aisle, followed by Jenny, Chrissie's bridesmaid and soon-to-be sister-in-law, who in any other company would have held every male eye in the church. However, at the moment, Jenny had a huge grin on her face and was frantically pointing back over her shoulder. Robbie craned to see what his sister was waving at, and saw a lone figure sliding into the back row of the church. It was Ian.

The small parish church had never seen anything like it. The priests were unaccustomed to requests for interviews from international media, or for space for newsreel cameras, all of which they rejected out of hand. Matters reached fever pitch when word got out that Noël Coward would be attending. The church doorkeepers were offered fat envelopes to allow journalists inside. Robbie fired their wedding photographer five days before the wedding when they found out he was holding an auction for exclusive pictures.

Realising she wanted some photographs of her wedding, and that she had to do something about the demands of the media, Chrissie walked in unannounced to the office of the *Clydebank Press* and caused huge consternation by offering the staff photographer, Ernie McPherson, exclusive access to the church in return for negatives of every photograph he took.

Ernie specialized in covering christenings and local school football teams; but in the event, he conquered his nerves and carried his duties off without a hitch.

The *Press* bought a new printing machine from the proceeds of the worldwide reprint fees.

The hysteria reached a crescendo when the newly married couple appeared at the church door. As a hundred flashbulbs exploded, they sprinted to their car and threw themselves in.

As they pulled themselves together, and prepared for arrival at their reception, Robbie turned to his new wife.

"Did you have anything to do with Uncle Ian?"

"Not me, my father. I wanted to kill him, but he insisted. As soon as mother and Jenny had left in their car, he rushed me into ours and told the driver to go to Ian's address. I don't know how he even knew it but thank God it was almost on the way to the church. Anyway, he wouldn't let me talk him out of it, said he knew what he was doing. Do you know, he made me come out of the car and go up to Ian's door with him? In my dress! We drew quite a crowd, I can tell you. Anyway, he told Ian he would regret not coming for the rest of his life. He reminded him what Alex had done for me all those years ago, then he pointed at me standing there, looking like a lemon in my wedding dress, and said, 'Are you really going to spoil my daughter's wedding day? Will you dishonour the memory of your brother's courage and kindness, over an idea you don't believe in anyway?'

"Well, at that point, Ian started to cry! Dad stood there a moment then announced we'd wait in the car while he got changed, but he'd better be quick because everyone was waiting. When Ian came running out, Dad made him empty his pockets and throw all his coins out the car window as we pulled away. Dad had already thrown all his change away, leaving our hotel. I had never heard of a scramble; Robbie or Hugh must have told Dad about it. Ian wasn't too happy; apparently it's usually pennies that are thrown, but Ian had lots of silver in his change. Dad was amused."

"Your dad is amazing, he really is. And by the way, Mrs Craig, you could never look like a lemon."

1959

NORTH CHANNEL OF THE IRISH SEA

The passage of the years had wrought further indignities on the *Empress*. Her two remaining funnels had collapsed over her decks, themselves now holed in many places. The crust of sea life was now complete and her outline had become blurred, ghostly.

The activity level around her bow section was considerably busier than around the main hull, which lay in much deeper water. Here and there, long strands of seaweed grew up towards the sunlight penetrating through the cold waters of the Atlantic Ocean.

Every year a large school of mackerel visited for several weeks to feed. In turn the mackerel were sought by predatory ling; fierce marine hunters.

An old fishing net festooned the shallowest section of the wreck. An unlucky fishing boat had caught hold of it and had been forced to cut away its gear. Juvenile fish swam in and out of the mesh, seeking sanctuary, but their larger cousins gave it a wide berth.

A giant conger eel had possession of the forward cargo hold. It was a true monster, almost two metres in length and as thick as a man's thigh. Sunset and sunrise were its preferred times to emerge and prowl its section of the ship. Occasionally the eel would find one of the huge skate patrolling the seabed around the *Empress*. Large though the skate were, they were no match for the eel.

Just above the bow, the school of mackerel moved as one. Every few seconds they turned, light glinting off their silver undersides. At these moments, the ball of fish seemed like an enormous single creature that might dominate the surrounding sea. The threat was illusory. Beyond the spinning silver sphere, six shadowy forms moved effortlessly through the water. The dolphins were herding the mackerel into an ever-tighter ball, the easier for taking turns scything through the mass of fish, taking five or six at a time. They wouldn't eat all the mackerel. When they were sated, the dolphin pod readied itself to move on to shallower waters. Later that day, the remaining mackerel also departed, heading for their spawning ground where they would replenish their numbers.

Before they left, the dolphins made a final leisurely circuit of the *Empress*, out of curiosity. They were familiar with the wreck, indeed, some remembered the ship from her glory days, as she regularly passed through their waters.

1960

HAMPSHIRE, ENGLAND

Philip Armstrong turned reluctantly from the window to sit down at his simple wooden desk. Before him lay another evening of tedium; manually updating Admiralty charts for a Southampton chandlery. If he worked steadily for four hours, he would make about twelve shillings; not too bad for a man earning less than £1000 a year.

Since Armstrong had obtained his discharge from the Merchant Navy in 1946, still a Second Engineering Officer, his life had spiralled steadily downwards. Initially, he had been able to blame his inability to find well-paying work on the post-war slump. However, when the economy began to recover, Armstrong was still unable to achieve what he believed to be his potential–and the standard of living he thought he deserved. In 1950 he had married a woman seven years older than himself but was divorced twelve months later when his wife at last found the courage to consult a sympathetic lawyer after Armstrong punched her a third time.

For the past six years, Philip Armstrong had been teaching science at Abbotsford College in Hampshire.

Abbotsford was the most minor of minor public schools, a status reflected in the meanness of its facilities and the mediocre calibre of its faculty.

He hated the school, he hated the boys and he hated his colleagues–in both latter cases a mutual sentiment. Since his divorce, he had become more and more solitary, although every three or four months he took the train up to London to visit his younger brother Jeremy and his family.

Philip would have struggled to articulate his feelings for his younger brother. It wasn't exactly affection, more a recognition of a faint residual bond that demonstrated there was at least one almost normal relationship in his life. It helped that Jeremy was even poorer than he was; eking out a threadbare existence from his salary from the haberdashery department of Debenhams.

Family visit over, he would spend the night in a seedy Soho hotel with a prostitute. Occasionally he had to pay the girl double money to compensate for a bruise or two.

The job of updating the stock of Admiralty charts was tedious and repetitious, but it required considerable concentration and attention to detail. Armstrong would only be paid for chart work that was accurate, neat and complete. After an hour he stood, stretched the kinks from his back and made himself a cup of tea. When he was finished, he would allow himself a large whisky, but for now, tea would have to suffice. Fifteen minutes later, he settled back into his seat and picked up the next Notice to Mariners and studied the list of changes it called for. A new survey had resulted in a more accurate profile of a slice of the seabed between Scotland and Ireland.

Carefully, Armstrong positioned his parallel rule and 'walked' it to the appropriate grid reference where the new contour line would start. Startled, he double-checked his data and positioning. There was no doubt about it. The depth contour line he was about to redraw was in the exact area where the *Empress* had gone down almost twenty years ago.

With mounting excitement, Armstrong digested the new information. The bow section of the wreck was lying, not in 500 feet of water, as had been thought, but in seas as shallow as 150 feet. And whereas only naval divers could operate in 500 feet of water, 150 feet was accessible to any well-equipped team.

Although Armstrong knew he was the only living soul who was aware there was gold in the *Empress's* bullion room, he also realised that it would only be a matter of time before someone else stumbled upon the significance of the Notice to Mariners he was holding in his hand. Even without the lure of gold, the *Empress* represented an irresistible challenge to daring divers seeking souvenirs and the glory of being the first person to dive on the famous wreck.

Immediately after the war, Armstrong had investigated the possibility of recovering the final bars of gold. He read the official report of the sinking and checked on the wreck's location. Then, as now, recovering anything from 500 feet would require considerable resources of specialised equipment, specialist divers and a lot of money to finance the required support infrastructure. The gold might as well have been on Mars.

But this new information changed everything. Rather than having to use traditional heavy diving suits with their massive copper helmets and surface air pumps, now dry suits and aqualungs would allow a diver to simply swim into the hull.

Although the task had become feasible, it hadn't become easy. Armstrong understood it would need competent trained people with skills he didn't have. He would need a small team and he would have to learn to dive.

***

First thing the following Saturday, Armstrong took an early train up to London to visit the huge WH Smith newsagent at Waterloo Station. Sure enough, he found a magazine catering to divers. In a nearby tearoom he skimmed the pages of the magazine before turning to the advertisements in the back pages. He soon had a list of three addresses of London outlets selling diving equipment and set off for the closest one.

He found what he was looking for at the second address; a small shop under the arches below Charing

Cross station. The shop sold diving equipment, but more important, it had a noticeboard with details of diving clubs and cards from instructors offering their services. He copied down the contact details of a club and two different instructors based in Southampton then rushed back to the station to make a phone call before catching the Southampton train.

At Southampton station he directed a taxi to take him to the address he had been given over the telephone.

The man who opened the door to Armstrong's knock was powerfully built, close to fifty years old Armstrong guessed, around six feet tall, with a shock of white hair.

"Turned white in the war, Mr Armstrong. Harbour mine clearance, that was my job. Took it out of you, I can tell you. Between the sea and the mines, most of my friends bought it one way or another. All I got, was white hair before I was thirty."

The two men talked for twenty minutes and reached an agreement. John Kennedy would give Armstrong a lesson each Saturday morning.

"The first lesson will be here in the house. We'll talk about safety and equipment and we'll make sure I have a dry suit to fit you. Then we'll use the public baths. The swimming pool doesn't officially open until nine o'clock, but I'll arrange for us to get in at eight. We'll have maybe three or four lessons there before we go to the harbour for your next two or three dives. Then, all going well, I'll take you out in my boat and show you a couple of wrecks from the war. How does that sound?"

"That'll be fine, Mr Kennedy, just fine. I'll see you here next Saturday, early."

The lessons went well. John Kennedy was a highly experienced diver and a good teacher. Seven weeks later, the two boarded Kennedy's thirty-three foot dive support boat, '*Sea Spray*'.

"This is Mike, Mr Armstrong. He'll stay up top and assist us with our gear and getting out of the water."

They motored out for twenty minutes until Kennedy took a bearing from the harbour lighthouse and a distant church steeple.

"OK, we're here. Look for a yellow ball, it should be around here somewhere."

Mike spotted the ball and used his boat hook to pull it onto the *Sea Spray*. The two divers suited up and, after careful safety checks by Kennedy and Mike, they dropped into the water and followed the line from the float thirty feet down to the dismembered wreck of a German U-boat. It was lying on its side and had obviously been well and truly plundered over the years. After slowly swimming around the submarine, John Kennedy signalled it was time to return to the *Sea Spray*.

"How was that, Mr Armstrong?" he asked over a cup of steaming cocoa.

"That was excellent, really dramatic. I can't believe the amount of damage; it must have been a gigantic explosion when she was sunk."

Kennedy laughed.

"Oh no, it wasn't the sinking that did all that. We're in shallow water here, and wrecks are a hazard to shipping and fishermen's nets, so the Navy goes about blowing them to bits. They'll be at it forever, I reckon."

They arrived back at the harbour and tied up *Sea Spray*. To his surprise, John Kennedy was invited to join Armstrong for lunch in the Blue Anchor pub. Armstrong had decided Kennedy could be the man he needed to help retrieve the gold. He was clearly competent, and just as important, Armstrong thought the diver would be up for an unofficial and possibly illegal venture.

When they had finished their ploughman's lunch, Armstrong took their dirty plates back to the bar and bought back two more beers.

"Do you mind if I call you John? And it's Philip. I have a proposition for you, one that could make you rich."

He gave Kennedy a heavily edited version of the events surrounding the sinking of the *Empress*, emphasising that no one else alive knew about the gold left aboard and that he alone could identify exactly where the gold was and how to get to it. He was deliberately vague about precisely how many gold bars had been left behind. He then explained about the Notice and the correction to the depth contour around the *Empress*.

"So you see, it won't be long before someone else realises the wreck is accessible to anyone looking for souvenirs from a famous ship."

"It isn't treasure hunters you need to worry about, Philip. She must have had a beam around 100 feet. If she's lying in only 150 feet of water, that means there's only 50 feet or so clearance above her hull if she's lying on her side. It's like I told you about the German sub, that's a shipping hazard. The Navy'll be blowing her up as soon as they figure things out."

"Well, all the more reason to hurry. Are you up for it?"

Kennedy took a long pull on his beer and thought for a long moment.

"Here's how I look at it. You say no one knows about the gold, so there's no one to miss it. It doesn't feel like stealing to me. So yes, I'm up for it. When do you want to try to retrieve it?"

"This summer. It's the middle of May now. Could you have the *Sea Spray* ready and up in Scotland by the first of July?"

"Don't see why not. We'll need a crew, mind. Mike and one more; the fewer the better I reckon. That'll be four of us. It'll be cosy, but we can manage. What's the deal with the gold, I mean shares an' that?"

"Half to me and half to you and the others. It's up to you how you divide your half. But you mustn't tell the crew their destination until you're on your way and at sea–I don't want any risk of tipping anyone off."

"I'll agree to that, but all the costs come out first. It'll cost a bit to get us all up there."

"OK, that's fair."

"How much do you think it's worth?"

"About as much as you or I make in 150 years."

***

It took a little more time than John Kennedy estimated. However, the fifth of July found the *Sea Spray* on a calm sea, holding station over the spot where Armstrong believed the gold would be found.

Armstrong had already explained how he had figured out the wreck's location.

"The *Empress* was being towed at between three and four knots when the torpedo hit. The main part of the ship would have started to scoop up huge amounts of water and must have slowed pretty quickly. However, the watertight doors were sealed, so she didn't fill with water right away. The general view is that she covered several hundred yards before she finally went under. That's what's generally thought of as the wreck site. But we're interested in the bow section, and all the witnesses say that dropped more or less straight down, so I think we're directly above her–or as near as dammit, anyway."

"Well, let's find out. Tommy, you help me. Mike, get Philip organised."

Tommy was another deckhand John Kennedy had used regularly over the years. He and Mike were regular drinking partners and occasional shipmates, but neither had ever dived. The three men knew each other well and they had had a pleasant trip bringing *Sea Spray* around Cornwall and up the entire length of the Irish Sea. Their trip had brought them all the way to Ayr on the west coast of Scotland, where they had collected Armstrong. After refuelling and re-stocking, they set off once again, for the channel between Mull of Kintyre and Rathlin Island, off the coast of County Antrim.

Notwithstanding Armstrong's confidence, it had taken them two days to find the bow section of the *Empress*. Armstrong saw it first and instantly realised they had been incredibly lucky. The hatch giving access to the cargo hold, the one they had used to extract the gold in 1940, had been a weak point in the ship. A planned weak point, carefully allowed for in the liner's design and construction, but a weak point nonetheless. When the fatal explosion had ripped the ship in two, she had broken right down the line of the hatch. The bow section had sheared off, exposing the decks and, more to the point, ensuring that now they had only to swim straight into the wreck to reach the bullion room door. A break further aft would have meant swimming along the hatch, then negotiating a right-angled turn in almost complete darkness—not an easy prospect.

John Kennedy had insisted on knowing everything about the bullion room and particularly its door; despite Armstrong's assurances that the door had been left open.

"I was told the strongroom floor was strengthened during the ship's last dry dock before the start of the war. At the same time, its door was replaced by a more secure version. The government anticipated having to move the gold, I suppose."

The new door came from a bank. When its handle was at three o'clock, the door was unlocked. At six o'clock the simple mortice-style lock engaged. This was used in the bank during the day, so the head cashier could access money as required, with only one key. Every night the handle was turned to the twelve o'clock position and the full, multi-point mechanism was engaged. Now it took two keys turning simultaneously to open the safe. The head cashier would have one key and the bank manager the other.

"When we were ordered to recover the gold, the Captain had one key and the Bank of England johnnie had the second one. MacDonald and Everett were given the two keys so they could open the door. When we left, we had more important things to worry about than locking the damn door, which was held open by two catches."

When the *Sea Spray* had picked up Armstrong at Ayr, he had two large canvas holdalls that had to be manhandled aboard. Now they would all see what was inside one of them. With Mike's help, Armstrong dragged the larger of the two bags onto the deck.

"Did you bring the wooden shipping pallet I asked for?" he asked.

The pallet was retrieved and laid beside the bag.

"The gold was originally in wooden boxes, but they may have rotted by now. One way or another, John and I will have to carry the bars along a corridor that's about thirty yards long. If the corridor is blocked, then we're finished. But even if it isn't, it will take too long to move the bars one at a time. And they're heavy. We'd be exhausted. So I designed this."

Armstrong wrestled a large sheet of heavy-duty rubberised canvas cloth from inside the holdall. With a lot of grunting and help from the others, he forced the cloth flat inside the slats of the wooden pallet. Now they could see the cloth was actually a sealed bag, with a valve and an attached rubber hose with a metal fitting at its end.

"Tommy, would you connect this to an air tank, please?"

When this was done, Armstrong nodded to Tommy, who opened the valve, allowing air to inflate the bag until it bulged from each gap in the slats of the pallet.

"Not too much, or the pressure will break the pallet apart. There we are. Now we can use this like a sledge. I reckon it's buoyant enough to lift two or three bars at a time. We can then easily push this along the corridor. Once we're outside the hull, we'll load them two at a time into this empty canvas bag, and you two," he indicated Mike and Tommy, "can lift the bag up to the boat, empty it, and lower it back down for the next delivery. We can let air out of the sledge as it gets lighter, and refill it when required. We'll have to take an extra tank with us for the sledge."

John Kennedy was clearly impressed. "That's very elegant, Philip. When you told me you had a system, I wasn't sure what to expect, but this will work well. I like that it's so simple, not much to go wrong."

Kennedy looked at his watch.

"We've got time and light for one more dive this afternoon. Let's go down for a recce; let's see what we're dealing with."

The two men were helped back into their dry suits and their dive equipment, before stepping off the stern platform into the cold water. As planned, John Kennedy took the lead, holding the end of a thick rope being paid out from the deck of the *Sea Spray*. When he reached the wreck, he carefully secured the line to a strong metal stanchion and gave it a confirmatory double tug, letting the men on top know they were firmly secured to the ship. The line would be their anchor as well as their guide, holding the *Sea Spray* in position.

Kennedy now signalled that Armstrong should take the lead and guide them to the right level on the slash in the wreck that was the loading hatch. At first, Armstrong was disorientated. The bow section of the ship was lying at a crazy angle. She was resting on her starboard side, but because the bow of the ship narrowed dramatically just forward of the line of separation, she was also tilted toward the bow.

Eventually, by turning himself to align with what had been vertical, Armstrong was able to count off the decks until he had reached the level of the bullion room corridor. He turned and motioned to his diving partner, indicating the opening they would have to negotiate.

By prior arrangement, they would only take a quick look today, not penetrating too far into the void. The corridor was wide enough to allow the two men to swim side-by-side, with the beams from their flashlights casting pale circles of light ahead of them. The passageway was still intact.

They peered into the gloom ahead for a moment, until John Kennedy reached out a hand to tap Armstrong's arm. With one last look around, they turned and made their way back to the surface.

The four men were sitting around the table in the cabin, cupping warm drinks as they discussed their plans for the next few days. Kennedy did most of the talking.

"The tell-tales on the line show that the shallowest side of the hull is barely over forty feet down. Add another thirty to the passageway opening, another ten for the slope inside and a margin for safety and I'd say we'll be working in 80 feet of water. So we'll plan on two dives a day, each with twenty minutes in the passageway. That should give us enough time to get a good few bars each dive, so it will take three or four days to get this done. Let's hope this good weather holds."

Later on, as they enjoyed a bowl of Mike's beef stew, which was to be their main sustenance every day, John Kennedy spoke again.

"I still can't believe no one has found this wreck. Forty feet is nothing, the *Queen Mary* draws fifty feet for instance. I hope we don't find an empty safe tomorrow. And for sure the Navy will blow this up as soon as they realise what's happened on the chart. I guess they used different sea lanes in the war, avoiding the Jerries."

Next morning, they were all up early, too excited to stay in bed. Once again, John Kennedy addressed them.

"I had a couple of thoughts in the night. After we send up the first bag with a load, we'll be hanging about, waiting for the bag to go up and come down again. We should unload the bars from the sledge at the edge of the passageway entrance then one of us will wait for the bag to come down and the other can take the sledge back along to the room and get started loading the next bars. When the bag comes down, it can be tied off at the entrance, and the next two bars can be dropped in. We'll take turns. One more thing. I'll take the sledge down with its own tank and we'll find somewhere to secure it, then we won't have to bring it up and down each dive."

By nine o'clock, the divers were in the water. Kennedy was handling the sledge and its tank, lashed to the pallet. Armstrong held the canvas bag, which had been securely tied to its lifting rope.

As they swam along the passageway, their spent air bubbles formed a silver ceiling above them. The fish, surprised to be caught in their lights, moved easily aside to allow them to pass. Finally, they reached the end of the passageway and hung, suspended, before the open strongroom, its door securely held above the opening. John Kennedy turned to signal OK: He had been more concerned than Armstrong that the door would have dropped and shut somehow and be difficult to open. It had been a close thing; the last ten or fifteen feet of what had been the corridor ceiling had been ripped out by the forces of the explosions. It was a miracle the strongroom door hadn't been affected.

Kennedy indicated that Armstrong should have the privilege of entering the room first. This was the real moment of truth. Was the gold still there after twenty years?

Philip Armstrong was aware of the beating of his heart. He could hear his pulse in his own ears, magnified by the water. Gingerly he drifted into the strongroom and shone his torch downwards, illuminating what had been the wall and was now the floor. He slid the beam down to the lowest corner of the room, but there was no reassuring glint of gold. Kennedy was now beside him and raised his hand in a signal to wait. He passed by Armstrong and approached the lowest corner of the room. Very slowly, he waved his open hand over the debris pile and pulled back. There was an immediate cloud of what looked like black smoke; four decades of rust, fish waste and other decayed organic matter that had steadily accumulated in an inverted pyramid in the lowest corner of the room. As the 'smoke' cleared, they could clearly see the shine of the uppermost bar of gold. The men clasped hands and pumped each other's arm. They had found the gold. They would be rich.

Kennedy backed out of the room once more and returned, pushing the sledge. Armstrong reached down into the pile of silt and slowly, so as not to disturb the debris any more than necessary, he eased the first bar up and onto the sledge. The bar was heavy, about twenty-five pounds he guessed, but manageable. Steadily they kept working, with Kennedy gradually introducing air into the flotation bag, aiming to suspend the loaded pallet just above the floor. When they had three bars securely placed in the centre of the platform, they worked together to guide it out of the room and along the passageway towards the bright opening ahead. As they passed the buckled wall on their way out, Armstrong pointed it out. This was the damaged floor that had slowed them down so much in 1941. This was the reason the gold was still on board when the *Empress* finally went to the deep.

When they reached the opening, they lifted two bars and placed them carefully into the canvas bag and tugged the line three times. Then they watched as the bag began its trip to the surface. Coming out of their reverie, they eased the remaining bar onto the floor to await the bag's return. As planned, Kennedy took the first shift of returning along the corridor with the empty sledge, while Armstrong waited to load the bag. Two trips later, he had just signalled that the bag should go up for the second time, when he felt his arm being tugged. Kennedy reached over and tapped Armstrong's watch. Time to get back to the surface.

Twenty-five minutes later, the four men stood in circle around four gold bars glinting in the bright sunshine. They were each wearing huge smiles but would wait until evening to toast their success: Kennedy forbade alcohol during the day.

"We'll be faster this afternoon," he observed, "now we know what we're doing."

And so it proved.

The first afternoon they learned that the sledge could support four bars and over three days they successfully extracted twenty-six bars of gold. On day four Armstrong went into the bullion room and fished around in the silt until he had passed out a further four bars which they raised to the surface. By now, both divers were feeling the strain, especially Armstrong, and so they had agreed to abandon the assembly line effort on the final day—they would need two final dives that day in any case.

The final afternoon they tidied the *Sea Spray* and prepared everything for their departure after the last dive. John Kennedy had brought along four army surplus ammunition boxes they were using to store the gold and would eventually use to carry the treasure ashore when they returned to Southampton.

At last the time came for their final dive.

"Ready, Philip?"

"Ready, John."

"Let's go then."

Once more they followed the guideline to the wreck of the *Empress*. The sledge had been left secured near the entrance to the passageway. When they arrived beside it, Armstrong signalled John Kennedy to proceed while he followed behind, pushing the sledge before him. By now they were expert at precisely managing the sledge's buoyancy and they quickly arrived at the doorway for the last time. Kennedy swam down to the far corner and gently fished in the accumulated silt, his fingers seeking the now-familiar smooth shape of a gold bar. Suddenly he felt a pressure wave pushing him into the corner. He twisted reflexively in time to see a cloud of rust falling towards him, dislodged by the strongroom door slamming shut.

He quickly swam to the door and tried to push it open. With nothing to stand on, or hold on to, all he did was push himself away. He turned back for another attempt, low down near the floor, trying to get some purchase with his feet. But by the time John Kennedy placed his hands back on the door, Armstrong had turned the door handle. It would move only to the first locked position, and then only with a little effort. Armstrong didn't waste time trying to double lock the door; the simple mortice lock would be more than sufficient. He quickly pushed the empty sledge back along the passageway, until he was once again at the entrance.

He untied the guide rope from its metal stanchion and secured it instead to the sledge, where it hovered, waterlogged, above the wreck. The *Sea Spray* was now free to drift. With a final look around, he rose at a measured pace towards the surface, matching the ascent rate of his own bubbles, until, for the final fifteen feet, he increased his speed so that he burst to the surface and pulled his mouthpiece away.

"Quick, quick, pull me in!" He yelled as loudly as he could. "There's been an accident. Pull me in!"

The two deckhands grabbed hold of Armstrong and pulled him aboard where he lay, gasping, on the deck.

"I was pushing the sledge in and it stuck in the doorway. John went around it, into the room and pulled hard to free it, but somehow the webbing caught the door and pulled it closed. I couldn't stop it and now I can't open it; it's too heavy for me, or it's jammed."

"So what the hell will we do?" cried Mike.

"I'm going back down, but with a line. You need to fix a grapple to a long line, Mike. I'll fix it to the door handle and you two can help to pull it up. The line will have to pass around the corner of the opening, but there's nothing else I can think of. Tommy, can you fix me a fresh tank, and another one to take down for John? I need a minute to catch my breath and get a drink, I swallowed a lot of sea water; to be honest, I panicked a little down there."

The two men rushed to carry out his orders, while Armstrong stumbled into the cabin to find water. When he came back on deck, Mike was securing a strong line to the winch, his back to Armstrong. Tommy meanwhile, was bent over a spare air tank, wrapping webbing around it so it could be carried down. Both men were totally absorbed in their tasks and failed to see that Armstrong now held a revolver in his hand and was breathing remarkably easily. He took two steps forward to narrow the range and said,

"Sorry."

Tommy heard him and turned around, and Armstrong shot him in the head. Mike heard nothing until the gun fired and he was only partly upright when he was shot. The bullet took him on the shoulder; not a fatal wound, but the impact knocked him backwards off the diving platform, into the ocean. A bright red stain quickly spread around him as he looked back at Armstrong.

He managed to spit out, "Bastard." before Armstrong shot him again, this time killing him.

Quickly Armstrong moved over to Tommy's body and pushed him into the sea to join his friend. He glanced at his watch–John Kennedy would be running out of air in less than forty minutes.

Armstrong hadn't known exactly how he would kill John Kennedy, just that he would if they found the gold. He had come prepared, with a choice of two knives in his holdall, plus of course, the revolver. He dreaded the thought of having to use a knife; John Kennedy intimidated him, and he was terrified that one stab wouldn't kill him. But in the end, Kennedy provided the means for his own death. By suggesting the assembly line process, he allowed Armstrong a few minutes alone at the door to the strongroom every time he took the sledge back. It had been relatively easy to work the dog catches loose, and to confirm how simple it would be to pull the door just enough for gravity to take over and bring it crashing down. He had been pleasantly surprised that the catches hadn't frozen in position, but the high quality brass had resisted oxidation and the few attached barnacles broke off easily, given the leverage being brought to bear. Even more surprising was the fact that the door handle turned when he had given it an exploratory tug.

Armstrong had deliberately misled John Kennedy into believing there were five boxes of gold, plus a number of loose ingots. This ensured Kennedy would enter the safe one more time to retrieve the phantom gold, giving Armstrong his opportunity.

His next task was to bring up the lines hanging from the boat. He soon had the canvas bag on deck and moved on to the line holding the sledge. He winched it up until he could thrust a knife into the airbag. He walked the line to the bow and tied it off. Once he was underway, he would cut the line and drop the sledge–with the tank still attached, it would sink far from the wreck. He wanted to make sure the sledge didn't get caught up in the wreck. He was being over-cautious, but he didn't want to leave anything on the *Empress* that might be traced back to himself. He was trusting that the dying man wouldn't have told anyone where he was going, and that the dead men hadn't known. Their deaths would soon be written off as another mysterious tragedy at sea.

Down below, John Kennedy was facing up to the terrible reality of his imminent death. When he saw the closed door, his first instinct was that there had been an accident, that something had caused the door to slam shut. He expected to hear sounds of Armstrong trying to open the door–and indeed, he thought he did hear faint sounds immediately after the door closed. However, as the minutes ticked by in silence, he faced the terrible alternative, that Armstrong had deliberately shut him in, and the sounds he had heard were the noises of the door handle turning, locking him in his tomb.

Afraid to know the truth, Kennedy nonetheless turned again and completed his check of the silt pile at the lowest corner of the room. When he was satisfied it was truly empty of gold bars, he had to accept the reality that he had been lured into the room one final time for the express purpose of being trapped.

From his vantage point at the lowest point of the room, he shone his light over the inner side of the door. It was, as he expected, completely smooth. Even unlocked, the door would have proved a huge challenge; locked, and with no point of leverage, he couldn't possibly open it. And the strongroom was empty; it could provide no tools or levers that could assist him. He would drown here, and soon.

Like most people who pursue dangerous activities, Kennedy had thought about the possibility of his death. Having survived the war, he had imagined some kind of accident; a severed air line, a faulty tank valve, or some other equipment mishap. What he hadn't contemplated was a situation like this, knowing death was approaching but with absolutely nothing he could do to stave off the inevitable. If he hung motionless, he would reduce his oxygen use and prolong his supply as much as possible, but eventually he would pull on his mouthpiece, and it would provide nothing. His reflexes would take over and he would gasp out the last toxic breath in his body, inhale salt water and die in excruciating pain; cold, alone and possibly in darkness; unless he conserved it, his light might fail before his tank was empty.

***

Armstrong sat on the *Sea Spray* in the darkness, as the silent boat slowly drifted northeast with the current. He had no regrets, no second thoughts. He had witnessed deaths in the war, dozens of them, even if not close-up, like today. Good people, bad people–all dead. What were three more? One day he too would die, so the only rational approach was to make your own life as pleasant as possible. He had played by the rules, more or less, all his life and where had it got him? Nowhere. A miserable job in a miserable school; a bitch for an ex-wife; a loser for a father–that's where it had got him. Playing by the rules was not its own reward and anyone who thought so, was an idiot.

In the years to come, Armstrong was never to lose a minute's sleep over his actions that day; would never experience a twinge of doubt or regret or guilt. He rarely thought about it at all. It was done.

At ten o'clock, he started the engine and motored due east for ninety minutes until he saw the Mull of Kintyre lighthouse. When he could see the faint outline of the shore, he turned and followed the dark coastline for forty minutes until he sailed through the tiny gap between the mainland and Sanda Island. With the moonlight showing him the outline of the surf breaking against the cliffs on his port side, it was a simple task to follow the coast until, around two in the morning, he saw the faint light of the tiny harbour at Carradale.

He cut the engine to almost nothing and crept in around the headland, until he tied *Sea Spray* against the low fishing pier. As soon as he stopped the engine he heard the sound of approaching footsteps.

"Hello, Jeremy. You made it then? Did you remember the place from our holidays all those years ago?"

"Yes, I made it, but I don't like any of this, I don't like it at all. And it's too dark to remember anything much."

His brother was nervous, which was no surprise.

"Nearly over; have you got the dinghy?"

"It's in the van. You'll have to give me a hand."

The two brothers were whispering, although there was not a soul around to hear them. The only witness was a scrawny cat who had been asleep under a tarpaulin loosely thrown over a nearby dinghy. After a brief inspection of the scene, the cat tucked his head back down, and went back to sleep.

Quickly, Philip followed his brother to where Jeremy had parked the Bedford van. Armstrong threw his holdall into the cab, and together they manhandled the little dinghy out of the van and into the water behind the *Sea Spray*. Philip went back aboard *Sea Spray* and tied the dinghy's painter to the larger boat's stern. Jeremy was sent back to the van to retrieve the simple Seagull outboard engine.

"Come on, let's get this lot off the boat."

It was a lot harder getting the boxes of gold off *Sea Spray*; each of the four ammunition boxes weighed nearly 200 pounds. However eventually they managed to transfer the entire load into the van, where they threw some old sacks over the boxes.

"OK, Jeremy, wait here. I won't be long, promise."

Armstrong reboarded *Sea Spray* for the last time and slowly motored out of the harbour, dinghy bobbing along in his wake. Once clear of the harbour, he picked up speed and sailed for fifteen minutes before cutting the engine. He went below and opened the hatch to the engine space. Moving quickly, he used his knife to cut the main cooling water intake to the engine and watched for a moment as seawater immediately gushed into the boat. He closed the cabin door, climbed into the dinghy, released the painter and started the ever-reliable outboard.

Between its engine, the compressor and the rack of air tanks, there was plenty of weight on board to sink the little vessel.

John Kennedy and his two deckhands would eventually be missed and someone might notify the police. When the *Sea Spray's* absence was noted, the coastguard would also get involved. Armstrong was confident the official conclusion would be a tragic fishing or diving accident, but somewhere off the south coast, many hundreds of miles from Scotland.

Kennedy was a bachelor and he had been deliberately vague about where exactly they were headed when he recruited Mike and Tommy, only mentioning the *Empress of the Oceans* when they were at sea, well on their way to Scotland. Armstrong realised there was some minimal risk that Kennedy might have told someone else where he was going and why; but on balance he thought it more likely that Kennedy had kept his plans absolutely quiet.

He retraced his route back to Carradale, this time aiming for the small launch ramp. When he finally reached it, he jumped out and pulled the dinghy ashore, leaving it turned turtle between two small fishing boats, its outboard underneath. It would be many weeks before it was stolen. He walked as fast as he could, getting back to the van and his nervous brother almost an hour after he had left him.

"You drive," he ordered, unzipping the holdall he had left in the van's cab.

As his brother drove slowly through the still dark hamlet, Philip unzipped his bag and found dry shoes and socks.

"Where are the other men who helped you at the wreck?" Jeremy asked.

"They had their own boat. They took their shares and headed home to Ireland." Philip replied easily, the lie already rehearsed. "But I didn't fancy that, I'm off somewhere warm."

They would drive non-stop, pausing only for fuel and toilet breaks, taking turns to drive. In sixteen hours or so he would drop Jeremy in London then head to

Dover. Somewhere between London and Dover, he'd find a safe place to stop for an hour and move the gold and his revolver into the space he had prepared under the floor of the Bedford van. He would sleep on the ferry.

1962

NORTH CHANNEL OF THE IRISH SEA

Both Philip Armstrong and John Kennedy had been correct with their predictions. It didn't take long for the relevant people to grasp the significance of the chart datum change as far as the *Empress* wreck was concerned. A Royal Navy ship was sent out to locate and investigate the wreck.

After a difficult operation, they found the main section of the ship in 450 feet of water, almost half a mile from where they then found the bow section. They marked the site with a temporary buoy and the Admiralty issued an emergency Notice to Mariners, warning seafarers to stay away from the wreck, from both wrecks. Treasure hunters were threatened with severe penalties if they interfered with either site.

Of course, the officials were well aware that this instruction would have limited impact, and so the shallower section was prioritised for a clean destruction, which would ensure there were no projecting parts to snag fishing tackle or an unwary propeller. However, seventeen years after the war's end, the priority list was still growing. There remained wrecks and unexploded ordnance near harbour approaches that required the attention of Navy divers. So Royce & Royce were contracted to deal with the *Empress*.

Royce & Royce was the leading commercial salvage company in Great Britain, and the Royal Navy contracted them to blow up this recently discovered wreck, a potential hazard to shipping. In return for this thankless task, Royce & Royce were granted the rights to salvage what they could from the entire *Empress* wreck, with the proviso that in the unlikely event they recovered any gold, it would be handed over to the British government in return for a reward.

Steve Royce was a methodical, careful man; but his patience was being sorely tried at the moment. Even after slipping a hardened steel tube over its handle, they couldn't unlock the bullion room door–a door that was supposed to have been dogged open. The Admiralty report had clearly stated the door had been secured by two brass dogs, a stupid name Steve thought, why not just call them catches? Anyway, the report had been very specific; the door was open and secured. When the new door had been fitted, dog catches had been installed so the heavy door could be securely held while fully open. No one wanted the door slamming on them in a heavy sea.

But here they were, looking at a closed and firmly locked door.

Steve and his colleague, Andy, were 90 feet below the unforgiving Atlantic waves, off the northwest coast of Ireland. Although it was night, bright underwater lights illuminated the scene. They now spent a day laboriously cutting an inspection hole in one of the walls of the submerged strongroom.

The other decks of the wreck, both below and above their level, were showing the unmistakable signs that would eventually lead to collapse, although not quickly enough for the authorities. Rust and decay, the weight of the ship's construction and battering from the regular storms that raged not so very far above, would, over time, fatally weaken the construction. However, the bullion room would be the last space to fail. Its walls and ceiling were constructed of two inches of solid steel and the floor was stronger still. The floor had been specially reinforced to carry the enormous weight of the room's wartime cargo of gold.

With the ship lying on it side, tilted towards the bow, the reinforced floor was now an almost vertical buttress, taking the weight of the structure above it. The strongroom was canted on its side, at the end of a passageway nearly thirty yards long. The room lay on its side and the door hinges were now on the top edge of the door.

The same report that insisted the door would be open, also confirmed that all of the gold had been removed from the safe before the ship had finally sunk. The fact that the government trusted them to report any gold they discovered was the strongest indicator that the Admiralty really was certain there was no gold to be found.

But one of the reasons Royce & Royce had become so successful so quickly, was that the brothers had learned not to trust anything people said about treasure until they had checked it out themselves. Before they blew the wreck to kingdom come, they would verify for themselves that the safe was empty.

From one point of view, the locked door had been a good sign. Why lock a door unless there's something to protect? And the door was definitely locked, not merely closed. Its handle was in the second position, at six o'clock; meaning only the simple mortice type lock was engaged, but that was academic at this juncture, simple or complex, they couldn't force or pick the lock.

Steve talked to his brother on the surface. "Taking a look now, Pete."

Up above, on the surface, Pete Royce tried to be patient, as he awaited his brother's report.

"Oh God! Oh God! Oh sweet Jesus!"

When Steve and Andy had fully recovered from the shock of discovering the dead body in the locked strongroom, they approached the inspection hole once again. Gingerly now, Steve again worked his head, shoulders and right arm into the huge safe. His flashlight quickly located the gruesome remains of whoever had died in the room. He examined the cadaver, but could see nothing to identify him. Once again, but more carefully this time, he swept his light over every part of the strongroom. He could see nothing of interest, although there was a small debris pile in the far corner of the room that might be worth investigating. He eased himself back out.

"Let's get a probe down here and we'll investigate that corner before we call it quits."

Back on their support ship, Steve described the situation to his brother. They discussed the next actions they would take. Recovering the body in one piece was not an option without significantly increasing the size of the hole—a major undertaking for no obvious benefit.

Pete wondered aloud. "But how did he get there? If the door somehow slammed on him by itself, how come it's locked? It was locked, wasn't it? I mean not jammed shut?"

Andy spoke up, "No, the lock was definitely engaged. Someone on the outside turned the handle while the guy was in there. The question is, was he already dead and they didn't want to bring the body back—or was he locked inside alive?"

The men around the table were silent, each contemplating the horror of being locked in an underwater box with no prospect of escape and your air supply inexorably running out. It was a diver's ultimate nightmare.

George Patterson looked at Steve. "Did you notice anything about his gear? I mean did it look old, dated? I'm wondering if we could figure out *when* he died."

"Looked pretty normal. Looked more or less like what we wear now. Look, let's get back down with the probe and a grab bag and see if there's anything in there. Then we'll decide what to do. Pete and George, it's your turn to go down."

Pete carefully worked the probe into the corner, trying to feel if there was anything more than rust flakes and organic junk. He could feel something, he was sure. He slowly pushed whatever it was until it was wedged against the far wall. Then he manoeuvred the long rod with its mesh grab bag tight into the corner, dropped whatever it was into the bag and slowly eased back. He could definitely feel there was something in the bag. He backed out very carefully, until the entire length of both rods emerged and George could remove the bag and tie it tight. They also studied the dead man but saw nothing to add to what little they knew.

Back on top, the bag was carefully tipped into a bucket of fresh water. The object Pete had felt was a watch, a Rolex Submariner—the same make and model of watch every one of them was wearing.

Pete thought they had to move on. They were spending too much time on this, and time was his and Steve's money. "Maybe this will tell us something. We'll have a jeweller look at it and see if it can be dated. There's no inscription, so I don't think we'll identify the guy from it, but you never know. OK, I think we need to get on and investigate the main section of the

Empress. Let's shift over to where the destroyer was stationed to have a quick search for any gold bars that went down with the launch. Tomorrow, we'll recover our gear and get this bow section demolished."

The entire diving team, eight men in total, all went down the following morning. No one had much expectation of finding a proverbial needle in a haystack. Seven small boxes of gold bars smashed up and widely scattered by a huge explosion over twenty years ago were not going to be easy to find. Add to that, the soft sandy bottom of this part of the ocean would in all likelihood have swallowed up the heavy bars.

And so it proved. Even though they quickly found three sections of the *Halifax's* launch, all massively damaged, the team failed to find any gold.

The following day they carefully placed explosives in and around the bow section of the *Empress* and retreated to the surface before detonating the charges. After a quick check to see that the job had been done properly, they moved on to the exploration and salvage of the main body of the ship.

Over the course of the next two weeks, the team removed everything of value that was readily accessible. The four huge propellers represented the bulk of their prize, but other pieces would bring money. Now that they were in much deeper water, they were working in traditional deep diving suits, with copper helmets and their air supplied from the surface. If the *Empress* had gone down in her halcyon pre-war days, there would have been lots of valuable high-end souvenirs– sculptures, crystal, fine china with the ship's logo, silver services and the like. However, almost everything that hinted of luxury had been taken off in 1939, when she was converted to a troopship. The little that remained in the much reduced first-class section wasn't worth a major effort, but they kept their eyes peeled none the less.

There was also little chance of finding valuable passenger possessions for precisely the same reason; there were no wealthy first class passengers aboard in wartime.

Steve Royce was again working alongside Andy, removing the ship's bell from its wood and brass stand. The stand had broken from its base and was lying on the seabed, making the bell easily accessible. As Steve shuffled his feet to position himself to attach the recovery line hanging from the surface, his foot disturbed something under the sand. He looked down and thought he saw a glint of gold.

The two men finished attaching the line and signalled topside to raise the bell. As soon as it was safely on its way, Steve bent down to pick up the gold object. Except it wasn't gold. It first appeared to be a section of brass tubing with relatively little marine growth encrusting it–perhaps being buried had protected it, was his first thought. He raised it up to his face to better see what the thing was, and realised it was a sealed container. He looked at Andy, who shook his head; he had no idea what it was either. Pete placed the item in the large recovery bag already containing a number of objects. When it was full, they would lift it to the surface using air bags.

Mission accomplished, the Royce & Royce team stowed away their kit and secured everything they had recovered from the *Empress*. Without a backwards glance, they fired up the powerful engines on the support vessel and set course for home. It had been a rewarding assignment, if not a stellar one. But they would dine out for weeks on the story of the gruesome corpse.

The body was still floating in the bullion room. Even after the demolition charges had done their work, the reinforced room was still intact. Now it sat on the seabed, in a nest of tangled metal.

With a new hole in one of the walls, fish and crabs could swim in to investigate. Their attentions, and the shifting ocean currents, caused the cadaver to shift position occasionally. By chance, every now and then an outstretched arm would seem to point to the inspection hole. An observer might have thought it was drawing attention to the words scratched on the wall inches above the opening, invisible from any vantage point except inside the safe.

If only John Kennedy had chosen another wall as the batteries on his flashlight began to fail. Before John died—cold, scared and alone in pitch darkness, he methodically scratched his final message: *'Philip Armstrong murdered me. John J Kennedy 11/7/60'*

Three weeks later, Steve and Pete were supervising the examination of the smaller items removed from the *Empress*. Alongside her massive propellers, the bell was by far the most valuable artefact. When they had finished cleaning it up, it would be sold and would take pride of place in some wealthy collector's display. The beautifully engraved ship's bell from one of the most iconic liners ever to set sail was a fantastic trophy. Indeed, anything labelled with the ship's name was valuable.

Even fairly prosaic items without an obvious connection to the *Empress* would be provided with a signed certificate, authenticating its provenance. This was where the sterling reputation of the brothers' company paid off; collectors worldwide respected a certificate under the letterhead 'Royce & Royce Ltd, Glasgow'.

Pete watched intently as Susan Duffy lifted the odd brass container out of the freshwater tank. Susan was one of the team who cleaned recovered items and prepared them for auction.

He observed for a while as Susan examined the object, before he went over to her workstation.

"What do you think it is?"

"I'm not sure. But, see here, it has a milled edge; someone worked this. But I can't see how it's sealed. I'm pretty sure it *is* sealed and watertight, because here, hold it. If you turn it around in your hand, you can feel things shifting inside."

Pete took the cylinder from her.

"I think it's a shell casing. I think it's been made to hold something. Can you give it a good clean and bring it to the office? I'm intrigued."

Soon after lunch, Susan appeared in the office the brothers shared. The brass container was unrecognisable now. All but one or two small areas had been cleared of the encrustations that had covered it. The firm had discovered that leaving some trace of the object's time on the seabed enhanced its value, so they rarely cleaned off every trace of marine growth.

"I found the join under the milled edge. This object was made by someone who knew what he was doing. But I can't open it; it's well and truly sealed by corrosion. I think it could possibly be forced, but that might damage it. It would be better to neatly cut the base out and remove the contents that way, then the bottom could be fixed back on–you'd have to turn it over to know it had been opened."

Susan turned the container around.

"And look at this; this was under the encrustations."

Steve and Pete looked at the markings on the brass then looked at each other.

The Square and Compasses were clearly visible, above a name, Alex Campbell.

Pete took the object from Susan.

"We'll take this one, Susan. It won't be too hard to find out who this belonged to. We'll return it to its owner. Thanks for your efforts."

Steve and Pete were both Freemasons and immediately accepted their obligation to a fellow Mason to return this container to its owner or his family.

"I wonder who Alex Campbell is, or was," mused Steve.

"I'm betting he was crew, not a passenger. It's too bulky an object for a soldier to be lugging halfway around the world. No, I'm betting Alex was a crew member on the *Empress*. It shouldn't be too hard to find out. I'll run over to the shipping office tomorrow, they'll have a record in Liverpool. If not, we'll get the Lodge secretary to track him down. We'll keep hold of this for now."

With that, Pete reverently lifted Alex's old container and placed it gently on top of the bookcase beside his desk.

Jim Craig's gift to his brother-in-law had miraculously re-appeared after twenty years. But neither man was there to hold it again.

Next morning, Pete was at the Empress Line office in St. Vincent Street when it opened at nine o'clock. He saw a sign indicating 'Crew' and followed the arrow to a long wooden counter staffed by four people. He went to the nearest position.

"Good morning. My name is Pete Royce, and my company has recently been salvaging one of your ships, the *Empress of the Oceans*."

Pete saw the instant effect his words had on the young woman, and more especially, on her colleague at the next position, a much older lady, in her mid-sixties, Pete guessed.

"Don't worry, we were appointed by the Admiralty; we're official salvage experts. I'm here because we found something we believe may have been owned by a crew member of the *Empress*. I was hoping you could contact your head office in Liverpool to help me track him down. We want to return the item to the gentleman in question," he paused before continuing, "or his family."

"Do you have a name?" the woman asked.

"Alex Campbell."

There was a gasp from the older woman, who turned to address Pete.

"Alex Campbell? You found something belonging to Alex Campbell of the *Empress of the Oceans*?"

"I believe so. It has that name engraved on it. We think it may be a container holding his personal belongings."

"Oh dear me! We don't need to ask Liverpool. I knew Alex Campbell. Everyone in here that's old enough, knew Alex Campbell. He was a lovely, wonderful man. He sailed on the *Empress* from the day she went to sea until the dreadful day she sank. I just can't believe this. You'd better come with me, young man. It's alright, Dorothy, I'll take care of this gentleman."

With that, the woman rose from her chair and led Pete down a short corridor, where she knocked once, before opening a door into a private office.

"Mr Edmonds, I think you'll want to hear with this gentleman has to say."

"Mr Royce, this is Mr Edmonds, Regional Director of Crew Affairs for Empress Line. He too was a colleague of Alex Campbell."

The mention of Alex's name ensured that Pete had Owen Edmonds' full attention, as once again he told his story. When he was finished, Edmonds spoke quietly.

"This is quite a story you've told us, Mr Royce. Alex Campbell was a steward on the *Empress of the Oceans* before the war. He was something of a legend around here when I joined the company. He had an outstanding reputation and was selected to serve as Senior Steward when the *Empress* entered war service. He looked after senior military and diplomatic figures, and important politicians from Britain and our allies. He was a remarkable man."

Pete decided to share more information with Edmonds.

"There's something else you might want to know, Mr Edmonds, as the *Empress* was your ship, so to speak."

He turned to the woman who had ushered him in.

"You may not want to hear this. It's a bit gruesome."

"Young man, I was an auxiliary nurse in the war. I doubt there's anything I haven't seen."

In an increasingly horrified atmosphere, Pete told them about the mysterious corpse they had found in the *Empress's* bullion room.

"We're baffled. The only way we can read the facts is that the man was deliberately locked in that safe. If so, it was a heinous crime. We recovered what we're pretty sure was the dead man's watch–it's with a Rolex retailer in Glasgow to see if he can tell us anything. I'll be calling on him when I leave here."

"Of course," he added, "the dead man was a diver, so nothing to do with the *Empress* or her crew. The Admiralty has our report, so it's up to them if they take it any further."

"Well, Mr Royce, you've certainly brought us some intriguing information. There has been no end of rumours about the *Empress* and gold, ever since she was lost–well, I'm sure I don't need to tell that to someone in your business! Coming back to Alex Campbell, not only did he serve on the *Empress* throughout all of her years' afloat, he helped build her. Before Alex was a steward, he was a boilermaker working on the *Empress*. You see, Alex Campbell lived just down the road, in

Clydebank. You won't have far to go to return his possessions."

Pete left the Empress Line office with the address of Alex Campbell's sister-in-law. He walked the short way down Buchanan Street to the 100-year-old shopping arcade where Glasgow's upmarket jewellers' shops congregated. Like most Scottish divers, Pete had bought his own Rolex from Arcade Jewellers, so they had been happy to help him with the mystery watch.

The manager greeted him and went to the back office to retrieve the watch.

"As you can see, we only had to clean it and wind it up to get it working again. We've given it a thorough exterior and interior clean and resealed the case. The serial number indicates it was made around the middle of 1956. Rolex will know which of their retailers sold it. But they're a pretty tight-lipped bunch in Switzerland. They might possibly tell the police, but they won't tell you or me.

"Other than that, there's nothing to report, Pete. It is a completely standard, stainless steel Rolex Oyster Submariner; no custom work at all to distinguish it. It has its original steel strap and has seen some wear and tear, but nothing out of the ordinary, except see here, this lug?"

The jeweller pointed to one of the lugs holding the watchstrap. One side had well-defined, almost sharp edges and shoulders, but on the other, one shoulder showed clear sign of heavy wear.

"I think this was used to rub or scratch something, with the watch off the wrist, the strap folded out of the way. I can't think of how else this part could be so badly worn. Odd. Anyway, I've written all the identifying marks on this card. If Rolex do want to help, this will be enough information for them. I hope you find out who he was, if it helps catch the bastard who killed him. What a way to go, eh?"

"So what's next?" asked Steve, as the brothers shared a sandwich lunch at their desks back in their office.

"We go to the address in Clydebank. It's twenty years old, but Edmonds was sure it's still the family home. He had to be a bit careful, but he did let on that, unusually, Alex Campbell's survivor pension didn't go to his children, but to his sister-in-law, and she has never submitted a change of address. It seems that, after the war, his surviving children requested that the money continued to be sent to their aunt. Mind, I don't suppose it's much. We could write, but I think we should go in person. Saturday morning might be best."

They found the address easily enough the following Saturday morning. It was shortly before ten o'clock when Pete knocked the door to Kate's flat. The family had long ago relinquished the unit next door that had been Alex and Annie's then Hugh's.

Steve was carrying a Gladstone bag.

The lady who answered the door was in her mid-sixties, short, with silver hair pulled back in a bun. She was dressed in a black skirt with a white silk blouse. She was wearing a striking pearl necklace; this was an extremely elegant lady.

"Mrs Craig?"

"Yes, can I help you?"

"I wonder if we could come in for a moment, Mrs Craig. There's something we'd like to show you."

Kate assessed the two young men. They looked friendly enough, obviously brothers. But still.

Pete held out his hand, palm down to show her the signet ring he was wearing.

"Mrs Craig, my brother and I are Freemasons." He paused, "Like your late brother-in-law, Alex Campbell."

Kate was startled to hear Alex's name from the young man, but she nodded her head and led them into her living room. Now it was the brothers' turn to be taken aback. Behind the modest front door was what could only be described as a luxury flat. The sofa and chairs were covered in the finest soft leather; a Bang and Olufsen radiogram sat in one corner, beside a television from the same company. The fitted carpet was luxuriant and a fabulous lacquered screen inlaid with mother-of-pearl had been mounted on one wall above a display cabinet containing antiques and intriguing objects made of jade and ivory.

"Please, take a seat."

As Steve settled himself on the sofa beside his brother, he realised he was facing a large and richly detailed oil painting of the *Empress of the Oceans* above the fireplace.

"That's a wonderful painting, Mrs Craig."

"My late husband and brother-in-law helped build that ship, right over there."

Kate was pointing out of her bay window as she continued, "and my brother-in-law was killed on her in 1941."

Pete cleared his throat.

"Yes, we know about Mr Campbell and the *Empress*. That's why we're here."

He nodded to his brother. Steve opened the bag sitting between his feet and carefully lifted out a bundle wrapped in a piece of red velvet. He gently placed it on the coffee table in front of him and unveiled the container, turning it so Kate could see the inscription.

Kate's hand flew to her mouth and for a long time she simply stared at the container in complete silence. The brothers had asked Susan to remove the rest of the marine growth and to give the container a high polish. It gleamed now in the morning sunlight that flooded the room.

"Where, where did you get this?" Kate finally stammered through a few tears quickly wiped away.

Slowly, carefully, the brothers told her about their work on the *Empress*, omitting anything about the strongroom. Finally, they described finding the odd object and bringing it back to Glasgow to be cleaned. They ended by passing on the good wishes of Owen

Edmonds. As they spoke, Kate picked up the container and turned it slowly in her hands, caressing its smooth surface.

"Mrs Craig, I'd like to finish by saying how sorry we are about your loss. But you should know that your late brother-in-law must have been a wonderful man. The people at the Empress Line office spoke most highly of him. And, if you don't wish to discuss it, we understand, but I wonder, can you tell us anything about how this was made? A real craftsman did this work."

Kate thoughts instantly returned to that day in 1941, the last complete day she and Jim had enjoyed with Alex. In her mind's eye the present room dissolved and she saw the three of them sitting in the same space, but in a much simpler, darker room.

Kate dragged herself back to the present and explained to the brothers how Alex needed something watertight to hold his personal things, and how her husband had the container made in the shipyard's metal shop. She also told them of the dreadful air raid that had taken her husband and cost Alex his daughter. As she spoke, she slowly turned Alex's container in her hands, feeling the contents rolling around inside; there was something large and heavy in there.

"They were great friends; I mean as well as being brothers-in-law. Family was everything to Alex. It breaks my heart to know he learned of Jim and his wee daughter's deaths just weeks before he died. The last thing he knew in life was terrible sadness. He deserved better. He was a good man."

After a while, the brothers made to leave, but first Pete spoke again.

"We'll be going now, Mrs Craig. I'm glad we were able to bring Mr Campbell's possessions back to his family. As you can see, we didn't open the case. I should tell you we don't think it can be unscrewed without damaging it. But we know how you could get inside it without ruining it. If you ever would like that, we'd be honoured to help, anytime at all. Here's our card, just get in touch."

He explained Susan's idea, tracing a line around the bottom surface of the container.

"The repair would be practically invisible. Anyway, as I say, get in touch if you wish."

"Thank you. I'll have to let Hugh decide. Hugh is Alex's eldest. He'll know what to do. I'll phone him in London, as soon as you leave. And thank you for taking the trouble you have, finding me, restoring this so beautifully. Alex was proud to be a Freemason; he would appreciate what you've done. So, thank you again, on his behalf."

***

"Hugh? It's Kate. Yes, I'm fine, son. And you and the family; all well? Good. Hugh, you'll want to sit down for this."

Kate cradled the phone against her cheek, so she could stroke the container, as she told Hugh the momentous news.

Between Hugh and Robbie, Kate had not had to worry about money for many years. Her son and nephew paid all of her bills, sent her money every month and brought her to their homes in Los Angeles and London two or three times a year. Jenny still lived in London, so Kate saw plenty of both her children—and of her grandchildren, which is how she thought of Hugh and Anna's children just as much as Robbie and Chrissie's two. Sometimes she broke her trip to Los Angeles with a detour to Chicago or New York, to spend time with Alan or Betty, both now American citizens with no remaining hint of their former Scottish accents.

She saw Wilbur and Joanne every time she went to LA, and the three of them had become closer as the years passed. They enjoyed the fact that they were now family; connected through their children's marriage.

They had all given up asking Kate to move to London or America, accepting that she would stay in Clydebank among her friends and her memories. Her bedroom walls were covered with photographs of her extended family. She missed her husband and Alex and Annie every day, but she felt blessed to be loved and cherished by the next generation. She was sure Annie and Alex would be proud and happy with their family.

"My God, Kate. This is incredible. Can you give me a while to think? I'll call you back in an hour or so."

It was only thirty minutes before her phone rang.

"Next month, Robbie and Chrissie will be in London. Chrissie's latest film is having its British premiere in Leicester Square. I think we should all get together in our place and open Dad's canister. What do you think?"

"I think that's a great idea. What about the Royces' idea about how to open it?"

"It sounds pretty simple. If you bring it down with you, I'll have arranged for a jeweller or someone to be ready. I'm sure we can have it back the same day with no trouble."

Hugh's meeting with Maurice Wilkes had proved to be serendipitous. His visit to Cambridge in 1946 led to him doing a PhD there, after which he followed some of the Computer Lab team to J Lyons & Co where they built the world's first computer to be used in business.

In 1951, Hugh met a young woman who was doing consulting work for his company. Anna Bartenstein was a ferociously smart mathematician from an Austrian Jewish refugee family. Her father had understood the threat of the Nazis even before Kristallnacht in 1938 and brought his wife and daughter to safety in London. Anna and Hugh had an unconventional relationship. Instead of going dancing, they spent hours discussing their respective work problems over cheap meals in Soho restaurants.

Under Anna's prompting, Hugh came to the realization that what he wanted to do, was to build a company. Not one that would employ his family, as his father had intended, but one that would provide financial security for them if required. The reality was that his siblings and cousins were all building successful lives and seemed unlikely to have to depend on Hugh for anything.

Just as important however, Hugh wanted to build a business that would reflect the principles his father had passed on to him. He would study companies and organisations that had developed forward-looking policies with regard to their employees and clients and build a company his father would be proud of.

Flush with the excitement of finally understanding his goals in life, Hugh proposed to Anna.

In 1956, he left Lyons & Co and, with his new wife, he set up Europe's first computer bureau, doing payroll and other tasks for some of Britain's biggest companies.

Hugh was by now a very rich man. He and Anna lived in Chelsea with their two children, a live-in nanny and two daily staff who cooked, cleaned and generally looked after them.

Robbie too had prospered. He and Chrissie lived mostly in Los Angeles, but they kept a flat in London to use on their frequent visits. Robbie had continued working as a journalist until, three years after their wedding, Chrissie had asked him to rewrite some of her lines for her latest film role, a romantic comedy. Chrissie had much preferred Robbie's version and, more crucially, so did the director and producer. From those beginnings, Robbie went on to become a successful Hollywood screenwriter; although he still contributed occasional humour pieces to British and American newspapers, mostly observations on the differences between life on either side of the Atlantic. When his movie career took off, they decided Chrissie would give up the movie business for a few years to enjoy time with their identical twin girls, born eight years ago. Even now, she only accepted parts where there was no location work that would prevent her from being home each night. Chrissie remained the most beautiful woman in whatever company she found herself. Robbie never tired of simply looking at his wife.

Alan and Betty had flown over with Robbie and Chrissie but without either of their American spouses. They both had infant children and no one relished the prospect of bringing them along on the long flight. Theirs would be a flying visit, as they would be returning home in three days, right after the premiere.

Robbie and Jenny were still as close as ever. In 1950, when she was 28, Jenny decided she was fed up being jealous of her cousin in America, and went to university.

"I loved Uncle Alex to bits, but he had no business sending you and the rest of the boys to Glasgow

Academy and university and not me. I hope he's looking down now to see me graduate!" She smiled at her brother as she said this on the day she was awarded a first-class degree in fine arts. Now she was a senior lecturer in the history of art, and a consultant to Christies auction house on Chinese and Japanese art and ceramics.

Six weeks after the Royces had visited Kate, the family were all sitting round in an expectant circle in Hugh and Anna's stylish lounge. The remaining Scottish branch of the family was also represented. Agnes had stayed home to be near their two daughters, both of whom were expecting babies any day now; but Ian and his two sons had arrived on the train from Glasgow earlier that afternoon.

As they sipped glasses of wine and caught up with each other's news, the mood was distracted. Finally, the doorbell sounded and Anna went to answer it. She returned with the now-empty canister and a black box file.

She handed the box to Hugh, put the container on the table in front of him and sat down beside him.

Hugh looked around with a nervous smile.

"Well, here goes."

He opened the box and took out the top sheet of paper, which was typed. He read the letter to the group in a clear, steady voice.

Dear Mr Campbell,

We are pleased to present the contents of your father's container, together with the object itself, which, as requested, has been resealed.

Your father was clearly an organised man. The canister contained a number of large envelopes, all unsealed and each bearing the crest of the Empress of the Oceans. As you will see, each envelope has an individual's name on the front. There is also another document which was not enclosed in any way.

The contents have taken on the curve of the container after having been constrained within for so many years; they should return to their original shape if stored carefully.

I trust you will find our work satisfactory. Our invoice will follow in due course.

Yours etc.'

Hugh finished reading and laid the letter on the low table in front of him. He reached into the box and pulled out the first envelope.

"Leckie," he read on its front, and reached across to hand the envelope to his cousin.

No one else moved as they waited to see what was in the envelope.

Ian and Agnes's son, Leckie, who went by Alexander since he qualified as a lawyer, peered into the envelope. Slowly he removed items, one after another: postcards of Melbourne and Cape Town, each with a scribbled sentence or two on the back; a rubber kangaroo, postage stamps and some copper coins from both countries. Alexander's hands had been shaking when he took the envelope, but by the time he was finished emptying it, he was smiling sadly. Jenny, however, had her handkerchief to her eyes.

Alexander looked up and nodded, and Hugh picked up another envelope.

"Betty," he announced and handed his sister her gifts from their long dead father.

The young woman took the envelope then started to cry softly.

She handed it back to her brother.

"You do it, Hugh, please."

Betty's gifts were similar to her cousin's: postcards, coins, stamps, a beaded purse and a miniature musical box that tinkled *'Waltzing Matilda'* when Hugh turned the tiny handle on its side.

Other than Ian, Robbie and Jenny, already adults and in uniform in 1941, every member of the family received an envelope. The contents were all much the same; little souvenirs of the two ports of call on Alex's final voyage. All were inexpensive, but each item testified to the love of their father and uncle. The only exceptions were the envelopes for Hugh, Agnes and Kate.

As Hugh handed an envelope to Kate, he thought at first it was empty. He gave it a little squeeze and realised there was in fact something inside. When Kate shook the envelope out, a little satin bag landed on her lap.

Inside was a pretty opal ring. Kate slipped it on, grasped Robbie's hand and squeezed it hard to help her maintain control.

"Oh, Alex!" was all she said.

Ian opened Agnes's envelope, to reveal a tiny gold nugget on a chain.

Finally, it was Hugh's turn. His envelope was at the bottom because it was, by far, the heaviest. When he looked into it, he could see that it contained no postcards or toys. He had been seventeen when his dad died, too old for childish things. Instead, he found a paperback novel, *Happy Valley*, which the cover described as a stirring tale of life in the Australian outback. The second item was a brochure, '*The Folly of Neutrality*' by the South African leader, General Smuts. On the front cover, Alex had written, 'You should read this, son. Smuts is a great man.'

Hugh smiled through his watery eyes. Here was his father, thousands of miles away, in the middle of a war, but still focused on Hugh's education. Hugh was aware that his emotions were barely in check, but there was one more item to get through. As he had lifted out his own envelope, he had seen that there was a final document at the bottom of the box, this one not in an envelope.

Hugh carefully put down his books and lifted the last item from his father's container. He turned it over, and quickly scanned the opening paragraphs of a handwritten letter. Then he stopped, and lowered the letter to his lap. His hand was shaking.

After a moment, he looked up. Robbie thought his cousin looked lost, frightened almost.

"What is it, Hugh? What's wrong?"

In response, Hugh's eyes darted around the room, finally settling on Chrissie. He held the letter out to her.

With a catch in his voice, he asked, "Chrissie, would you, would you read it, please? Read it to the end and decide what to do."

He saw that Chrissie was confused.

"I trust you; you decide." Hugh insisted.

The others were by now completely bemused. But Chrissie took the flimsy papers from Hugh and read the letter in silence. There were four pages, on two sheets of thin blue paper. She read to the end then looked at Hugh with her eyes shining and a soft smile on her face.

"It's OK, Hugh. It's beautiful, actually. Would you like me to read it out?"

Hugh nodded.

In her lovely trained voice, Chrissie read out Alex's final letter.

437 Fairway Court,
Geelong,
Victoria,
Australia

25th May, 1941

My Dearest Alice,

I've just come down from looking towards home as we steam past Scotland. It was too dark to see anything, but knowing how close I am, filled me with happiness at the thought I'll see my family again very soon and will be able to hold my babies in my arms once more, even though they're no longer babies of course!

And yet, at the same time, I long to be 10,000 miles away, holding _you_ in my arms. I so desperately want my family to meet you and love you as much as I have come to love you in such a short time. I know you'll love them, because they are all so loveable.

I told you about Hughie, about how clever he is. Even though I wanted him to finish his studies, I'm proud he pushed back and wanted to put on a uniform and fight. I really think he'll do something wonderful one of these days.

I'm so sorry you'll never get to know Jean, at least in this world. She was such an affectionate wee girl and idolised her big brother, who I must say, protected her every day, especially after Annie's death. I still can't believe she's gone.

I maybe never mentioned that we had another son; our first, Willie. He was only two when he passed away. He was such a funny wee boy, just starting his life; I would love to know how he turned out.

I feel most guilty about Betty and Alan; I've missed so much of their growing up. I often wonder if I made the right decision to go to sea. Times were hard, but maybe they paid too high a price. I hate this war for keeping me away from them even longer. By rights I would be leaving the Empress now and we'd be opening our family hotel, me and Ian and Agnes and Kate and Jim. Instead Jim is dead, I'm still not home and Ian is learning how to kill people. It's a terrible world.

Well, of course it isn't all terrible, and I shouldn't say it is. You saved me after I got that awful telegram and I'll never forget it. I'll never stop missing Jean and Jim, any more than I'll forget Annie; but you've given me hope for the future and I'm more determined than ever to do whatever tiny things I can to make this war shorter so we can all be together.

I love you with all of my heart. Maybe it's something about wartime that makes us fall in love faster than before. Maybe it's getting older and realising life isn't as long as it seemed when you're a teenager. Whatever it is, I know my love for you is as deep and strong and real as it would be if we had known each other for a hundred years.

I'll post this tomorrow in Liverpool. I need to go to the office to sign my papers and withdraw some money to get my watch back from a real - well I won't write what I think of Armstrong, some people are parasites, preying on others. Anyway, then Johnny and I will be off to the station and home to Scotland, where I'll write to you again. I'm not sure how long I'll be at home this time, it won't be long enough.

Give my regards to your father and think about me every day – as I will of you.

I was on deck a few minutes ago, looking at the stars and thinking how very, very far away you are. When this war is over, we'll be together and never again do I want you far from my side.

Ever yours,

Love,

Alex

XXXXX

P.S. I just realised I've got no more envelopes. What a nuisance. I'll borrow one in the morning.

After Chrissie finished reading, she handed the letter back to Hugh. Everyone was utterly stunned, several of them were quietly weeping. It took an age before anyone spoke; it was Kate who broke the silence.

She looked around at her family and spoke softly, but with passion trembling in her voice.

"When the men who found this canister came to give it to me, I told them about Jim and Jean. And I told them how I had always hated the fact Alex heard about their deaths before he died. I said something about how that meant Alex's final weeks were spent in terrible sadness, and how that wasn't what he deserved. Well, now I can be happy that in the midst of his despair, he found love and happiness too. *That's* what he deserved."

None of them was in the mood to talk about the bombshell yet. Ian took Hugh aside as everyone stood up and refilled their drinks or chatted about their gifts.

"I know there's a lot to take in, but did you pay attention to Alex's comment about his watch? Do you mind if I read that part again?"

Ian then Hugh re-read the final section of Alex's letter. Hugh was relieved to be talking about anything other than the most important information in the letter.

"I wonder what he meant, I mean about the parasite thing?" Ian pondered. "I think the Johnny he mentions is probably Johnny Fraser. He was a friend of mine and …"

Hugh interrupted his uncle.

"I met Johnny Fraser, years and years ago, with Kate. We must have forgot to tell you."

Hugh told Ian about meeting Johnny in the Cunard office in 1946 and his kindness in getting them upgraded to first class.

Ian was intrigued of course. "I wonder if he's still there? He was only a year or two older than me; he's probably still working. I bet he knows about this Armstrong."

Later that night, when everyone else had gone to bed, Hugh, Robbie, Chrissie and Jenny sat together in the lounge. Hugh had opened a bottle of single malt whisky and now he poured them each a glass.

"To Dad," he toasted.

"To Alex," the others responded in unison.

Hugh looked at his cousins.

"It'll take me a while to digest that letter. It was just about the last thing I would have imagined."

Jenny put her hand on her cousin's arm. "Mum was right though. It's good he found happiness at a time when he must have been devastated. I think it's lovely. But I wonder about the girl, woman I suppose, Alice? I imagine she heard the news at the time, but it must have been devastating for her."

"I never even thought about her, but you're right. The poor girl must have been so hurt. Do you think we should send her the letter? It is addressed to her after all."

Jenny was thoughtful for a moment, then decisive. "I'm going to take it to her. I know we could just post it, but I don't think we should. We don't know her circumstances, she could be married. Maybe she never mentioned a wartime romance."

Now Robbie spoke.

"I think that's a great idea, Jen, but its a long way to go, to Australia."

Jenny smiled as she replied. "I'm not that much of a hero. I'm going to Japan in May; I'll add Australia to my itinerary. Can you get someone to find me an up-to-date address?"

"I'm sure I can. I'll make a call tomorrow." Robbie continued, "What about this business with the watch? Will we pick that up and try to find it?"

Hugh answered him immediately. "Yes, let's find Johnny Fraser first. That should be easy. We can take it from there."

Up until that moment, Chrissie had been silent, but now she spoke up.

"I have to say just how remarkable your father was, Hugh. All those envelopes! He must have been thinking about every one of you every single day. I thought Alex was a special person when I met him as a teenager. In the years since, I keep learning more about him and he seems still more remarkable. As I looked around you all tonight, I thought how proud he would be. Not only at what you've all achieved, but how close you've stayed over the years. I think he'd have been delighted to see you all, together."

***

While all this was going on, Pete Royce had decided to get some publicity, in an effort to stir up some information on the dead man. The Admiralty had been singularly uninterested in pursuing the matter, and he was pretty sure he was being fobbed off by the police as well. They took his statement and promised 'someone will look it into it'; but he was unconvinced.

So, he called a journalist on the *Daily Mail* in London. At first the man was distracted, obviously doing something else while Pete talked. However, as soon as Pete mentioned finding the *Empress of the Oceans*, he had the journalist's full attention. When Pete told him about the corpse in the strongroom, the journalist stopped him.

"Mr Royce; by the way, is that like the cars? No relation I suppose? No, well, never mind. Look, if I come up to Glasgow tomorrow, will you give me an interview, on the record? An exclusive?"

***

Johnny Fraser was still working for Cunard, in London now, and was happy to meet Hugh for lunch.

"Philip Armstrong was a complete bastard, simple as that. He loaned people money at exorbitant rates and demanded collateral."

When Hugh told him about the reference to Armstrong in Alex's last letter, Johnny realised that Alex must have been forced to hand over his grandfather's watch to get the cash to bail him out in Cape Town.

He was upset he hadn't thought to ask Alex where the money had come from.

"I had no idea. It was just like Alex not to mention what he had to do to get the money. I can't tell you how sorry I am, Hugh. I was weak and a fool. And I realise how unbelievably selfish and thoughtless I was. If it wasn't for me, your father would never have had to hand over his watch. Or I should have taken over the debt and Armstrong would have been holding my stuff and not your dad's. I'm so sorry."

"Don't worry about it. We'd have lost the watch anyway. Do you have any idea where we could find Armstrong now?"

"None. I was ill for a long time and anyway, we were never going to be friends. Our paths never crossed again during the war—I don't think I even heard his name mentioned again. To be honest, I completely forgot about the whole business with Armstrong. You see, thanks to Alex, once I got home from the hospital, I fought to hang on to my marriage and deal with other family problems. I was a mess for quite a while. But I came through it somehow, thanks to Stephanie and, I don't know, I didn't want to face it all again, I suppose."

The two men stared at their plates for a while, until Johnny continued. "Have you read the official report, about the sinking I mean? They're usually not completely reliable, but you never know, there might be some useful information buried in there. And the shipping line might have records."

The official report was dry and uninformative. His father was mentioned only once, and then only in passing. Armstrong's name appeared often however, in connection with the efforts to recover the 'specialised war matériel' being carried by the *Empress*. The account of the recovery effort was, in truth, confusing, but Hugh noted that the only other survivor of the final transfer was a Henry Brown. He had been the boatswain of the *Halifax's* launch that brought Armstrong and the last recovery crew back to the destroyer. Henry Brown hadn't served with Armstrong, but they had shared the trauma of the destruction of the launch; Hugh was hoping this might have established a connection between the two men.

He had made a note of the names of the other officers of the *Empress* who had survived the sinking. He also realised he could go to the Empress Line offices and try to discover what ships Armstrong had served on after the sinking. His to do list was getting longer, and he decided he would employ a private detective to do this work.

But before he had taken any further action, Kate called him.

"I had a call from that nice Pete Royce, you know, the diver who recovered your dad's things. He told me there will be a story in the *Daily Mail* tomorrow about the *Empress*. He warned me what it's about—it's a horrible business!"

The newspaper's story was all about the gruesome discovery of the corpse in the *Empress's* bullion room. Beyond the bare facts, the article was all speculation about how the corpse came to be there and when the diver must have entered the strongroom—sometime after 1956, judging by the age of the watch found with the body. The story was illustrated by photographs of the *Empress* before and during the war and a close-up of the Rolex watch. It was a disturbing story, but no help to Hugh's quest for his family's watch.

In light of the *Mail's* article however, Hugh decided to track down Henry Brown and talk to him, before handing the job over to a professional.

Henry Brown had been Royal Navy, so it was relatively easy to find him. Now 70, he lived with his wife in rural Sussex. The Browns had no phone, so one fine Sunday afternoon Hugh and Anna simply drove down and knocked on the door of Henry's cottage. He had come to discover if Henry Brown had maintained contact with Armstrong after the war, given their shared experience of surviving the destruction of the launch. However, as soon as he mentioned Armstrong, the Navy veteran went off in a different tangent altogether.

"It's strange you coming here with these questions after all these years."

Henry Brown was clearly in the mood to talk.

"I was interviewed by that Merchant Navy captain, I forget his name now. My own captain was in the room of course; he explained this was only a preliminary, informal enquiry. You need to understand there's no such thing. The Navy pays attention to everything when there's been a sinking. Anyway, they had already interviewed Armstrong, and so the captain read from Armstrong's version of events. 'Mr Armstrong reported all of the gold had been recovered.' Then he says, 'The final seven boxes were on the launch when it was hit. Is that your recollection, bosun?'

"Well, one thing you learn right smart in the Navy, is don't be caught on the wrong side of an argument with an officer, even if he's only Merchant, not Royal. I reckoned Armstrong had got the wind up and left some of the gold on board. And I thought, '*Can't really blame him.*' It was only government money after all, and what's the point in dying for that? So I nodded and agreed. I knew we didn't have seven boxes that last trip, but I went along."

"And did you ever see Armstrong again after that episode?" Hugh asked.

"Never. We took the survivors back to Liverpool and that was that."

From his silence on the subject, Hugh decided Henry Brown had not seen the *Daily Mail* article, so he filled him in on the information about the dead diver. Henry became extremely agitated.

"So they must have gone back for the gold! But why wait all those years? That's odd. But, maybe it was simple lucky chance. Folk are always finding sunken ships. Still, it's strange."

Someone else became extremely agitated when they read the *Daily Mail* story.

Jeremy Armstrong and his wife Sarah had added a daughter to their family the previous year. The daughter was unexpected, coming almost ten years after her brother. Jeremy had not progressed in Debenhams and money was still tight. He and Sarah had earlier decided that when Alfred went to secondary school, Sarah would go back to work—but the baby's arrival had scuppered their plans. The £1000 that Philip had sent over two years ago had been a welcome boost; they had even managed a week in Blackpool. But the last of the £1000 had been spent a while ago. If Sarah had known about the money, she might have made sure they saved at least some of it, but Jeremy didn't want to tell her what had transpired during his 'fishing trip' to Scotland with his brother. Sarah had never liked or trusted Philip, had actually been afraid of him, especially after her then sister-in-law told her why she wanted to divorce him. And, in his heart, Jeremy knew the whole business was shady.

So when the money turned up, in cash, Jeremy had hidden it, and for eighteen months he lied, explaining he was receiving bonuses for good performance. The money had eased the tension in the marriage, hence the arrival of a new baby. With the windfall now gone, he had been forced to begin a new series of lies to explain why the 'bonuses' had dried up.

Since the birth of their daughter, Jeremy and Sarah's marriage had descended into a state of grudging toleration as each tried to endure the disappointment of their lives. Sarah's affections were transferred entirely to her children.

That evening, as soon as the children were in bed, Sarah retrieved the *Daily Mail* and handed it to her husband, who was watching the television—one of the luxury purchases from twelve months ago.

"Look; isn't that the ship your brother was on, when it sank I mean?"

Jeremy read the article and understood immediately that his brother had murdered the man in the strongroom. He knew it with absolute certainty. He was pretty certain that his brother must have murdered the other men; there were more than two of them involved in the salvage dive. He also realised if the authorities ever connected him to what had happened, he would be in dire trouble. Jeremy had long since come to terms with the fact that he was weak. But he also intuited that the police would never believe that someone would be so passive as to accept his brother's flimsy story about his accomplices.

That night Jeremy lay awake, unable to sleep, his thoughts circling round and round, the overwhelming feeling of despair and guilt growing stronger and stronger by the hour. Whether the police came knocking or not, he had facilitated the murders. He was guilty.

The next morning, Jeremy left for work at his usual time. When the 7:55 express came hurtling through his train station, he stepped in front of it. His death rated a small piece in the local newspaper, while the London papers covered the story of the disruption to rush hour commuting service due to 'a body on the line'.

Jeremy's small life insurance policy didn't pay out in the event of suicide.

***

Hugh felt certain there was a connection between the missing gold in the final transfer on Henry Brown's launch and the dead man in the *Empress's* wreck but couldn't figure out the links in the chain. He needed some current information about Armstrong. It was time to use a professional.

Kingsbay Associates was one of the world's most prestigious security and investigative agencies. Brian Houston was a senior operative in their London office. He met Hugh in a conference room high over Euston Road.

"Your brief is straightforward, Mr Campbell; and your notes give us several good start points. I'm confident we'll be able to trace Philip Armstrong within a reasonable timeframe. I'll report back to you this time next week. Should I require anything else from you, I'll be in touch. Assuming we do find him, do you want us to maintain a trace on him?"

"Yes, at least until we decide what to do next."

A week later, the two men met again, this time at Hugh's office.

"We have a fairly complete record of Armstrong's life and movements until two summers ago. You'll find the details in my report. In short, he is the middle of three brothers, both parents dead, the father a suicide after a financial scandal. His older brother was killed in the war. After his discharge from the Merchant Navy early in 1946, Armstrong drifted between various jobs, none well-paying or high status. He married and divorced; his wife sued on grounds of cruelty–physical abuse in this case. He finally wound up teaching in a small public school. In the summer of 1960, he resigned his position, by letter. Since leaving his teaching post, there is no record we can find of him working in the UK. So far, we have found no trace of him whatsoever for the past two years or so, but I'm sure we will. I'll keep you informed."

The following week, Brian Houston was clearly embarrassed by the lack of progress in the case.

"We still have no trace of Armstrong since he resigned his teaching job. He had use of teachers' accommodation, but never returned for his possessions, or asked for them to be forwarded. The school still holds them, although apparently they don't amount to much. Assuming he is alive, he's only 47, so years away from drawing a pension.

"Oddly enough, his younger brother, Jeremy, died recently; a suicide like his father–although there was no suggestion of scandal with the brother. According to his widow, the brothers hadn't been in touch for at least two years, maybe longer. They were never especially close; there was a ten-year age gap between them. Armstrong seemingly had no friends, no girlfriends, not even casual acquaintances. No one knows what he did with his weekends, although he apparently spent more time away from the school in the months leading up to his resignation.

"To be frank, Mr Campbell, we are coming to the conclusion that he may have died, changed his name, or gone abroad. Only a few hundred unidentified bodies turn up each year, so unrecorded death is highly unlikely, unless it happened overseas. If he has changed his name, we will probably not find him, and if he has emigrated, I'm afraid our investigation would become much more complicated and, frankly, much, much more expensive. Without a lead to his destination, he could be literally anywhere."

For the next two weeks, Brian Houston visited Hugh, and each time there was absolutely no progress to report whatsoever. For all intents and purposes, Philip Armstrong had completely vanished in July or August 1960. There were records Kingsbay Associates couldn't access—tax records and passport information in particular. These would only be available to the police if they became officially involved, but there were no grounds for anticipating that. As it happened, it was easy enough to access police records with an envelope slipped into the right hands, but this too had come up empty. Armstrong had no convictions or charges and was not a suspect in a crime, at least in England.

"I am sorry to have let you down, Mr Campbell. We feel there is no point in further efforts at this time, when we have no prospects for success. However, in light of the fact that we have achieved essentially nothing for the past two weeks, my firm has agreed to add Armstrong to our persons of interest file. All of our worldwide offices will know we are interested in this man, and if he does surface, I'll be contacted and will be in touch."

***

Meanwhile, the time for Jenny's trip to Japan came around and she made arrangements to travel to Kyoto via Australia.

She wasn't precisely sure how she would handle the situation with Alice Murray, but she was confident she'd figure it out at the time. A local journalist contact of Robbie's had found a current address and phone number and confirmed she was still Alice Murray, so presumably unmarried.

Jenny gave herself a day to get over the long flight from Los Angeles via Hawaii. Early the following morning, she plucked up her nerve and telephoned the number she had been given.

"Miss Murray? Alice Murray? My name is Jenny Craig. You don't know me, but I wonder if you would agree to meet with me in the next day or two. If you don't mind, I'd rather not discuss the matter on the telephone, but I have a message for you, from an old friend."

Alice thought the request more than a little odd, but decided to agree to meet. She arranged to join Jenny for a drink at six o'clock the next evening, in the Hotel

Windsor, across the square from where she worked in the parliament building.

The two women had no trouble finding each other. Jenny had arrived early, to make sure she could secure a seat in a secluded area; Alice, she was sure, would want some privacy for their encounter.

After some pleasantries, Jenny turned to the subject at hand.

"Several months ago, and quite out of the blue, my mother was contacted by two men who had recovered an object which had belonged to our family. The men were deep-sea divers, and they had been salvaging the wreck of the *Empress of the Oceans*. The object was a brass container, and it had belonged to her brother-in-law, my uncle–Alex Campbell."

Jenny paused and watched for the reaction of the woman opposite. Alice was younger than Jenny had anticipated, and she had quickly seen why Alex would have been attracted to her. Now she watched as a succession of emotions played over Alice's face and her startling green eyes, as she absorbed Jenny's surprising news.

"I don't understand ..." Alice began.

Jenny reached across the table between them and gently touched Alice's arm.

"There's more. We had the container opened. And this was inside."

With that, Jenny slid the letter over to Alice.

Alice read the letter slowly, in total silence. Tears began to flow, and she blinked, trying to clear her vision. Eventually, she held the letter out to Jenny.

"No, no, its yours. I came here to give this to you. I know we could have sent it, but, well, I didn't think that was the right thing to do. I don't think Alex would have wanted that. He was a wonderful man, but I think you knew that. I hope you don't mind that I've taken so long to deliver your letter. And, well, it wasn't in an envelope, so I'm afraid we read it. But, that's how we found out about you, about you and Alex."

Alice was composed now, although her eyes were still bright.

"Thank you very much for such kindness. You can't know how much this means to me. He had sent me several letters from Cape Town, but then nothing. Of course I learned about the ship then about Alex, but I wasn't sure exactly what…you have to understand, we were together for such a short time. I believed with all my heart that he loved me totally, but I wondered if maybe…well, you understand, I'm sure."

"You wondered if he would still love you when you were apart? Well, the letter is clear. I must say, we were absolutely amazed when we read it. But, do you know what my mother said? For all these years she had fretted that Alex's final weeks had been filled with nothing but pain and sorrow after hearing about his daughter and my dad. But now she is happier, more at peace, knowing

Alex's last weeks were also filled with love. My family feels we owe you a great deal, Alice."

The two women spoke for hours over dinner. Alice wanted to know about Hughie and the rest of the family.

Jenny laughed, "He's Hugh now, very successful and very rich." She went on to tell her about Alan and Betty and their move to America and how that had led to her brother marrying Chrissie.

"Christina Fredericks, the film star, is your sister-in-law? Oh, my God!"

Alice was clearly amazed by this news.

"Alex talked to me about Christina. He mentioned her name in connection with Noël Coward and Dorothy Parker. I had completely forgotten her name until it started popping up all over the place years ago.

"He would entertain me with stories about the celebrities on the *Empress* before the war. Oh, how Alex would have loved knowing that Christina married his nephew. He talked about his family all of the time. I felt I knew you all. He was so proud of you, Jenny; you and your brother. You know, he once admitted he may have made a mistake not insisting that the girls had the same education as the boys; and here you are, a professor!"

"And what about you, Alice, what have you been doing?"

"Oh, nothing much. It took me a long time to get over Alex, years. I still work in government service, I run the Prime Minister's office, which is very interesting. You know, our PM in the war, Robert Menzies, knew Alex, and even that we were having an affair, if you can believe it! Things were different during the war of course. I never married, for one reason or another, but I'm seeing someone now. He's a widower, very nice, so we'll see. It isn't a soaring passion, not like with Alex, but, just maybe, you never know."

"The letter mentioned your father. Is he well?" Jenny asked.

"Absolutely! Alex was there the night he had his first date with my stepmother, Doreen. They're still very much in love, very happy. She keeps him young."

Three days later, the day before Jenny left for Japan, the two women met again for a final lunch. Afterwards, as they walked out together into the Melbourne sun, Alice embraced Jenny to say farewell.

"I can't thank you enough for your generosity in coming so far out of your way for me. The last few nights I've finally been able to think about Alex without getting upset. Reading the letter and hearing all about his family has changed things in my heart now. It all feels more like a warm memory of a lovely interlude, and less like an open wound. I think I'll be able to move on now, and maybe … well, we'll see. So, thank you, with all my heart. And please tell all your family there will always be a welcome for them in my home. Do you think it would be OK if I wrote to Hughie, Hugh I mean? There are things I would like to tell him about his father."

"I think Hugh would like that very much. Here, let me write down his address for you. And I'm sure Alex would have wanted nothing but your happiness; as I do. I'm glad we met. I know now, that despite everything, Alex's last weeks must have been happy indeed."

1964

CANNES, FRANCE

Almost a year after Hugh's final meeting with Brian Houston he heard from him again, by telephone.

"Mr Campbell, Brian Houston here, of Kingsbay Associates. Mr Campbell, you may recall me saying we would add Philip Armstrong to our list of persons of interest? Well, I can tell you that he may have turned up at last.

"Our French office provides security services to the Majestic Hotel in Cannes, in the south of France. As part of their service, they were vetting the guest list for the opening reception for next week's Cannes Film Festival, and Armstrong's name seems to be on the list. I say 'seems to be', because we haven't yet verified our information. Initial enquiries in Cannes suggest that their Philip Armstrong is a wealthy expat Englishman, invited by a local importer of luxury cars who is presumably well connected in the area. Our local contact says the Englishman turned up in the area over two years ago, buying an expensive villa above the village of Èze. No one seems to know anything about his background, but this isn't unusual in that part of the world, where lots of shady people with murky pasts seem to gravitate. Would you like us to make some more enquiries to ascertain whether this is your Armstrong?"

"Yes, please. And quickly. Members of my family are attending the Festival, this could be our opportunity to confront him."

"Yes, I asked for a copy of the reception guest list and saw that your wife and your cousins were on the guest list for the reception."

Robbie and Chrissie were currently in London, visiting for a week or so before travelling on to Cannes.

Over the past two years, Robbie and Chrissie found themselves enjoying London more and more. Chrissie, who had more of an outsider's perspective of the UK, picked up ever more indications that Britain in general, and London in particular, was well and truly recovered from the war and the austerity that followed. The signs were everywhere; new restaurants were opening, there were more cars in the streets, people looked happier. In particular, the fashion and music scenes in London were incredibly dynamic and exciting. During their last trip, they had seen a great new band called the *Rolling Stones* and she found herself buying more and more of her clothes during her London visits. They could see a time coming when they might move to London for a year or two with the children, to immerse them in their father's culture.

Robbie had a short film in competition in the Cannes Festival. It wasn't a commercial venture, but it was his first foray as a producer, so he and Chrissie were attending. Jenny and Anna were already scheduled to go with them. They claimed they were going to support the family, but everyone knew they were both thoroughly star-struck. It greatly amused Hugh that his cerebral mathematician wife, who cared nothing for her own appearance, was besotted with the glamour of Hollywood films. He often teased her that she had married the wrong cousin. She was quick to agree with him on that, and made no secret of how much she enjoyed the access to Hollywood stars she obtained thanks to her husband's cousin and Robbie's world-famous film star wife. Anna and Jenny often travelled to California together to attend premieres and award shows. Hugh was generally too busy building his company.

There couldn't have been a greater contrast between the women. Chrissie was a world-famous beauty and Jenny too turned heads wherever she went. Anna in contrast, was short, slightly overweight, completely uninterested in fashion and a stranger to make-up beyond a light touch of lipstick. She wore her hair unflatteringly short, and she refused to dye it. Life was too short and her interests too absorbing, to waste time primping herself. However, her intellectual brilliance and mischievous sense of humour endeared her to everyone she met, including a growing list of Hollywood celebrities who numbered her among their friends.

Hugh called Robbie and Jenny and they agreed to come round for supper the following evening.

Hugh filled everyone in on his call from Kingsbay Associates.

He challenged the group, "So, what are we going to do? Assuming that is, that they confirm we have the right Armstrong."

Robbie answered him. "Well, this started with us wanting to recover Alex's watch—and that should still be our first priority, I think. But now there's the business with the gold and the dead body. It does seem Armstrong is connected somehow, although I still can't make sense of it. If Armstrong knew there was gold left on the ship, why wait fifteen years after the war to get it? Someone else could have sought it out, or stumbled across it in that time. I don't understand that piece of the picture. Oh, and I called the journalist on the *Mail*. They didn't get any follow up on the story. No one came forward with information about a missing person who might fit the story."

Jenny offered an idea. "Maybe Armstrong delayed going for the gold because he didn't have the money? It must cost something to hire a boat, people to help, all the equipment."

"I hope you're wrong, Jenny." said Anna. "If he spent the time raising money, there's every chance he sold the watch. Although, let's be realistic, its highly probable he sold it anyway, it had no meaning to him except its monetary worth."

Hugh had wrestled with this reality ever since his father's container had miraculously turned up. In all likelihood, the watch had gone down with the *Empress*. He also realised that if Armstrong *had* somehow brought the watch safely off the ship and later sold it, during or soon after the war, then even assuming he told them where he had sold it, the trail would be cold now, and the chances of finding the watch, remote in the extreme.

"You're right, darling, but I think we press on anyway, I feel like I owe it to Dad to do the best I can to get it back. And now with this other thing, I'm even more determined. If we can just meet Armstrong, and get the measure of him, we may be able to convince the authorities to investigate his wealth and maybe they'll turn up something that would bring him to justice."

***

It was fortunate Anna already had a room booked, as Cannes was full for the Festival. As it was, they were all staying at Hotel Le Majestic; and with her industry contacts, Chrissie had no trouble adding Hugh to the guest list for the reception.

Soon after they had checked into the hotel, Hugh received a message that someone wanted to come up and see him. Two minutes later, there was a soft rap on his door.

"Good afternoon, monsieur; and welcome to Cannes. I am Serge Morel, a colleague of Brian Houston, based in Nice."

"Yes, he told me you would be in touch."

"Indeed. I will be attending the reception tomorrow evening, so I will be able to point out to you, the man Armstrong. We still cannot be absolutely certain he is the man you are seeking. However, our Armstrong did buy a motor yacht here in France, and the salesman says the buyer claimed to have been an officer in your Merchant Marine. He explained that he preferred motor yachts to sail because he had more faith in machines than in the wind. Naturally, this is not conclusive proof, but with everything else we know, I think we can be confident that he is the same man."

"I'm inclined to believe he is." Hugh replied.

"One more thing, monsieur. We have many expatriates here, from England, Russia, Italy, even a few Germans now. Between tax authorities, police forces, former business associates, lawyers acting for ex-wives and so on, most of these expatriates live quiet lives. Keeping a small profile, I think you say. This is not so with Monsieur Armstrong. He has joined the yacht club; he is often seen at parties and receptions in the company of attractive young women; he drives a very expensive automobile. Nor, of course, has he changed his name. In other words, monsieur, he gives every sign of not fearing that someone is pursuing him. For a man with no past, this is intriguing, is it not?"

The following evening, Hugh and Robbie wore tuxedos, and even Anna was in an evening gown, as the five of them went down together to the reception, which had been underway for an hour. Robbie and Chrissie were soon whisked away to meet members of the competition jury. Hugh, Anna and Jenny were still on their first glass of champagne, when, as if from nowhere, Serge Morel appeared at Hugh's elbow. After an appreciative glance at Jenny, he leaned in and spoke quietly to Hugh.

"The man in front of the pillar opposite. He is talking with the redheaded woman in the blue dress with no back."

"Got him. Thank you, Serge."

Hugh pointed Armstrong out to the two women. As they watched, a man came up to Armstrong's group and placed a glass of champagne into the redheaded woman's hand, slid a possessive arm around her waist and joined in the conversation.

"You two leave me," instructed Jenny.

"OK, but we'll be keeping an eye on you."

"Relax, Hugh, he's not going to molest me here!"

Anna and Hugh walked away and Jenny drifted slowly into the middle of the room, closing the distance to Armstrong. As a waiter passed by, she placed her empty champagne glass on his tray. She was about to reach for a fresh drink, when a voice from behind said, "Allow me to get that for you."

She turned to accept the glass, somehow knowing it would be Armstrong in front of her.

"Did I see you come down the stairs with the ravishing Miss Christina Fredericks?"

"Yes, you did. Mrs Craig is my sister-in-law," replied Jenny, emphasising the Mrs.

"Ah! Your husband's sister?"

"No," she smiled, "my brother's wife."

"Excellent! And are you visiting Cannes for long, Miss Craig?"

"It doesn't seem fair that you know my name, and I don't know yours," she teased.

"How terribly rude of me. Philip Armstrong, at your service."

"Jenny," she replied, shaking his hand. "And are you a visitor too, Mr Armstrong?"

"Please, Philip. And no, I live here; well, a few miles inland. It's cooler in the hills and the views are magnificent. You should come up for a visit while you're here."

Jenny didn't want to put Armstrong off, but neither did she want to appear too easy, so she chose to ignore his invitation, for the moment anyway.

"And have you lived here long, Philip?"

"Two years, more or less. I looked at Spain, but this area suited me better. The climate is almost perfect and the social life is much more sophisticated."

They chatted for a few minutes, Jenny trying to concentrate on his questions and come up with polite answers while her brain feverishly tried to figure out what she should do.

Finally, she had it.

"Philip, earlier you suggested a visit to your home in the hills. That sounds delightful. Would it be OK if I brought my brother and …"

He interrupted her just in time.

"Of course! It would be my great pleasure. How about tomorrow for an aperitif before dinner? There's a wonderful restaurant in Èze with a spectacular terrace. I'll make a reservation. Say about six o'clock? Let me draw you a map with directions."

He took a small notebook from his pocket and quickly sketched a map on a blank page, which he tore out and handed to Jenny with a smile.

"Thank you, Philip. Now I must go and find my family, I've monopolised you long enough. Until tomorrow, at six?"

She offered him her hand before turning away to look for Robbie or Chrissie. She guessed Armstrong would be following her with his eyes, and didn't want to raise questions in his mind by bumping into Hugh and Anna first.

Fortunately, it was easy to find her sister-in-law; there was always a crowd around her. Jenny pushed her way through and leaned in to whisper to Chrissie.

"Look over my shoulder. I'm supposed to be inviting you and Robbie to dine tomorrow with Armstrong. He's in the centre of the room and probably watching us. Smile and nod if he is."

It wasn't hard for a professional actress to summon up a charming smile and nod to Armstrong, who was indeed watching. He looked delighted as he gave her a little salute.

At ten past six the following evening, their car pulled into the driveway of Armstrong's villa. When it stopped, Jenny stepped out, followed by Robbie and Hugh. The driver would wait; they had told him they would probably be no more than twenty minutes. Serge Morel had provided the car and driver, in case there was any trouble; although they were confident they could handle Armstrong themselves, no matter what transpired.

Armstrong opened the door and couldn't hide his disappointment.

Without waiting for an invitation, Jenny eased past him as she said, "Good evening, Philip."

Caught unawares, Armstrong waved the two men in and followed behind.

"Philip, this is my brother, Robbie. And this is my cousin, Hugh Campbell."

Armstrong had recovered by now and offered each man his hand.

Robbie opened the conversation. "My wife sends her regrets, but she thought you might prefer to meet Hugh here."

Armstrong was clearly mystified.

"As I mentioned, my name is Hugh Campbell. My father was Alex Campbell, of the *Empress of the Oceans*."

Recognition dawned at last. Armstrong was clearly taken aback to hear a reference to his history.

"I see, so your father was Alex Campbell? Well, I'm sure I'm pleased to meet you, Hugh. I didn't know your father very well, I'm sure he was a good …"

Hugh interrupted him, "You knew him well enough to steal his watch. I want it back."

At this point, Armstrong made his major mistake. If he had looked blank and confused, they would have been easily persuaded that he truly had forgotten all about the watch, just one of a thousand inconsequential transactions in wartime. Or he could have expressed regret, explaining that he had sold the watch years and years ago.

Instead, he became instantly defensive.

"I didn't steal the watch. Your father borrowed money, which was never repaid. The watch was collateral. It was forfeit."

"You bastard. My father was dead, and you knew it. You could have contacted his family easily enough, but no, you kept a valuable watch, worth infinitely more than the £50 you had lent him. You were a fellow officer, you had a duty to return that watch and you damn well know it. Well, now you can."

"Or what, you'll beat me up? I don't think so. I've no intention of handing over the watch. Now get out of my house."

"I tell you what, Armstrong. I'll offer you something in exchange, another watch."

Hugh reached into his jacket pocket and produced a Rolex Submariner.

"You can have this watch in exchange. You're shaking your head. Well, this Rolex is much more interesting than it first appears. You see, this watch was found next to the dead man who is floating in the bullion room of the *Empress of the Oceans*. Interested now?"

Armstrong's face turned white, but Hugh wasn't finished.

"Your brother, Jeremy, committed suicide the day after the *Daily Mail* ran a story about the discovery of the dead man. You didn't know that, did you? A coincidence? Maybe; I wonder if the police will think so. And another coincidence: you, a complete loser and failure, turning up here with masses of money, soon after a diver is murdered on the wreck of your old ship. And did you know that your old naval colleague, Henry Brown, is still alive and well and in full possession of his memory? Name not ringing a bell? Henry was the boatswain on the launch that was torpedoed. He was the other survivor. And he is certain there were only two boxes of gold on that launch, not seven. And he isn't afraid to call an officer a liar anymore."

Hugh stepped closer to Armstrong.

Hugh couldn't have known it, but Armstrong was experiencing an instant flashback, to a day years before, when a slightly older man, but one who looked a lot like the person before him, had also stood toe-to-toe with him—and he had been afraid that day as well.

"So no, we're not going to beat you up. Well, not unless we have to. You see, Armstrong, Jenny is going to leave now, and take that car back down to Nice. The driver works for a well-connected security company, mostly ex-police and secret service people. He has a complete dossier on you. With his connections, I'm guessing the police will be up here within an hour or so to have a conversation about where your money came from. Robbie and I will keep you company while we wait. I see you have some wine chilling. Excellent!"

"OK, OK, you can have the damn watch. I'll go get it."

"No, we'll come with you. In case you have any crazy notions."

Hugh and Robbie accompanied Armstrong to his bedroom and stood over him as he opened a drawer. The lovely pocket watch was sitting in a suede and velvet tray, its heavy chain nestled beside it. Hugh reached in and picked it up, its weight instantly familiar in his hand. His father had often allowed him to hold his watch on Sunday mornings. He opened the watch's gold back. The engraving was still there. He felt the emotions stirring within him, but pushed the feelings away. Now was not the time.

Hugh took £50 from his pocket and threw it at Armstrong's feet.

"We'll be leaving now, Armstrong, but we'll be going straight to the police. We'll see ourselves out. Come on, Jenny, let's go."

"The Rolex was a brilliant idea, Hughie."

Hugh smiled as his cousin used his childhood name. Robbie was experiencing the same wave of memories as he was.

"Thank God one second-hand Submariner watch looks like any other! There are dozens for sale in Bond Street."

Twenty minutes after they left, Armstrong threw two heavy suitcases into the back of his Rolls Royce. The Silver Cloud was his pride and joy; he had taken delivery of it only four weeks earlier. However at this precise moment, he was in no mood to appreciate his car. Armstrong was frightened, terrified. He had no doubt Hugh would indeed go to the police and he saw his carefully constructed life unravelling.

Why had he left John Kennedy's body in the strongroom? If he had stuck to his plan and used a knife, ocean currents and scavenging fish would have transported the body away from the wreck. He had known someone would dive on the *Empress* sometime.

They were bound to open the safe and find the body. Kennedy's name would eventually turn up.

Deep down though, Armstrong knew he had been scared witless at the thought of stabbing Kennedy. He might not kill him immediately; there could be a struggle. Or Kennedy might turn around as he was about to stab him in the back. There were too many scenarios where he wound up having to fight with John Kennedy if he had tried to kill him with a knife. The slammed door was a much cleaner option.

'Damn, damn, damn!' he swore as he put the car in gear and drove out of his driveway.

The body was the problem. Even if the authorities suspected he had found the gold, it would be next to impossible to prove it, and he was not certain it was a crime anyway. But murder was murder in any jurisdiction.

And why did he not keep more money in the house safe? He had less than 12,000 francs in cash. 'Fuck, fuck, fuck!'

Armstrong was becoming more and more agitated as he contemplated his situation. He had no plan beyond driving into Italy. But what then? They would likely freeze his bank accounts.

These thoughts were tumbling feverishly through Armstrong's mind as he navigated the sweeping curves of the Corniche road, banging his fist on the steering wheel in sheer frustration.

The coast of this part of France is the fabled Côte d'Azur; but a few kilometers inland, there were still a few surviving family farms. As the Rolls came around another fast corner, a tractor from one of those farms was painfully reversing onto the road, with zero regard for other road users. Armstrong saw it much too late to stop, and his instinctive swerve carried him over the edge of the roadway. For a second or two, he thought he had made it, but with a sudden lurch, the verge crumbled and the driver's side of the car dropped sickeningly. The last recognisable image Armstrong's brain processed, was the precipitous drop down the almost vertical hillside.

The heavy car barrelled through the few shrubs and saplings that clung to the tiny rocky ledges. It rolled across the bend of the road far below, finally coming to rest in an explosion at the bottom of a dry stream bed, over 150 feet below the gaze of the farmer, who reached the side of the road just in time to witness Armstrong's fiery death.

The cousins were sitting down for dinner in Cannes. Serge had decided it would be easier if he delivered the dossier himself to his old comrades in the police the following morning. The family would make themselves available for questioning if required. Meanwhile, Hugh, Jenny and Robbie were being cross-examined by Chrissie and Anna, who wanted to hear every detail of the encounter.

When they had had all their questions answered, Hugh took out the gold pocket watch, enjoying holding it again. After a while it was passed around to be admired. Finally, it arrived at Chrissie, who glanced over at Hugh with a strange look in her eyes.

"Hugh, come sit beside me, there's something I need to show you; a secret, from your father."

Hugh looked puzzled, but came around the table to sit beside her, as Chrissie slowly turned the beautiful watch over in her hand. She looked around the table; at her husband, Alex's nephew; his niece Jenny, Chrissie's sister-in-law and closest friend; and finally at Alex's son. She thought again how much Hugh resembled his father, on that long ago evening in the silver room of the *Empress of the Oceans*.

Chrissie opened the back of the watch.

***

The young girl looked gratefully at the steward. They had spent half an hour in the Empress's silver room. Alex had explained about the finger bowl then he had talked her through an entire silver service, with all the specialised implements for oysters, snails, strawberries and so on.

At first, she had been embarrassed by her stupidity, until Alex corrected her.

"It wasn't stupidity, Miss Christina. This is all just etiquette, nonsense really. But, what Mr Coward did when you made a mistake; that was real class. Good manners, consideration for the

feelings of others; these things are much more important than etiquette."

He checked his watch, it would soon be time to organise pre-dinner drinks for his passengers.

"That's a lovely watch, Alex, may I hold it?"

"Of course; here you are."

"Gosh, it's heavy! Heavier than I expected anyway. It's very beautiful."

"Aye, it is beautiful indeed. It's heavy because it's made of gold. And see here; here is the story of the watch."

With the nail of his thumb, Alex carefully opened the hinged back of the watch and showed her the engraving. Under the Square and Compasses, she read, 'Presented to Brother William Hugh Campbell, 27th March 1899, by his fellow Brethren. In recognition of exceptional service.'

"He was my grandfather. My first sons were named for him. When Hughie is 21, I'll add a new engraving on the other side."

"What will it say?"

"It will say, 'Given to Hugh Angus Campbell, by his loving father, Alex; son of Angus, grandson of William'. That way, one day his sons and grandsons will know their family history."

Alex wasn't finished with this young woman he had become so fond of.

"But look, see here? This watch is much, much older than you may imagine, and it has a very special secret. I haven't shown this to Hughie yet. It'll be a nice surprise when I pass on the watch."

Alex slowly turned the watch around and felt carefully until he found a certain spot that he pressed firmly. Chrissie gave a little gasp as a cunningly hidden cover popped open. Once again, Alex used his nail to carefully prise open the secret hinged back. Christina could now see the workings of the watch; tiny wheels and delicate levers moving in an endless silent symphony. On the inside of the secret cover she could make out another engraving, in an older script, but one she could read with little difficulty. She read aloud, "Presented to Caledonia's bard, Bro. Robt. Burns, on his app'tment Poet Laureate, Grand Lodge of Scotland. 10th Feb in the ^{yr} of our lord 1787, at Edinburgh."

The young woman looked up in utter amazement.

"This watch belonged to Robert Burns! Really?"

"Really. This watch is the treasure of our family. Now every New Year's Eve when you sing his song, Auld Lang Syne, you'll remember you held Robert Burns' watch in your hand."

"No, Alex," Chrissie replied softly, "I'll remember you."

END

If you have enjoyed this novel, please take a moment to leave a review on Amazon or Goodreads. Thank you.

Author's notes follow

Author's Notes

This novel was inspired by the tragic and enigmatic story of the *Empress of Britain*.

Launched by renowned Clyde shipbuilders, John Brown & Co. in 1931, the *Empress of Britain* was commissioned by the Canadian Pacific Railway Company to serve the route from Canada to Europe during the summer season, and the emerging market for luxury world cruises in the winter, when the St Lawrence River was frozen over.

In 1939, the UK government requisitioned the *Empress of Britain* as a troopship. In August 1940 she transported troops from Liverpool to Egypt via Cape Town. On her return journey she stopped again in Cape Town.

At 9:20 a.m. on Saturday, October 26th, 1940, when she was off the NW coast of Ireland and thus almost home, the ship was spotted and bombed by a long-range German weather reconnaissance plane. An uncontrollable fire ravaged her entire mid section and within half an hour the signal to abandon ship was given. In extremely difficult circumstances, around 600 of the 647 passengers and crew were saved. A few hours later the still burning ship was taken in tow in an effort to bring her to where she might be repaired.

However, around 2 a.m. on Monday 28th, a U-boat fired three torpedoes at the stricken liner. One was a dud, one narrowly missed, and one was a direct hit. In less than ten minutes, the *Empress of Britain* turned on her side and slid beneath the waves, finally coming to rest upside down in over 500 feet of water. She was the largest civilian ship sunk in World War II.

In the years after the war, rumours persisted that the *Empress of Britain* had been carrying gold from the mines in South Africa. In fact, between 1939 and 1942, dozens of shipments of gold were sent across the Atlantic to Canada to pay for food and munitions. And gold was only a small fraction of what was the greatest movement of wealth in human history, as all of the negotiable financial instruments of the United Kingdom were transported in complete secrecy.

Rumour characterises everything that follows in the tale of the legendary liner.

In 1949 the *Daily Mail* ran a story announcing there was to be a salvage attempt to recover millions of pounds in gold from the ship. No other newspaper carried the story, and it was never followed up. In 1985 a prospective salvor was apparently advised by the UK government that any gold that may have been aboard had been recovered. Finally, in 1995 a reputable salvage company cut through to the bullion room of the wreck and entered it. It was completely empty.

Except for a skeleton.

No one knows how or when the skeleton got into the strongroom. No one can even confirm the skeleton was really there.

Recall that the ship stayed afloat for around 40 hours after being bombed. The post-war testimony of Hans Jenisch, captain of the U-boat that sunk the *Empress of Britain*, reported he saw lights moving on the liner when he found her being towed. Yet the official Admiralty reports insist there was no one on board at that time.

Only naval divers and an exceeding small number of commercial dive teams were capable of recovering materials from deep inside a wreck in 500 feet of water. (The *Empress of Britain* sank in one piece.)

It is important to note that, while the story of the *Empress of Britain* was the inspiration behind this tale, the *Empress of the Oceans* is a completely different and wholly fictitious vessel whose voyages, passengers, crew and ultimate fate bear only a passing resemblance to the real thing; or to the *RMS Queen Mary*, some of whose early story and characteristics I also exploited.

Similarly, I took extensive liberties with other historical figures and events. To give one example, BOAC flying boats to Asia and Australia would typically have a single male steward, not two female stewardesses (who were yet to be termed flight attendants).

I have accelerated considerably the development of diving equipment. It is difficult to comprehend how relatively recently recreational divers gained access to wet suits, regulators, dive computers, even decent diving fins. In reality, Armstrong would have found it practically impossible to carry out his raid on the *Empress* before about 1970, and certainly he would not have succeeded in 1961 in the manner portrayed in the novel. Diving limitations also explain why I shifted part of the wreck into unrealistically shallow waters.

Maurice Wilkes was indeed a computing pioneer during and after the war. He collaborated with, and trained, the team who went on to build LEO, the world's first commercial computer, for J. Lyons & Co.

Tom Honeyman was the most influential director of the Glasgow Art Gallery (although several years later than depicted); buying many paintings, including most notably, his friend Dali's *Christ of St. John of the Cross*.

Rabbi Louis Rabinowitz was the Senior Jewish Chaplain of the British Army during World War II.

Jimmy Walker, Betty Compton, Noël Coward, Mr & Mrs Dorothy Campbell, and Clare Boothe Luce are all historical figures.

The letter to Joanne Fredericks' neighbour on page 198 of the paperback edition consists of verbatim extracts from a letter in my possession sent from a Cornish writer (and a remarkably far-seeing lady) to her correspondent in California. The original letter was written on December 29th, 1940.

For the record; unlike the great Robert Burns, I am not, and never have been, a Freemason.

ABOUT THE AUTHOR

Brian McPhee lived in Glasgow, Scotland until he was 21, when he moved to London. In his early 40s, following a year in New York, he moved with his wife and daughter to a community near Annapolis, Maryland. He holds UK and US passports.

Since 2010, he and his wife have lived in Monpazier, in southwest France. *Empress* is his second novel.

ALL VISIBLE THINGS

When Lauren Patterson, an American PhD student, discovers the diary of an assistant to Leonardo da Vinci, we are immediately immersed in the personalities and intrigues surrounding the greatest genius in history. A series of dramas—extortion, murder, defamation, betrayal and bitter artistic rivalries—play out against everyday struggles to extract money from clients, find lost pattern books, deliver on rash, wine-fuelled boasts and, amidst everything, create timeless masterpieces.

The enthusiastic diarist is Paolo del Rosso, thrilled by the vibrant city and completely enamoured by Chiara, Leonardo's goddaughter and the model in some of his greatest paintings. While their tender relationship is the constant thread of the Renaissance tapestry, the complex saga of the *Mona Lisa* and the scandalous secret behind her enigmatic smile weaves through the narrative.

The chronicle also records the memorable day when, with the encouragement and assistance of Leonardo, Paolo created a charming portrait of Chiara.

At the centre of everything, is the maestro himself—animal lover, vegetarian, contrarian, dandy and genius. When not executing the commissions of ungrateful clients, he is constantly juggling finances, friends and rivals while trying to find time for his true love—his scientific enquiries.

The discovery of the diaries is a once-in-a-lifetime opportunity for Lauren, an opportunity threatened by academic jealousies, unwanted media attention and personal insecurities. However, a fruitful partnership develops between the young researcher and an English art dealer as they work to complete the diary and track down Paolo's drawing—a trail they will follow from Renaissance Florence to Nazi Germany and the Holocaust to a thrilling dénouement when the portrait gives up its remarkable secret and our protagonists embrace their future.

BUNCO

Bunco is an engrossing, international tale of deception, retribution and romance. Four women, aged from 25 to 65, close neighbors and closer friends, undertake a quest for justice when their close-knit community is attacked from within. The journey takes them from their idyllic neighborhood on Long Island, NY, to Barcelona, a city of seduction, beauty, elegance and passion – just like its men and women.

The Kingsbay men play poker and sail their boats, the women play bunco, take trips to Las Vegas and organize an incredible social calendar for children and adults alike.